Peralta's Bike Shop
© 2016 Mark A. Roeder

Cover Photo Credits: Model: Curaphotography on Dreamstime.com. Background: Joe Mabel via Wikimedia Commons

Cover Design: Ken Clark

ISBN-13: 978-1533679352

ISBN-10: 1533679355

Need A Great Book Cover?

Covers By Ken created the cover for this novel. Check Out The Website at coversbyken.com. Ken will design a great cover for the best price you'll find on-line.

Acknowledgments

Ken Clark, James Adkinson, and David Tedesco have once again put in a great deal of effort pointing out mistakes and correcting errors. In addition, Ken has created another great cover.

Other Novels by Mark A. Roeder

*Also look for audiobook versions on Amazon.com and
Audible.com*

Blackford Gay Youth Chronicles:

Outfield Menace

Snow Angel

The Nudo Twins

Phantom World

Second Star to the Right

The Perfect Boy

Verona Gay Youth Chronicles:

Ugly

Beautiful

The Soccer Field Is Empty

Someone Is Watching

A Better Place

The Summer of My Discontent

Disastrous Dates & Dream Boys

Just Making Out

Bloomington Gay Youth Chronicles

A Triumph of Will

Temptation University*

The Picture of Dorian Gay

Yesterday's Tomorrow

Boy Trouble

The New Bad Ass in Town

Bloomington Boys—Brandon & Dorian*

Bloomington Boys—Nathan & Devon*

Bloomington Boys—Scotty & Casper*

Bloomington Boys—Tim & Marc*

Peralta's Bike Shop

Hate at First Sight

A Boy Toy for Christmas

*Crossover novels that fit into two series

Other Novels:

Fierce Competition

The Vampire's Heart

Homo for the Holidays

For more information on current and upcoming novels go to markroeder.com.

Chapter One
Bloomington, Indiana
July 1995

I opened the door to my dreams and stepped inside. I paused and took in the empty retail space that would soon be the home of my shop. The location was perfect. The building was located on Kirkwood Avenue and so close to Indiana University I could walk there in under thirty seconds. I had worked eight years for this, twelve counting my college years and at last it had become reality.

The shop was a blank canvas. I smiled as I pictured rows of bikes on display and "Peralta's Bike Shop" painted on the window. On the wall behind the counter I would display my prized possession; the bike that the Alpha Alpha Omega team rode to victory in not one, but two Little 500 races. My dream was about to come true, but first I had to get to work.

I locked up and walked around back. I unhitched my Camaro from the large U-Haul moving truck. It was not the 1970 model that I drove in high school and all through college. I had upgraded to a blue 1980 Camaro with racing stripes and a wide white stripe on the hood. That might not sound like much of an upgrade, but my old Camaro could best be described as decrepit. It would take far too long to describe everything that was wrong with it by the time I graduated from IU. It died not many months later. My "new" Camaro was a beauty and everything worked.

I climbed in and headed for my old fraternity, Alpha Alpha Omega. I was due to pick up four of the current brothers who I had hired to help me move in. I had met none of them. It had been eight years since I'd graduated so even those who were freshmen my senior year were gone.

I drove the few blocks to Alpha on 3rd Street. It looked exactly the same as the day I left. It was mostly empty at the moment. Not many brothers stayed over the summer. Come August and the beginning of the fall semester the house would begin to fill.

I walked up the steps and opened the door. There was no one in sight, but I was a few minutes early. I walked into the lounge and admired the Little 500 trophies I had helped win. Next, my eyes went to the photo of the team my sophomore year. There were Hunter, Conner, Jonah, and me. We all looked so young. I couldn't believe I had turned thirty. My eyes went to the photo for the next year's team and there he was—Alessio, my little frat brother and the boy who had stolen my heart. I hadn't forgotten him after all these years and I still wasn't over him. Alessio and Hunter were still together. I'd kept in touch with them, but had not seen either since I graduated. Perhaps it was better that way for I still had feelings for both of them.

My thoughts were disturbed by the sound of footsteps.

"Are you Marc?"

I nearly gasped for the boy who approached looked so much like Alessio that he could have been his brother. He had the same curly black hair, hazel eyes, and tanned skin. All that was missing was the Italian accent.

"Yeah."

"It's nice to meet you. You're legendary."

I laughed.

"I mean it. This is only my sophomore year, but every year the captain of the Little 500 team tells the story of how you single-handedly won the Little 500 your senior year."

"I didn't do it by myself."

"Very nearly."

"Are you on the team?"

"No. I only pledged last year, but I hope to make the team this year."

"Great. I'm always glad to meet another biking enthusiast. Which one are you?"

"Cameron, but everyone calls me Cam."

"Are you guys ready?" I asked.

"Yeah. I'll go grab the others."

I realized as Cam walked away that my heart was pounding. He reminded me so much of Alessio. I fought the surge of memories that threatened to overwhelm me and reminded myself that Cam was not Alessio. He was most certainly an attractive boy. Did I ever look that young? I suppose I did, but didn't realize it at the time. When I went to IU I didn't give it any thought.

A couple of minutes later I shook hands with Michael, Kevin, and Aaron and led them all out to my Camaro.

"Sweet ride," Kevin said as he climbed in the back. "My car sucks."

"You should see what I drove when I went to IU. I had a 1970 Camaro with no air conditioning, seats that were mostly duct tape, a door that wouldn't open and a window that wouldn't close, a tendency to overheat, and... well, you get the idea."

"A 1970? Oh man. I love vintage cars."

"It was vintage when I drove it. I think it would qualify as antique now."

"What happened to it?"

"It completely fell apart. I had to give it up once the transmission burned out."

"That is a shame."

"Yeah, I loved that car even though it was a piece of crap."

We soon arrived at the small building I had purchased with my savings and a loan. I parked directly behind it in my own private parking area, which was a true luxury in Bloomington. We climbed out of the car and I unlocked the back of the U-Haul.

"You guys will be doing most of the carrying and I will direct traffic," I said, grabbing a box.

The boys followed, each carrying a box or small item of furniture. The heavier stuff was buried under boxes.

I unlocked back door of the shop where the stairs to the upper story were located. We ascended into what would be my new home. It was a rather spacious apartment with two bedrooms, a kitchen, a bathroom, and a large living area that overlooked Kirkwood Avenue. I gave the guys a quick tour and then we headed back downstairs for more.

I helped with the unloading some, but mostly directed the guys to place boxes and items in the proper rooms. Soon, they began to bring up the furniture. I had planned in advance where I wanted each piece because I could not move most of it myself.

Over the next couple of hours or so my apartment slowly took shape. I had picked up a lot of second hand furniture since my college years so I wouldn't need to purchase much. The furniture I had was quite nice and much of it was painted red so it gave my apartment a unified feeling. I think it looked better here than in my old place.

I had time to check out my young frat brothers as they worked. They all possessed the beauty of youth that no one realizes they have until it slips away. At thirty, I wasn't exactly old, but I was also no longer twenty. Kevin and Michael, who were only average looking, still possessed the beauty I had lost; their bodies were young and firm, too. Aaron was quite good-looking and Cam... I wouldn't have minded hooking up with him at all.

The boys set up my bed and even my TV and audio-visual equipment. While they worked I further organized boxes, which I would unpack later. I was very pleased to get the U-Haul unloaded. It would have taken me hours to unload even what I could move myself.

When the last box, lamp, and table had been brought in I pulled out my wallet and handed out cash.

"How do you guys feel about pizza? I'm buying," I said.

"Hell yeah!"

"There's only one catch. I need to return the truck and we'll go from there. Want to drive my Camaro?" I asked Kevin as I shook the keys.

"Fuck yeah."

I tossed him the keys and we all headed downstairs.

Cam climbed into the truck with me and the others piled in my car and followed.

"Did you make the Little 500 team the first year you tried out?" Cam asked the moment we were on our way.

"Yes. I pledged in my sophomore year and tried out for the team my junior year."

"How long did you train?"

"For over a year."

"Seriously?"

"Yes. My big brother at the frat got me into biking. He convinced me to pledge Alpha Alpha Omega. Hunter and I rode a great deal before I pledged and then I trained with the team during my sophomore year and all summer at home after that."

"Damn. I rode a lot this summer, but I haven't exactly trained."

"Do you know how many spots are open this year?"

"Four."

"Four? No one is back? What happened?"

"Three riders last year were seniors. The fourth transferred."

"Wow. I don't know if there has ever been zero returning riders. The new team will need a damn good coach. Experienced riders are critical."

"Yeah it's not a good situation, but at least it gives me a better shot at making the cut. I've got to make the team. Any tips?"

"Train hard. Start now and push yourself. Don't overdo it, but work to increase your endurance and speed. Back in my day we worked on endurance some days and on speed others. You should also hit the gym. Focus on your legs, but don't neglect the rest of your body. You have to take it seriously if you're going to have a chance to make the team."

"Okay. It sounds like more work than I was anticipating, but I can do it. Maybe it will give me an edge."

"That depends on the competition."

We pulled into the U-Haul rental location. I returned the truck and Kevin surrendered my keys.

"Damn, I want this car," Kevin said.

"You can get your own someday. Once you graduate and begin earning money it's much easier. Believe me. I'll let you in on a secret. College is great, but it's actually more fun being my age."

Kevin grinned.

"I'm going to park at the frat and we'll walk to Mother Bear's. I assume there is still no parking there. Right?"

"Yeah. One of the advantages of living in the house is being able to walk everywhere. There is never a place to park," Michael said.

"I guess some things never change."

I drove to the frat and parked the Camaro. We walked the short distance to Mother Bears Pizza, claimed a booth, placed our drink orders, and browsed the menus.

"What does everyone like?" I asked.

By the time our waitress returned I knew what everyone wanted so I ordered three large pizzas; one pepperoni, one sausage, mushroom, and green pepper, and one with everything.

"Do you guys still do paddling during initiation?" I asked

"Yeah and I'll admit I was scared. When you think an entire frat is going to beat your ass it's a frightening experience," Michael said.

"Hearing screams in the next room doesn't help either," Kevin said.

"During my first initiation as a brother, one of the pledges went off on me during the paddling initiation and walked out," I said.

"Really? He left?" Cam asked.

"Yeah and everyone was glad to see him go. He was a dick."

"I bet you have a lot of stories," Kevin said.

"Quite a few. Have you guys met your roommates yet?"

"None of our roommates show up until next month," Michael said.

"Let me tell you about my roommate. He was known for being odd. No one wanted to room with him so the council pulled a name out of a hat and I lost."

"Ouch! That sucks!" Kevin said.

"Yeah. That's what I thought, especially when I opened the door to a wardrobe and he was inside hanging upside down like a bat."

"Seriously?" Cam said.

"Yeah. He did a lot of strange things. It wasn't usual to walk in and find him listening to three pieces of music at once or reading three or four books at the same time. He stared at me a lot too."

"What a freak," Michael said.

"That's what I thought at first, but I grew accustomed to his oddities and gradually realized he was brilliant. Then, he asked me to accompany him to an event. He led me to the art museum on campus where he unveiled a full-sized nude statue of me in front of scores of people."

"Nude? Was he a homo?" Kevin asked.

"Dude," Cam said, elbowing him.

"No. He wasn't, but I am."

"Oh. Shit. Sorry. I didn't mean... It's just..."

"We're not monsters you know," I said, grinning at Kevin's discomfort.

"I know I'm just..."

"Being a dick?" Michael suggested. Kevin reddened.

"I'm sorry," Kevin said.

I nodded.

"Wait. I've heard about this. Are you taking about Adam Abernathy?" Michael asked.

"Yeah. That's him."

"*The* Adam Abernathy carved a sculpture of you?"

"We just called him Adam back then, but yes, he carved a nude statue of me posing with a bike without my knowledge. It's in the Cincinnati Art Museum now."

"Were you pissed?" Cam asked.

"Dude! That's a huge honor," Michael said.

"You'll have to forgive Michael. He gets a hard-on for famous artists," Kevin said. I laughed.

"I was embarrassed, but yet I felt honored. I also had no idea why he chose me as a subject. Are you an artist Michael?"

"Graphic artist, but I have a great interest in traditional art as well."

Cam pretended to yawn. Michael reached across the table and smacked him in the head.

"Hey!"

"I knew Adam Abernathy was a brother of our chapter, but you actually roomed with him. That's incredible! That's like... hanging out with Andy Warhol or Jackson Pollock."

"He was bizarre, but there was a reason for everything he did. He's actually a genius when it comes to art. He's also a really great guy. We asked to room with each other the next year. When he sold the statue he gave the frat and me each $10,000."

"Holy shit!" Michael said.

"Yeah, I put it in the bank. It was the beginning of my savings for the building you were just in."

"So you own that?" Cam said.

"I own most of it. The bank owns the rest. I'm opening a bike shop downstairs and living upstairs."

"A bike shop?" Cam said, growing more interested.

"Yeah, opening a bike shop has been a dream of mine since college. I'll probably add skating equipment later."

"Do you keep in touch with Mr. Abernathy?" Michael asked.

"Why? Want a date?" Kevin said, then reddened. "Sorry, I didn't mean anything by that," he said, looking at me.

"Relax Kevin. Yeah. I haven't seen him since I graduated, but we write or call now and then and exchange Christmas cards."

"I would love to meet him."

"If he comes to Bloomington, I'll introduce you."

"Thanks!"

Our pizzas arrived and the boys dug in. We didn't talk nearly as much for quite a while. If there is one thing college boys excel at, it's eating.

We talked and laughed more frequently when half the pizzas had been demolished. It wasn't quite like being with my old frat brothers, but I enjoyed myself.

There was very little pizza left when we were all stuffed, but we had it boxed up and I told the guys to take it. We walked back to the frat, said our 'goodbyes' and then I drove the short distance to my new home in Bloomington.

I didn't go inside immediately, but instead crossed Indiana Avenue onto campus and then walked along the path by the stream known as the Jordan River. I remembered all the fun times I had experienced in Dunn Meadow playing Frisbee and football and sometimes doing nothing more than sunning on the grass. Bloomington and especially the IU campus was filled with memories.

Soon, the IMU, short for Indiana Memorial Union, came into view. It is the largest student union in the world but I had been inside so often that I no longer got lost. I considered walking to my old dorm, Briscoe, but it was several blocks away up near the stadium. I lived there at the beginning of my college years with my boyfriend Dorian. We kept in touch, but I missed him.

I missed all the Verona boys; Brandon, Jon, Brendan, Casper, Ethan, Nathan, Dorian, Shawn, Tim, Dane, Tristan, and Scotty. I kept in touch with all of them. Some of them still lived in Verona, but others had spread out across the country. None of them were here and it made me feel lonely. None of my old frat brothers were here either. I especially missed Hunter and Alessio. I wished we could all be together again, but that time had passed and would never come again. That was all the more reason for enjoying the present. This time would never come again either and I was about to embark on a new adventure. No doubt much had changed in Bloomington during the years I was away, but at last I was back.

***

I returned to my apartment. It was time to get to work, but first I took a moment to gaze out the large windows that looked down on Kirkwood Avenue. I had a great view of the restaurants and shops directly across from me. Down the street I could see Kilroy's on Kirkwood, better known as KOK, which was the bar most frequented by the IU crowd. Just beyond was Jimmy John's, one of the best sub restaurants anywhere. I was certainly going to enjoy having a huge selection of restaurants close at hand again.

I turned from the window and my eyes fell on the stacks of boxes in the living room. I left those for the time being and set to work in the kitchen instead. I would need dishes and silverware before I would need anything else.

My microwave already sat on the counter. The microwave was my best friend. I rarely cooked anything that could not be nuked. I unpacked a few pots and pans, plastic storage containers, glasses, plates, and bowls. As I did so I made a list of items I needed, mostly food. I had brought such things as plastic wrap, paper towels, and such from my old place so I didn't have to worry about any of that, but I had almost nothing to eat in the apartment. I needed to hit Kroger to stock up on cereal, bagels, cream cheese, bread, peanut butter, Pop-Tarts and other items I considered necessities.

I felt strange being in a new place. I had checked out the apartment and retail space thoroughly when the realtor gave me the grand tour and again with an inspector, but I had forgotten many of the details. The kitchen was the smallest room, apart from the bathroom, and that was fine by me. A serious cook wouldn't like the space, but I much preferred having more living room and bedroom than kitchen space. The extra bedroom was going to come in very handy while I was unpacking because it was a great place to stash boxes as I emptied them one by one.

The kitchen slowly took shape as I emptied the boxes. I tried to organize as I went along because I hated having to search for things. Next, I turned my attention to setting up my TV and DVD player. My apartment was too quiet despite some traffic noise coming up from Kirkwood. I also set up my laptop and checked to see if the Internet connection was working. I had arranged for service to be turned on before I arrived and had splurged on high speed Internet because I could use it for both my apartment and business. I was going to enjoy high speed Internet. Back in Verona the Internet speed was slow. I had a feeling the online world would become more and more important in the coming years and, if so, I was prepared.

My connection was up so I checked several orders I had made for the shop. The first delivery was scheduled for the next day and I had more coming in daily for the next several days. Tomorrow, I would focus on getting the shop downstairs ready for stock. There were more tasks to be completed than I cared to think about, but I would soon have help. I had received several applications for the few positions I needed to fill and the first interviews were tomorrow afternoon. The window and sign painter was coming tomorrow as well. I might have been wiser giving myself a couple of days to settle into my apartment before busying myself with the shop, but I had waited for years to open my own bike shop and I didn't want to wait any longer.

Satisfied that there were no imminent disasters to head off I got offline and began unpacking and putting away everything I might need the next morning. That reminded me that I needed to put up the shower curtain, which reminded me to unpack the towels and washcloths, which led me to seek the box that contained soap and shampoo, and so on. The time slipped away and it was midnight before I knew it.

I walked to the windows and peered down at Kirkwood Avenue before turning in. Kilroy's was busy and cars passed on the street below. This was not New York City, but Bloomington never slept. I, on the other hand, did. I yawned and turned toward my bedroom.

It was then I realized I had not made my bed, but at least the boxes with sheets, pillows, and blankets were sitting in the bedroom. It was only a matter of a few minutes work before my bed was made. I climbed in and lay listening to the quiet sounds of life outside. I smiled. I was beginning my dream at last.

Chapter Two

I laughed to myself as I sat at the table eating blueberry Pop-Tarts the next morning. How many times had I toasted Pop-Tarts in my dorm or frat room during my college years? It was almost as if no time had passed and nothing had changed and yet it was eight years later and everything was different. I had my own place instead of living at the frat. Instead of classes, I had my own business to run. This is what I had worked toward during those years, although it had taken me a year or so to figure out what it was I wanted. I finished my Pop-Tarts and hot tea and then put my plate in the dishwasher.

A few minutes later I headed downstairs. My footsteps echoed in the empty space and I could still smell the fresh paint. I was pleased with the way the walls had turned out. It was exactly what I had pictured when I sketched out my plans for the painters. The walls were cream with bold dark crimson borders at the top and bottom. The effect was pleasing and reflected plenty of light from the large picture windows that faced Kirkwood Avenue and the People's Park next door. Crimson and cream were the colors of Indiana University and many, perhaps even most, of my customers would be students.

The only item of furniture in the shop was a large counter, which had been painted to match the walls. I could already picture the cash register sitting on top and racks of bikes on display in the shop. Near the rear would be the repair area where I would repair and restore bikes.

I walked into the stock room. It was mostly empty, but there were plenty of sturdy metal shelves as well as a set of old gym lockers for employees to store their personal belongings. I wasn't sure how many people I would have working for me. I hoped to have someone in the shop with me most of the time and have someone present who could repair bikes. In order to have two helpers in the shop most of the time, I would have to hire four or more, depending on when those I hired could work. I would likely hire students so I anticipated difficulties in working around their class schedules.

I unlocked the door and swept up, but there wasn't that much to do in the virtually empty shop. The situation changed a few minutes later when UPS arrived with a large order. By the time the UPS driver finished carting in boxes there were nearly two dozen of them in a large stack. Before I could even begin to think about digging into them a large truck pulled up with my shipment of bike racks.

I was kept busy the rest of the morning accepting deliveries and checking off invoices against orders. Before I knew it lunch had rolled around.

I put a sign on the door that read "Back in 15 minutes" in case any deliveries showed up in my absence and walked the short distance to Jimmy John's, where I ordered a country club sandwich, which was made with turkey breast, apple wood smoked ham, provolone cheese, lettuce, tomato, and mayo.

Jimmy John's had not changed. It seemed like yesterday when I had eaten there with Hunter and various other friends and frat brothers during my college years. I almost expected Dorian to come walking through the door, but Dorian was far away, living his dream of being an actor in New York City. I needed to email him some pictures of the shop once I got everything set up.

I took my sandwich and drink back to the shop and sat at the counter and ate. I couldn't wait to get the place up and running, but it would take time to get the shop manned, stocked, and ready for business.

Another delivery arrived before I could even finish my sandwich and it was a big one. It was my order from Trek, one of the brands of bikes I intended to offer in my shop. I was picky about the bikes I sold. After years of riding, I knew the good from the bad. The shop would offer bikes in different price ranges, but anyone who wanted a cheap, inferior bike would have to head to Target or K-Mart.

Before my bike order was unloaded, the sign painter arrived to begin work. He was painting "Peralta's Bike Shop" in large cream letters bordered with dark crimson on the window that faced Kirkwood and another smaller version on the glass entrance door. He was also painting "10% discount with IU Student ID" in smaller letters at the base of the large window. In addition, he was going to create a few special signs for me inside the shop and even an "Open/Closed" sign for the window and door. I had found a painter who was quite an artist and I knew his work would give the shop extra flair.

My first job applicant arrived at one and I interviewed him while we both sat on cardboard bike shipping boxes. I had never conducted an interview before, but my classes at the Kelly Business School at IU had taught me most of what I needed to know about operating a business.

I really liked Jake, the first applicant, and not just because he was a handsome young man. He sounded sincere, mature, and dependable. When we concluded the interview I told him I intended to interview all the applicants before making a decision. He seemed pleased when I told him I would call him by eight p.m. if I intended to hire him.

Most of my afternoon was taken up by interviewing potential employees. They had varying levels of retail experience, but what interested me most was their knowledge of bikes. I wanted those working for me to be able to help customers choose the right bike. I would often handle that myself, but I wouldn't always be in the shop.

I only had one female come in for an interview. She showed up forty minutes late. I told her I wasn't interested in interviewing her because if she couldn't make it on time for the interview she likely wouldn't be on time for work either. I didn't want to deal with someone like that.

I had hoped for a few female applicants. I knew there were girls interested in biking. There was a women's Little 500 in addition to the men's. If any females had applied, and shown up on time, they would have stood a good chance of being hired.

I worked on inventory in the few spare minutes I had between interviews and receiving deliveries. The empty space in the shop was now mostly filled with packages large and small. It would take a great deal of time to sort it all out, but soon I would have help. There would never again be such a huge influx of deliveries, so once I got on top of the situation it would be easier to control.

I made myself a fine repast of macaroni and cheese for supper. It was one of the few things I could cook with my limited supplies. I added extra cheese so it was especially good. I ate at the table while browsing applications and thinking about prospective employees. I had ten applicants, not including the girl who showed up late. I decided to begin by hiring four. I would see how things ran and then hire more if necessary. I was able to eliminate three applicants easily, but picking four out of the remaining seven was difficult. I thought long and hard before I could make a decision. Once I had my list, I began making calls.

***

The newly installed bell on the door rang. I looked up and smiled.

"I'm glad to see you."

"Thanks for hiring me," Travis said.

"You know a lot about bikes and you obviously love riding. That's the kind of person I want working here. The fact that you know about bike maintenance and repair is a bonus."

"So, what's first?" Travis said.

"Paperwork. A W-4, so I know how much tax to withhold from your pay, an I-9 to prove that you're a US citizen, and several other forms and such. Then you can help me assemble bike racks."

I had worked assembling bike racks, both the floor and wall-mounted models since breakfast, but once Travis joined me the work progressed much faster. Jake showed up an hour after Travis and with his help we moved along nicely.

"Have you ever watched *Breaking Away*?" Jake asked as we worked. I laughed loud enough both he and Travis stared at me.

"When I was on the Alpha Alpha Omega Little 500 team, I drove my teammates insane the first year by pretending to be Dave Stoller. I sang in fake Italian, badly I might add, to amuse and annoy them. My little brother in the frat was from Italy so I had him teach me a few phases. I would pretend to go off on one of my teammates in Italian, but I'd be saying something like, 'My pasta is cold.'"

The boys laughed.

"You raced in the Little 500?" Jake asked.

"Twice and we won both years."

"Damn," Travis said. "I didn't know you were famous."

"I don't think that makes me famous. My ex-boyfriend is famous, or at least well known in New York. He's done a lot of Broadway shows."

"Wait. Ex-boyfriend?" Jake asked.

"Yeah. I'm gay. I hope you don't have a problem with that."

"Nah. It's cool. I'm just surprised."

"My older brother is gay," Travis said.

"Is he single? Just kidding," I said.

"You wouldn't like him." Travis smiled.

"So what's it like racing?" Jake asked. That was it for questions and comments about the fact I was gay. I liked these guys.

"I loved it. Training is a huge amount work, but even that is enjoyable. The only negative was the anxiety over screwing up an exchange or making a mistake. During qualifications the first year our team captain jumped off the bike for an exchange and the bike went down with him because his shoelace was caught in the chain. If we had only been allowed one try at qualifying we would have been stuck back in thirtieth place for the race. My first year, we won by a fraction of a second so the tiniest error can cost a team the race. In fact, my first year the times for the top three places were all within the same second."

"I don't think I could handle that on top of school. I love to ride, but that sounds like work."

"It is and it isn't. I played soccer in high school. I looked upon biking as my sport in college. Hunter, our team captain, was on the IU wrestling team and the Alpha Alpha Omega Little 500 team. I didn't think about it at the time, but I'm not sure how he had time to study. Which reminds me... as soon as you guys know your fall schedules and when you'll be able to work let me know. I want to schedule things well in advance. I've hired two other guys as well. I'll be here most of the time, but I hope to have one of you here as often as possible."

"I registered online, but don't have a schedule yet," Travis said.

"Me too."

The afternoon slipped away, but our progress was evident. We assembled and mounted all the display racks and then started unpacking bikes and other inventory. We slowly filled the racks with new Trek bikes and the shelves with bike parts, books, and related supplies. We kept at it until 6 p.m. and then called it a day.

I gazed around the shop after the boys departed. It was beginning to look like an actual bike shop. Most of the racks and shelves were empty and I only had Treks in stock so far, but the shop was beginning to match the store of my dreams. I smiled when I read "Peralta's Bike Shop" on the window and behind the counter. Part of me couldn't believe this was really happening. I wished Dorian was here to see it, but I'd send him photos as soon as it was finished.

The shop began to take shape over the following days. At times, all four of my new employees were setting up at once. I wouldn't need that much help once the shop opened, but for now there was enough work to keep everyone busy. The boys were available more now than they would be once school started so the timing was perfect.

The selection of bikes increased dramatically as more shipments arrived. Beside the Trek bikes stood those made by Cannondale, AMF, and other lesser known, but high quality manufacturers. I mostly stocked bikes suitable for urban riding, but also stocked mountain bikes, and, of course, the single speed AMF Roadmaster required for the Little 500 race. All of the bike brands had one thing in common; I had test driven each brand and found it to be among the best. I had tried more bikes than I could count over the years and many did not make the cut.

I was well aware this was a college town, so I stocked a good selection of quality, but reasonably priced bikes. There were bikes in the shop that cost more than $1,000, but the vast majority were not out of reach for college students. I did not stock cheap bikes because they were cheaply made, but I did have a wide selection of affordable bikes. It wasn't that long ago that I was a student.

I had little time to get out and enjoy Bloomington, but I allowed myself an occasional break from setting up the shop and getting my apartment in order. I took walks on campus, admiring the scenery and the boys. Dunn Meadow, located only a block away from my shop was the best place to check out college guys. It was there that many IU boys tanned or played pickup games of Frisbee, soccer, and football. Viewing all the shirtless hotties in the summer sun reminded me that I hadn't hooked up in a while.

After another day of unpacking, stocking, and arranging I locked up and walked the short distance to campus to unwind. I caught sight of three shirtless boys playing Frisbee on the near end of Dunn Meadow so I headed that way for a closer look.

The boys looked like they belonged in high school, but then the college boys who worked for me did too. I guess the youthful appearance of the college guys was a sign I was getting older. I didn't remember anyone looking so young when I attended IU, except Anton, but then the boy genius actually was fifteen his freshman year.

I surreptitiously checked out the boys playing Frisbee. One of them reminded me somewhat of my ex-boyfriend, Dorian. He had long blond hair and a slim, sexy body with defined abs. His companions were somewhat muscular and gazing at them made the front of my shorts a little tighter.

"Hey, wanna play?"

I turned my head. A boy with curly black ran toward me holding a soccer ball.

"Sure. Why not?" I grinned.

"I'm Laurent."

"Laurent? That's not a name I hear often, or at all."

"Yeah, it's a little unusual."

"I'm Marc."

"Nice to meet you. Come on. With you we'll have ten. Know anything about soccer?"

"A little." I grinned.

I followed Laurent to the group playing soccer a little further up in Dunn Meadow. It was a little after six, but July was nearing August and the sun was still high. It was an especially hot day as well with afternoon temperatures near 100 and it was still in the low to mid 90s.

The others had their shirts off, so I pulled mine off as well. I had kept myself in shape so I wasn't ashamed to do so. I was not in my late teens like the others, but I didn't look too bad for an old guy of thirty.

"Those are the goals," Laurent said, pointing out shirts arranged on the grass at the ends of our makeshift field. "The base of the hill on our left and the path on the right are the sidelines."

"Got it."

I was on Laurent's team along with three other equally young and hot looking boys. Their hard, youthful bodies were a distraction, but I had the ability to focus during a game. The other team was just as alluring, but for now they were the enemy.

It had been years since I played, but my old skills snapped back into place. I never considered myself one of the top players on my high school teams, but I was good. The college boys quickly learned I had moves when I stole the ball from a hunky redhead on the other team, booted it over the heads of the enemy, then dashed in, kicked the ball, and scored.

The guys on my team cheered and slapped me on the back. Our opponents eyed me warily.

"You've played before," Laurent said with a grin. "I thought you looked like a soccer player."

"I might have played a little."

Our game was friendly, but fierce. I could tell some of the guys knew each other, while others had merely joined the game. There was some pushing that would not have been allowed in a real game, but no one got violent or angry.

I was slightly more winded that my younger teammates and opponents, but I kept up well. I had my bike riding to thank for that. I wasn't in condition to race the Little 500, but I hadn't let my skills deteriorate, mostly because I loved to ride. I worked out as well and walked a great deal. It all helped while I played with the younger crowd.

I intercepted the ball and raced down the field, but couldn't get a shot. I kicked the ball backwards with my heel to a blond boy with spiky hair. He zipped around the side, but got hemmed in, and booted the ball back to me. I spotted Laurent near our opponent's goal and booted it over the head of the other team and dropped it right at his feet. He kicked it in for an easy goal.

I had almost forgotten how much fun it was to be a part of a team. I didn't even give the sexy bodies of the boys around me much thought as we played. I was all about soccer. I loved having the chance to play again.

We won 6 – 3. As happy as I was to play, I was glad we called it quits. My chest was heaving and I was starving.

"Laurent, we're going to get a pizza. Want to come with?" called out a boy who had been on the other team.

"No thanks. I have other plans."

Laurent turned to me.

"Want to get something to eat?"

"I thought you had other plans," I said, grinning.

"Eating with you is my plan. So... you wanna?"

"Yeah, I'm starving, but I need a shower."

"Me too. Want to meet back here in say, half an hour?"

"Sounds good."

Laurent sprinted off. I turned and headed back to my apartment.

I walked upstairs and hopped in the shower. I was sweaty, smelly, and nasty. I usually preferred a good hot shower, but I settled for lukewarm and the relative coolness of the water was refreshing. I'd had a blast playing soccer and now I was inordinately excited to have a date with a college boy. Of course, this wasn't actually a date, but a very young and handsome man had asked me to go out with him.

I climbed out of the shower, dried off, and put on some of the cologne I purchased at Aeropostale. I picked out a nice, but casual blue polo and cargo shorts. I wanted to look good, but not like I'd made an effort to look good. Of course, anything was an improvement over the clothes I'd worn during the game.

I walked back to Dunn Meadow where a different group of boys were now playing football. There were some quite attractive boys on the field, but even the least good-looking possessed the beauty of youth. I was still handsome I guessed, but I did not possess the beauty I did in college. I suppose it's relative. I likely appeared young to those who were forty, fifty, or sixty. I was not greatly concerned about it, but my youth had begun to slip away. I missed being one of the college boys, although truthfully I would not have traded places with them. My life was just now truly taking shape.

I spotted Laurent in the distance. He was wearing khaki shorts and a pink polo. Was he trying to tell me something or did he just like pink? Dorian adored pink and he was the most stereotypically gay guy on the face of the earth, so I couldn't help but associate the color with being a homo.

Laurent grinned as he neared. He looked particularly boyish as he did so. How old was he anyway? He certainly couldn't be more than twenty and didn't even look eighteen. He was at least a decade younger than me in either case, but I didn't mind if he didn't.

"Hey, where do you want to eat?" Laurent asked when we reached each other.

"About anywhere, but I'd like to avoid Jimmy John's. It's near my shop so I've eaten there too often lately."

"How about Bub's?"

"Sure, but if you think I'm eating one of their huge burgers forget it."

Laurent laughed.

"I usually go for the quarter pound version. My photo will never be up on the wall. So, you said you had a shop?" Laurent asked as we turned and started walking in the opposite direction.

"I will have a shop when it opens. It's not quite ready yet, but I'm setting up a bike shop near KOK."

"Peralta's? I noticed it."

"Yeah, that's it."

"You own your own shop? That's impressive."

"We'll see how impressive it is after it opens. Most businesses fail."

"So, you must be into biking."

"I love it. I raced in the Little 500 when I went to IU."

"I've heard of that. It's a big bike race. Right?"

"Yeah."

"I'm a freshman so I'm just beginning to find my way around."

"If you're a freshman, why are you here so early?"

"My brother started last year. He has an off-campus apartment and is letting me stay until the dorms open if I get lost when he has a girl over."

Laurent wrinkled his nose with such obvious distaste I could barely keep from laughing. I smiled instead.

"So, are you?" Laurent asked, gazing into my eyes.

"Gay?"

"Yeah."

"Yes. I am. Why do you ask?"

"Because I hoped you were and because I saw you checking out those guys playing Frisbee."

I laughed.

"I hope you don't find that creepy."

"You were merely admiring male beauty. I do that too and I like older guys."

"Well, I am definitely older."

"How old?"

"Thirty."

"Ouch! That's ancient! Just kidding. I find older guys sexy."

"You don't like boys your age? How old are you?"

Laurent wrinkled his nose again.

"I'm eighteen. Guys my age are too immature, not that I can claim to be completely mature either, but older guys are more settled. They know who they are, where they are in their life, and what they want out of life. Like you, you have your own bike shop. Your life has direction while I have no idea what I'm going to do with mine."

"You'll find your way. I did. When I was a freshman I seriously thought I'd go into media and perhaps become a sports anchor, but then I fell in love with biking. I graduated from Kelly."

"Sweet. Older guys have wisdom too. I'm sure I can learn plenty from you."

"Perhaps."

"You've already taught me that I'll figure out what I want to do with my life. Even if you taught me nothing, you seem like a fun guy and you're uber sexy."

"Thanks."

"So, do you like younger guys?"

I grinned.

"Yeah."

"Like, eighteen?"

"It depends on the guy, but yeah."

"Do you like me so far?"

"Yes. What's not to like?"

Laurent grinned and wiggled his eyebrows.

I felt a tad perverted for flirting with a boy barely out of high school, but then he started it.

We walked across the town square, passing places familiar from my college days such as Opie Taylor's and the Bakehouse. I was glad they were still here. When time allowed I would see how much they had changed inside.

A couple of minutes later we arrived at Bub's Burgers & Ice Cream on Morton Street. The sight of the pavilions across the street near the town hall reminded me I wanted to attend the farmer's market on Saturday.

Laurent and I were shown to a booth. We browsed the menus while waiting on our drinks.

"I can't believe so many people can manage to eat an entire Big Ugly burger," I said looking at the scores of photos that covered the walls. The Big Ugly burger patty weighed a pound, after it was cooked.

"I can't believe they named it that. Seriously. Big Ugly does not make one think, 'Mmm, I want one of those.'"

"True."

When our waitress returned we both ordered a 'Settle for Less Ugly" burger which weighed a quarter pound. I also ordered a large order of sweet potato fries with marshmallow dipping sauce to share.

"Marshmallow dipping sauce? That seems unnatural," Laurent said after our waitress departed.

"Trust me. It's great. Are you excited about school?"

"Yes! I can't wait! That's why I'm here early. I wanted time to explore and to check out guys."

I laughed.

"Unless Bloomington has changed, there will be plenty of guys to check out. Once the fall semester begins they will be everywhere."

"I don't want you to get the idea I sleep around a lot. Some, but not a lot." Laurent smiled.

"I don't see anything wrong with hooking up. When I came to IU as a freshman I had a boyfriend. We even roomed together. We broke up after our freshman year so we could play the field. There were too many temptations here."

"Are you seeing anyone now?"

"No. I just moved here and I have too much going on. I'm not against dating, but I'm not especially looking for a boyfriend either."

"Still playing the field?"

"It's more a matter of being spontaneous and seeing who I happen to meet. It doesn't really matter if I end up with a boyfriend, a hookup, or just a pleasant afternoon. All experiences are valuable."

"I like the way you think. I'm not especially looking for a boyfriend. Part of me wants one, but then I feel like this is my time to experiment."

"You're right. It is. There is time to get serious about someone later. I know you haven't quite started college, but four years passes quickly. You never know where you'll end up after you graduate. When I left IU, I hoped to return to Bloomington to open my shop, but that plan was never carved in stone and it took me eight years to get here."

"Yeah. I get what you're saying, but here you are. I'm glad you returned. Otherwise I would have missed you."

Our food arrived and we tackled our burgers. Laurent's eyes widened when he tried a sweet potato fry dipped in marshmallow sauce.

"Oh my god! This is orgasmic!"

I lost it. I hadn't laughed so hard in quite some time.

"At your age that means a lot," I said, when I could once more speak.

"What? Orgasms aren't fun anymore when you're thirty?"

"Oh, they are, but they aren't as intense and the new has worn off by the time you reach my age."

"That's nearly impossible to imagine. I could... but I probably shouldn't talk about that while we eating. You are still interested in sex. Right?"

"Oh, most definitely. I'm older. I'm not dead."

"Good." Laurent grinned mischievously.

I began to breathe a little harder. It had definitely been too long, but I wasn't going to swoop in on this boy like a chicken hawk. I intended to content myself with enjoying his company. I had been a little lonely since moving back. Bloomington seemed empty without my friends and frat brothers. I had the sense of returning to a party only to find that everyone had gone.

"What dorm will you be in?"

"Briscoe."

"Yeah? That was my dorm my freshman year. It's kind of far from main campus and there is no dining facility, but I liked it. Distances aren't a problem with the campus buses. Do you have a bike?"

"No."

"You should get one. It's the best way to get around campus."

"Do you try to sell a bike to every boy you meet?"

"What? No! My shop sells better bikes than you need just to get around campus. Unless you're into biking you're probably better off buying a cheap bike at Target."

"You're not a good salesman."

"Oh, but I am. It's all about matching the right bike with the buyer. Someone who rides several miles a day needs a different bike than someone who merely rides to classes. Someone who rides in town needs a different type of bike than someone who rides off road."

"How much is the most expensive bike in your shop?"

"$2,500."

"Whoa!"

"There are bikes that cost much more. Only a very serious rider will shell out over $1,000 for a bike. Most of the bikes I have run from about $350 to $700. I don't handle anything that isn't high quality. You can't find the bikes I sell in K-Mart."

"How much did the bike cost that you ride the most?"

"I think I paid $650 for it. My dream bike at the time was $1,200, but I was saving up to get my shop going. The Trek I purchased was a big splurge. If the shop is successful I'll trade up."

"At least you can give yourself a discount."

"True. Bikes are my passion. What's yours?"

"Boys, chocolate, and music, in that order."

"Boys were usually at the top of my list in college, until biking knocked them down to second."

"Wow, you really are into bikes. Where do boys rate now?"

"Hmm. Biking is still on top. My shop comes next, although it's related to biking. Boys might come third, although chocolate might edge them out, depending on the chocolate."

"And the boy?"

I nodded. Laurent grinned.

"I'll admit, I'm a little boy crazy, especially now that I'm away from home. I come from a small town where there weren't that many options. Here, the options are extensive."

"Just wait until the semester begins. Your options will increase from extensive to nearly unlimited."

"How *will* I have time to study?"

"You have to make time for that. I did so I'm sure you can. Even my ex-boyfriend managed to study and no one was more boy crazy than him."

"You haven't had a boyfriend since college?"

"No one that significant. No one that meant as much to me."

"Do you miss the boy-crazy boyfriend or have you forgotten about him?"

"I miss him, but we keep in touch. I don't see him often, but we're still friends."

"Wow."

"Yeah. We did what everyone says they'll do when they break up. We remained friends. He lives in New York City. He's an actor and singer."

"What's his name?"

"Dorian Calumet."

"Are you *serious*? You dated Dorian Calumet? Oh. My. God. When my glee club traveled to NYC we saw him in *Cats*. He was phenomenal. Some of us waited by the stage door and he signed autographs for us! He's so handsome! Will he ever come to Bloomington to see you? If he does will you introduce me? You *have* to. Please. Please. Please!"

I began laughing. I couldn't help it. Laurent looked mildly hurt.

"I'm sorry, but you actually sounded a little like Dorian just then. Yes. I'm serious. We began dating in high school. We were even in *Peter Pan* together. Dorian had the lead. He always got the lead when he tried out for it."

"You're an actor as well?"

"No. I only tried out because Dorian convinced me to do so. I didn't think I'd get a part, but I ended up playing Captain Hook."

"So. Will you introduce me?"

"Sure, if you're here. It could be years before he comes to Bloomington. He's rather busy these days."

"That is so amazing you know him and *dated* him."

"I have a life-size painting of him in my apartment if you want to see it. It was painted by a friend of ours as a prop when Dorian had the lead in *The Picture of Dorian Gray* in high school."

"I think you just want to get me to come home with you."

I laughed.

"I don't move that fast these days."

"Pity."

"I'll show it to you if you like."

Laurent raised his eyebrows.

"Oh will you?"

"The *painting!*"

"Ohhh. Yeah. I would love to see it and *anything* else you care to show me."

"You are a shameless flirt."

"It's one of my hobbies."

I spent the rest of our meal answering questions about Dorian. I didn't mind. It allowed me to relive the good times with him. The more I told Laurent, the more I remembered.

"Is this together or would you like separate checks?" our waitress asked when we'd finished.

"Separate," Laurent said quickly.

"I don't mind paying. I know what it's like to be a poor college boy. I used to be you," I said when our waitress had departed.

"I don't want you to think I'm looking for a sugar daddy, not that you're that old."

"I think I'm old enough to qualify. I'm just not old enough to be your actual father."

"Since you were about twelve when I was born I'd hope not!"

We paid our checks and walked back to my apartment. We talked the entire way there. I was glad I'd met Laurent. I enjoyed his company.

I unlocked the shop and we stepped inside.

"It's not all set up yet, but this is my shop."

"This is nice. It's a great location too."

"Location is everything. Plus, I live upstairs so I get a great location for my apartment *and* I have my own parking space. Having a parking space near the university is a big deal here."

"I've heard about the parking, but I won't be bringing my crappy car until next year."

"I had a crappy car when I went to IU too. Perhaps it's a tradition. It was a Camaro and I loved it, but it had... let's just say several problems. Come upstairs and I'll show you the painting."

We climbed the stairs to my apartment. There were still a few boxes scattered about, but I was mostly unpacked now.

"Nice place. Oh, I love the view," Laurent said, walking to the window and gazing down onto Kirkwood Avenue.

"It's not the New York skyline, but then I would hate to live in NYC."

"Have you been?"

"Yeah. I went to visit Dorian. NYC is filled with things to do, but I was glad to leave. It's too big and too crowded. Dorian loves it."

"He must be bold."

"He is. Dorian is probably the most stereotypically gay guy I've ever met. I actually mistook him for a girl when I first heard his voice. In high school, he was fearlessly himself even though some guys gave him a rough time. I've always admired his strength and courage."

I led Laurent into my bedroom and turned on the light.

"Wow."

"Yeah. It's incredible, isn't it? The artist considered it a rush job, but I think it's fit to hang in a museum. He perfectly captured Dorian as Dorian Gray."

"It's beautiful. So is Dorian."

"Yeah. I think he's the most beautiful guy I've ever met and that goes for his personality as well as his physical appearance. A lot of guys would consider him too feminine, but to me he is perfect."

Laurent turned and looked at me.

"You still have feelings for him. Don't you?"

"Yes. I've never stopped loving him, but we make better friends than boyfriends."

Laurent gazed at the painting.

"Man, I'd like to... sorry that's crude."

I laughed.

"I have, many, many times."

"Jerk."

I laughed again.

I led Laurent back into the living room because I didn't want him to think I was trying to seduce him. I sat on the couch and he sat close beside me.

"I really like you Marc and not just because you know Dorian Calumet."

"But that's a plus. Right?"

"Oh, hell yeah! You get bonus points for that, but I like you regardless. I was attracted to you the moment I spotted you. That's why I asked you to play. Now that I've spent time with you I like you all the more."

We grew quiet and gazed at each other. Laurent leaned in and kissed me. I returned his kiss and wrapped my arms around him. We sat on the couch and made out for several minutes. Laurent drove me mad with desire.

"Would you like to go to your bedroom?" Laurent asked when we pulled away at last.

"I don't think we should."

"Why not? I'm into you and I know you're into me," he said, gazing meaningfully at the bulge in my shorts.

"Oh, I want to, but I don't want to take advantage."

"You won't be."

"Let's take things a little slower. Okay? I am interested. Part of me wants to... but I'll feel more comfortable if we don't move straight to sex."

Laurent sighed.

"You know this only makes me want you more."

"I'm evil that way."

"Mmm. Okay, as long as I get you eventually."

"I promise, unless you lose interest."

"Oh, I won't."

We made out for a while more and then I showed Laurent out. Part of me regretted not jumping into bed with him, but I needed to make sure I wasn't take advantage.

After Laurent departed, I made myself a cup of hot tea and sat down at the table near the windows. Had I done the right thing? Laurent was obviously willing to hook up with me. In my college years I would not have hesitated, but I couldn't shake the feeling that I was taking advantage of him. I knew it was nonsense. I could tell Laurent was disappointed. He was most certainly interested. His shorts were about to rip from the strain of his obvious excitement. Why couldn't I shake a feeling I knew was illogical?

Laurent was young. In college, eighteen didn't seem young, but now it seemed extremely young. The idea of hooking up with an eighteen-year-old seemed perverted and yet extremely hot. I guess the age difference bothered me. I was thirty, and while not nearly old enough to be Laurent's father, I *was* twelve years older. I suppose it was best to make sure I didn't harm him, but I knew no harm would have come of it. There was no use in second guessing myself now. I had made my decision. I might never see Laurent again because of it, but even that wasn't so bad. I had spent the evening with a handsome young man. If that was all there was to it, then that was good enough. If there was more, all the better.

I opened my laptop and checked on the status of orders. Bikes and accessories arrived daily now. A few of my orders were delayed, but it was nothing that would cause a problem. There were a few orders I wanted to receive before I opened, but they were due in the coming days. I could have almost opened the shop now, but I wanted it fully stocked. If customers found a poorly stocked shop they might not return.

The grand opening was scheduled for Saturday, August 5. The students would begin to arrive that week and Bloomington would be teeming with people that weekend. It was the perfect time to open my shop. I had partnered with Mother Bears Pizza and Dagwood's and was going to offer a certificate for a free large pizza from Mother Bears with the purchase of any bike and a certificate good for any sandwich from Dagwood's with a purchase of $50 or more. There would also drawings for a new Trek, a helmet, bike maintenance, and gift certificates. In addition there would be free cookies, lemonade, and other goodies. I would also have a sale, but the drawings and free stuff would hopefully draw in people to check out the shop.

I went through my notes and records, trying to figure if I'd left anything out. The flyers and posters were being printed. I had ads coming out in both the *Indiana Daily Student* and the *Herald-Times*. I had already placed orders for cookies and other goodies. Everything seemed to be in order. If it weren't, I would deal with it on the fly.

I gazed out the window and down the street. KOK was busy. Bloomington was already beginning to come back to life after its summer slumber. Soon, the population of the town would double and I would open my shop. I couldn't wait.

Chapter Three

The Grand Opening of Peralta's Bike Shop was about to begin. All four of my employee's were working all day today. I didn't expect a big crowd, but on this day I would much rather have too much than too little help. I quickly ran a last minute check. The cash register and credit card machine were up and running. The cookies and other goodies were in place as were the cards and the box for the drawings. The shop looked incredible. It was hard to believe, but I had over 200 bikes on display. My dream was about to come true.

I unlocked the door and turned the sign to open. No one entered at first, but in less the five minutes the bells on the door rang, then rang again, and again. The shop began to slowly fill.

Travis, Jake, Aaron, and Todd mingled with the customers, being helpful, but not pushy. When I entered a shop I liked to have help available, but didn't like anyone hovering over me. I strived to create the atmosphere in my shop that I wanted to experience in others.

Our first sale was a copy of *Breaking Away*. This wasn't a video store, but I couldn't resist handling the film that meant so much to me. Besides, it was all about biking and Bloomington.

I sold my first bike within half an hour, a Cannondale road bike that was $1,200 on sale, which was quite a good price for that particular bike. Not twenty minutes later I sold a $500 Trek. I hadn't expected to sell two bikes so quickly.

I enjoyed talking to the customers and giving them information and advice on bikes. During the morning Aaron, who was a current Alpha Alpha Omega brother, introduced me to four others, all of whom were into biking to some degree. Two of them wanted me to tell them about the Little 500 races I had participated in and a small audience gathered each time. I felt a bit like a celebrity.

"Just look at him, now he thinks he's really something."

I looked up.

"Brendan!"

I gave Brendan a hug and then hugged Casper.

"You know that sounds like something Brandon or Jon might say," I said.

"That was a message from Brandon. I talked to him on the phone yesterday. He also said to tell you he wished he could be here, but that he'll visit Bloomington sooner or later."

"I'm so glad you guys came!"

"We couldn't miss this so we drove down for the day. We're going to visit a few of our old haunts while we're here."

"Your bike from the Little 500," Casper said, looking at the display high on the wall behind the counter.

"Yeah, I've never been able to part with it."

"A *Breaking Away* poster, why am I not surprised?" Brendan said. I laughed.

Among the memorabilia on the wall was a copy of the photo of Hunter, Conner, Jonah, and myself with the Little 500 trophy as well as posters I'd saved from the years I participated, my helmet, and other pieces.

"I wonder what Brandon would have to say about that," Casper said, pointing to the photo.

"Probably something about an enlarged ego or being a has-been. I wish he could be here to say it in person," I said.

"This is bigger than I expected," Brendan said, looking around.

"Yeah, that's one thing I like about the building. There is plenty of room for stock and bike repair."

"This is great, Marc. Congratulations," Casper said.

"Thanks. What time are you guys heading back?"

"Probably about four."

"I wish I had time to go to lunch with you."

"Hey, we didn't expect you to have time for us today. We'll come down again and we can all go out to eat. We're here today to wish you luck and Casper needs a bike," Brendan said.

"You don't have to buy anything."

"No. I really need a new bike and who better to buy it from? Show me the mountain bikes. In fact, show me the one you would buy for riding around Verona," Casper said.

I showed Casper three different bikes that would be good for town and country riding and then the one I would purchase myself.

"It's blue so it's perfect, unless it comes in purple," Brendan said.

"Purple isn't currently a Trek color choice."

"Pity," Brendan said.

"We'll take it and no giving us an extra discount. It's already on sale," Casper said.

"Okay, but you do get a gift certificate for a free large pizza at Mother Bears. Everyone who purchases a bike today gets one."

"I guess we know where we're eating lunch," Brendan said.

"So what are you guys up to while you're in town?" I asked as I rang up Casper's bike.

"We already visited the stadium, drove by our old apartment, and went to College Mall. Next, we're going to walk around campus and go to the art museum. I'm not sure what we're doing after that. It depends on how much time we have," Brendan said.

"Sounds like fun. I walk on campus often, although I've been a bit busy lately."

"I bet. The next time we come down we can all have lunch in the Tudor Room together. Oh, that reminds me Casper, we have to pick up some cupcakes and no bake cookies at Sugar & Spice."

I grinned.

"It was good to see you guys. Thank you for coming today," I said, giving them both a hug.

"We'll see you again soon," Casper said.

Brendan opened the door and Casper wheeled out his bike. I hadn't been away from Verona long, but I had already missed those guys.

"Marc, can you help me with a customer? He's asking questions about a Cannondale I can't answer," Travis said.

"Be right there."

The rest of the day was busy. My guys each took a lunch break, but I had a sandwich delivered from Dagwood's and ate between helping customers. We sold mostly accessories, but also several bikes. I had no idea how much business to expect during our grand opening, but sales exceeded my wildest dreams. I knew we would probably never have such a day again, but the shop was off to a great start.

When closing time came I divided up the few remaining cookies between the guys, except for two I kept for myself.

"Great job today guys. Thanks," I said.

"I'll see you in morning," Jake and Todd said.

"Have a good evening guys."

When the boys departed, I turned the sign to "Closed," locked the door, and shut off the lights. I took my cookies upstairs and collapsed on the couch. My sole plans for the evening were to eat supper and do absolutely nothing. My feet ached and I felt like I could go to sleep right then, but it was only a little past six. My first day was a great success. I hoped it was a sign of things to come.

***

The bells on the door rang. A handsome young man entered. He nodded at Aaron as if he knew him, then stepped to the counter.

"Mr. Peralta?"

"Yes, but call me Marc."

"I'm Jens Meriwether. I'm the head of the Alpha Alpha Omega fraternity council. Could we have a word?"

"Of course."

"I'd like to talk to you about the Little 500."

"Oh, one of my favorite topics."

"Great. Our team has been decimated. We had three seniors last year and the only rider who wasn't a senior transferred to Notre Dame."

"I heard about that. I don't think that's ever happened before."

"It hasn't as far as I know, but we're in a fix. We need someone experienced. I've come on behalf of the fraternity to ask you to be our Little 500 coach."

My eyes widened.

"This is... unexpected."

"I know you have a business to run, but the team can train around your schedule. If you accept, the team will be yours with no interference. The council will choose the team members as always, but I can almost guarantee we will pick whomever you recommend. I know it's a great deal to ask, but we need you. You reputation is legendary."

"You don't have to flatter me," I said laughing. "I would love to help. Besides, how could I turn down Alpha?"

Jens smiled broadly and shook my hand.

"This is great news and so generous of you. I don't have to tell you about the time involved."

"I'm glad you asked. I live and breathe biking."

"That's exactly why we want you. I wasn't flattering you. You are legendary at the frat."

I smiled.

"If we're going to do this, we had best get started. How many guys are interested in trying out for the team?" I asked.

"Ten."

"Great. That will give us some options."

"Think about when you'd like to meet with the riders and we'll go from there. In the meantime, I'll gather up the manual and entry forms and have it all ready."

"I'd like to meet with them tomorrow. Do you think most of them can make it at 7 p.m.?"

"I'm sure most can, probably all."

"Then I'll come to the frat tomorrow at seven."

"Thank you so much for this Marc."

"Thank you."

Jens departed and suddenly I felt as if I was back in college again.

"Well this just sucks," Aaron said, looking up from a case of bike tubes he was unpacking.

"What sucks?"

"Here I have the perfect opportunity to suck up to get on the Little 500 team and I'm not a racer."

I grinned.

"Sucking up wouldn't help you. You can try out for the team. We haven't started yet."

"No thanks. I heard stories about the training sessions last year. I love to ride, but training for the Little 500 is too intense and I don't think I could handle the pressure if I made the team."

"It does take dedication and there is a lot of pressure."

"I'll stick to leisurely rides, thank you very much, but I will say I think our chances for a win just increased dramatically."

"Brown-noser," Todd coughed into his fist.

"I will beat you with one of these tubes, Todd and you'll never be able to prove a thing."

I laughed. I enjoyed working with all four of the college boys I had hired. Jake turned out to have great skills in bike repair. He was so good that I generally let him handle them when he was in shop. All four were easy to work with and got along well with each other. Not one of the lot was ever late. Todd had to change his work schedule because of a class switch, but it wasn't difficult to accommodate him. So far, I had no problem getting along with my four employees.

My mind was on the Little 500 as I unpacked a new shipment of bikes. I would not be racing, but that didn't matter. In fact, I had no desire to race again. Okay, maybe a little, but I doubted I could compete against college boys. I was far from old, but I wasn't twenty anymore either.

I was excited to coach. There was much I could teach the team. Usually, an experienced team member would coach and pass on his knowledge, but this year there was no current frat brother who had actually raced in the Little 500.

I had never stopped riding. I was not in the shape I was when I was training for the race, but I was reasonably sure I could handle whatever I put the potential team members through. As I slowly built them up, I would build myself up.

The next day at closing, I pulled my old bike down off the wall. No more would it be a mere reminder of past glories. It was going back into action. As the coach, I could have ridden my multi-speed Trek, but I didn't intend to ask the boys to do anything I wasn't willing to do myself. I had learned from Hunter long ago that the best way to lead was by example.

My old Roadmaster was in great shape. I had ridden it little since my college years, but I had maintained it. A little oil on the chain and it was good to go.

I went upstairs and fixed myself a bowl of cereal. I ate out often, but sometimes I liked to "cook." My specialties were cereal, Pop-Tarts, toasted cheese, and any soup that could be microwaved. I actually could cook if I wished. It's just that the desire rarely struck.

After supper, I went back downstairs and wheeled my Roadmaster outside. I climbed on and headed toward the Alpha Alpha Omega house on the backstreets. It had been a long time since I rode a single-speed bike, so I knew I would need time to grow accustomed to it. A single-speed bike was required for the Little 500, so that was what I had trained with back in my day. It paid off. There was a world of difference between a single-speed and even a three-speed.

Riding was difficult at first. I had grown soft. My twenty-one speed had spoiled me. Even so, I knew I would quickly get used to it again. Until the race I would ride only my Roadmaster.

I parked my bike in the rack at the frat and walked inside. Part of me expected to see Hunter, Alessio, Adam, Jonah, and all of my brothers, but they were all long gone and had been replaced by new faces. I reminded myself that these new boys were my brothers too. Once a member of AAΩ, always a member, except for the very rare few who were kicked out.

"Marc, they're all gathering in the lounge," Jens said as he came down the stairs.

"Great."

We walked in together. My eyes were drawn to the Little 500 trophies and framed photos displayed on the wall for a moment, but then I gazed at my younger brothers. There were a dozen of them. I hadn't expected quite so many. I didn't recognize any of them except for Cameron, whom I'd met on my previous visit to AAΩ. He smiled at me.

"Brothers, I would like to introduce Marc Peralta, although I don't think he needs an introduction to those of you familiar with AAΩ Little 500 history. Marc has graciously agreed to coach the team this year."

The guys clapped.

"Now, since I'm not a biker, I'll get out of here."

I stepped forward.

"It's been several years, but I once sat where you do now and before that I had to face the terrifying paddling ceremony."

The boys laughed.

"Only four of you can make team, but you're actually in an enviable position. Most years, there are only one or two open spots and some years none. Most of you won't make the team this year, but those of you who don't will have a better chance the following year. It takes two tries for most to make the team so don't give up.

"We're going in with a disadvantage. To my knowledge AAΩ has never been faced with the prospect of zero returning team members. Not only that, but I'm told there is no one who tried out for the team last year either. That lack of experience may hurt us, but whether or not it does is up to you. I trained for two years and raced in two Little 500s. I know what to do and, more importantly, what not to do.

"I would like to begin training today. You can use any bike to train, but if you're serious, you need to train on a single-speed because that is what you will be using when you race. If you don't have one I do happen to own a bike shop, but that's not why I recommend a single-speed. Really!"

Some of the guys laughed.

"I'm not here to promote my shop, but AAΩ members do get an additional discount and if any of you do want a bike, I will cut you an even better deal. Okay, enough of that. Questions?"

"When will we train and what do we do if we have a class or a sports practice during a scheduled training session? I'm on the soccer team," said a boy with spiky blond hair.

"Excellent question. Most of the sessions will be after six throughout the week. That will avoid conflicts with most classes and some practices. On weekends, we'll have sessions earlier in the day. I know how you guys hate anything that cuts into party time."

All the guys laughed or smiled.

"You will not be penalized for missing a training session, but if you do I suggest you make up for it on your own. I also suggest you train on your own or with others in the group as well. I know all of you have classes and some are on sports teams. You also have lives. I will say that if you miss too many training sessions you won't have a very good chance of making the team because you won't be ready."

"What will we do during the training sessions?" Cam asked.

"Mostly, ride. We will begin with a relatively easy ride and increase the difficulty and length as we go. Some days, we'll ride for distance, others for speed. I will teach you how to make an exchange during the race, which is absolutely critical. We will spend quite a bit of time on that. A single bad exchange can make the difference between winning and losing. The first year I raced, not only did AAΩ win by a fraction of a second, but the time for first, second, and third all occurred within the same second."

"Shit," said on of the boys.

"We will do some weight training, especially on the legs. That is something I encourage you to do on your own as well as with the group. In the winter months, we'll train in the SRSC on stationary bikes, but whenever possible we will ride outside."

"Who decides if we make the team?"

"The fraternity council, based on my recommendations. Anything else?" No one spoke. "Okay, I'd like to start today with a short ride, does anyone not have a bike?" No one raised their hand. "Okay, I suggest a helmet, which you will be required to wear during the race. It's very wise to wear one in any case because sooner or later you will go down and your head won't feel good after it hits the pavement."

The blond raised his hand.

"Yes?"

"Does your shop sell helmets too?" he grinned.

"Thank you for asking. Yes, it does!" I laughed. I liked the blond and that he wasn't afraid to mess with me.

"Let's meet at the bike racks in ten minutes. Also, if you want to have a chance to make the team, you'd better be familiar with *Breaking Away*. There might be a quiz."

Most of the guys headed outside. Cam approached me.

"Thanks for pulling our asses out of the fire. We would be screwed if you weren't here."

"I don't know about that, but I have a lot of tricks to teach you."

"Yeah, I bet those tricks will gain us those fractions of a second that can make the difference between winning and losing."

"They might."

Cam kept talking to me as we walked outside. His eyes also subtly roamed over my body making me wonder if he was gay. He was certainly a very attractive young man. I couldn't get over how much he reminded me of Alessio, my crush and more during my frat years.

I pulled my bike out of the rack.

"This guys, is an official Little 500 bike. It's an unaltered, single-speed Roadmaster. This is what those of you who make the team will be riding."

A couple of the boys looked discouraged, but no one backed out.

"Today, we'll do an easy ride of about ten miles. Don't be afraid to bunch up and ride close, even though it may result in a collision. During the race, the bikes are often so close they touch, so you need to get used to it.

I put on my helmet and gloves and climbed on my bike.

"Let's head out. Hopefully you can all keep up with an old man."

Some of the guys laughed. We rode out of the AAΩ parking lot onto 3rd Street and headed west. We turned right on Indiana Avenue, and rode toward the stadium. As we rode, the years melted away. I almost expected to see Hunter, Alessio, Jonah, Conner, and the others riding by my side.

We rode through Bloomington at a leisurely pace, passing the Mather's Museum and homes rented out to students. After a few blocks we reached the northern end of Indiana Avenue, which stopped at 17th Street across from Memorial Stadium where my friends Brendan, Shawn, and Tim once played football. We turned left on 17th, then right on Dunn Street and rode it past the stadium, across the bypass, and into the country.

It had been years, but I had followed this route more times than I could remember. I rode here when I was trying out for the team, then with the team, and often on my own. As I gazed at the young boys riding beside me I could almost forget that most of a decade had passed and that I was no longer a student at IU. Part of me wished I could remain in those years forever, but there was much to be said for being older. It was easier being thirty than it was twenty. My life was more settled now and yet not in the least boring. I no longer temporarily lived in Bloomington wondering where the future would take me. This was my home now and I never planned to leave.

I often almost forgot it myself, but I was born in Bloomington and lived the first years of my life here. I even attended grade school here, but my memories of those times were fragmentary at best. If I had thought about it then, I would have probably thought my life would go on and on and I'd never leave Bloomington. That's what it's like as a kid. One never thinks things will change then, but they always do. My family moved to Verona and I did not return to Bloomington until college. By then, my memories of the place I was born were so vague it was as if I had never been here before. Now, I was back again.

We rode well out into the country. The temperature was warm enough to work up a sweat, but not uncomfortable. I had ridden in blistering heat, horrible humidity, and torrential downpours when I was trying out for the team. All that might come yet and oddly enough I didn't mind.

After some five miles I turned us back toward town, choosing the route through the valley that passed Cascades Park. Exactly as I remembered, the temperature dropped by about ten degrees as we entered the valley. The difference was sudden and noticeable. It was almost like walking in from the heat into an air-conditioned room. After a while, the park appeared on our right. We rode past a large stream that cascaded down in many small waterfalls. The winding road roofed by trees was a beautiful place to ride. I wanted to share it with these boys as Hunter had shared it with me.

We passed beyond the park and later came to College Avenue. I followed it to 17th Street and we headed east, beyond the stadium and Assembly Hall to Fee Lane. We rode past my old dorm, Briscoe, then McNutt where Brandon and Jon roomed and then Foster, on the left side of the street, where Nathan and Anton once lived. Everything looked the same.

A few of the boys were winded, but none of them were in too bad of a shape. I was pleased to find I could handle our first ride with relative ease. I wasn't doing at all bad for the eldest of the group. I turned left at the bottom of the hill past Foster Quad and tormented the boys with the steep uphill grade. I turned on Jordan Avenue and we rode south, passing the main library and other campus buildings until we reached 3rd Street. There I turned right and in a few blocks we were back at my other old home, Alpha Alpha Omega.

"Not bad guys. That was approximately ten miles. We will work our way up to fifty, which is the length of the race. For those of you who can make it, we'll ride again tomorrow at say 6:30."

The guys put their bikes in the rack and most headed inside.

"What time are you open tomorrow? By the way, I'm York," asked a boy with spiky blond hair and blue eyes.

"We're open 10-6 every day, except Sundays when we open at noon. We're closed on Mondays."

"Great. I want to buy a single-speed. I intend to make the team."

"I like your determination."

"See you tomorrow."

"Sounds good."

Cam eyed York as the handsome blond departed. I had the feeling he didn't care much for him, but he smiled again as he looked back at me.

"Are you busy? I'd like to hear about some of your Little 500 experiences. I watched the race last year, but actually racing must be incredible."

"There are invoices at home with my name on them, but they can wait. Thanks for giving me an excuse not to work. That's the problem with working for yourself. It's hard to fool the boss."

"Hard to fake being sick for a day off too I bet."

I laughed.

"I haven't tried yet, but I doubt I'd believe me. I know how sneaky I am."

"Let's walk to the IMU. I'll buy you a Coke," Cam said.

"Sounds good, but I'll buy. You don't want anyone to accuse you of trying to bribe me for a spot on the team."

"Like anyone would ever know."

"It's harder to keep secrets than you'd think."

Cam and I crossed 3rd Street and walked onto campus. As I walked beside him I sighed.

"What?"

"Nothing."

"Come on. Tell me."

"It's just that you remind me of someone I knew in college."

"A special someone?"

I nodded.

"Boyfriend?"

"No. During my senior year he was dating one of my best friends."

"Oh, the plot thickens."

"It's not a tale of intrigue and betrayal if you're hoping for an exciting story. It's merely a case of unfulfilled longing and regret. I doubt you want to hear about my feelings for a guy anyway."

"Why's that?"

"You wanted to hear about the Little 500 and it's unlikely that you are gay. Most guys aren't, you know," I said, smiling.

"I do want to hear about the Little 500, but this sounds even more interesting. As for being gay, I never said I wasn't."

Was this young frat boy flirting with me? I thought I detected some interest, but I wasn't sure. I put it out of my mind. I was his coach. There was nothing unethical about getting involved with him because I would not show him favoritism, but still...

"So, what happened?"

"I'll give you the short version. In my junior year I met a boy from Italy at the Alpha Alpha Omega rush party. I was very impressed with him and sponsored him. When he was selected, I chose him for my little brother."

"Did you guys..."

"No. I was attracted to him and had a crush on him, but I didn't want him to feel pressured. I didn't reveal my feelings until he was a brother."

"What happened then?"

"I found out he was already involved with my frat big brother who was also one of my best friends."

"Ouch."

"I didn't blame either of them because neither had done anything wrong. It was merely unfortunate. I really *liked* Alessio, but I couldn't act on it once I discovered he and Hunter were involved. I tried to push my feelings to the side and I succeeded for a while, but my senior year was even more difficult. I don't want to go into details, but it was a hard time for me, but also a wonderful time. It's just that being around Alessio and not being able to have him was rough."

"Yeah, I bet."

"So that's the story. I've kept in touch with Alessio and Hunter. We're still friends."

"They're still together?"

"Yeah. They're as good as married. I'm very happy for them, but yet I feel a little left out. I could have spent my life with either of them."

"And I look like Alessio?"

"Very much so. If you had an Italian accent I could almost believe I'd stepped back in time."

"It's probably a good thing I don't have an Italian accent then."

"True, but enough about that. Let's talk about racing."

We had passed Lindley and Kirkwood Halls by then and were nearly to Wiley Hall. I turned to the left and led Cam to the Rose Well House.

"Do you know the significance of this place?" I asked, indicating the small limestone pavilion.

"I know that those who kiss inside at midnight on Valentine's Day are destined to marry or stay together forever or something like that."

"True, but it's also where part of *Breaking Away* was filmed."

"You mentioned that movie during the meeting. It's really about the Little 500?"

"Yes. It's my favorite film. You *have* to watch it."

"I'm eager to see it."

"Remember this place. You'll recognize it when you see it." I laughed.

"What?"

"I drove those who were trying out for the team crazy my junior year by pretending to be Dave Stoller, the main character. I sang in mock-Italian while we rode."

"Dave was Italian too?"

"No. He was from Bloomington, but pretended to be Italian to impress a girl. I had Alessio teach me a few Italian phrases so I could mess with the other rider's minds. I pretended to insult them in Italian, but I was actually saying something like, 'It looks like rain today.'"

Cam laughed.

We turned and walked toward the IMU. Soon, we stepped inside and walked down the hallway that led to the South Lounge. There were only a handful of students in the lounge, but during the day there usually wasn't a seat available. I gazed at the fireplace as we walked past. No matter the time of year, there was also a fire going. This winter, I wanted to come over and sit by the fire and read.

We left the South Lounge and walked down another hallway.

"Have you eaten in the Tudor Room?" I asked as we passed it.

"No."

"You have to try it. It's wonderful or at least it was when I went to school here."

"I will sometime."

We walked past the bookstore, then down the stairs to the next level.

"I kept getting lost in here for my first two years at IU," I said.

"I still do get lost."

"It is the biggest student union in the world."

"Yeah, and what's up with the names of the floors? Lobby level, mezzanine... I mean what's wrong with 1st, 2nd, and 3rd? Cam asked.

"I think it's an intelligence test. It was probably the psychology department's idea. They probably have hidden cameras and watch students and visitors try to deal with finding their way.

"Ah, here we are at another of my favorite places on campus. Sugar & Spice."

I ordered a large drink and a chocolate chunk cookie. I was hungry after my ride. Cam ordered the same.

We filled our enormous cups, then walked down to the Commons and found a table not far from Burger King. Most of the restaurants were closed at this hour so there were plenty of places to sit.

"Is this place still crowded at lunchtime?" I asked.

"It's crowded from about 9 a.m. until 5 p.m. It's hard to get a table most of the time."

"I see little has changed."

"So how does it feel to race? I bet it's exciting. Is it frightening? Did you feel like hurling because you were so nervous?"

"It is exciting. I was anxious each time I waited for our rider to come in so we could make an exchange. I was keenly aware that if I screwed up the exchange I could lose the race right there. Once I began to move, all that went away. I focused entirely on my bike and the other riders. I could hear the crowd cheering and was aware of my teammates in the pit each time I passed, but my focus was on those thirty-three bikes or at least those around and in front of me. While I was riding I was always looking for an opportunity to advance while keeping an eye out for danger. There are usually a few wrecks and being involved in one can cost a team the race. When I was on the bike, the race was my entire world. I think you'll have to experience it to truly understand."

"I hope I get the chance."

"You have a lot of competition, but there are four spots open so that increases your chances. You could be competing against as many guys for one or two spots."

"True."

"Some will drop out before the actual tryouts for the team."

"Yeah?"

"Every year there are usually at least a couple who decide they can't handle it. Practices can be rough and training is rougher. Some guys figure out they can't spare the time or aren't willing to put out the effort. Most will go the distance, but not everyone."

"I'll go the distance. If I don't make the team it won't be because I didn't put everything I had into it."

"I like your attitude. It will help you."

"I don't mind telling you I want this bad."

"You sound like me when I tried out."

"Yeah and you made the team and won the Little 500. Twice."

"Well, I did have a little help. I wasn't the only Alpha rider out on the track." I grinned.

"True, but I think you were the best there ever was."

"I doubt that."

"The guys still tell the story of how you won the race your senior year. You are legendary. That can't be said about anyone else."

"I'm glad I don't have to race again. I'm not sure I can live up to my reputation."

"Come on. I bet you'd love to get on that track again."

"Yes. I would love to race again, but I'm a decade older than most of the guys who will be racing. I couldn't do what I did when I was in school."

"You look like you're in great shape."

"I am, for my age, but that still doesn't make me twenty."

"I think there's something to be said for older men."

The expression on Cam's face at that moment made the front of my shorts grow tighter, but I tried not to let on.

"Not when it comes to racing."

"I'm sure your experience makes you very talented at *other things*."

The boy was definitely flirting. I pretended not to notice and took a bite of my cookie.

We kept talking about training and racing, but there was a slight undercurrent to our conversation. Perhaps Cam was merely a flirt, but I was fairly sure he was interested in me. First Laurent. Now Cam. I guess I hadn't completely lost my sex appeal.

I had a rather pleasant evening sitting in The Commons talking with Cam. Our cookies were gone and our cups empty long before we ceased. It was dark when we headed back to the frat. I didn't like to ride at night, so after I bid Cam goodbye I walked my bike home. Using the most direct route, it was a less than ten-minute walk.

I didn't have a problem with self-esteem, but having two young men express interest in me since I returned to Bloomington made me feel rather good about myself. Everything was going well. I was back in Bloomington, the shop was a success so far, and I was coaching the AAΩ Little 500 team. I don't think I could have come up with a better life.

Chapter Four

"Do you sell tricycles?"

I looked up from the receipt I was writing out for York's Roadmaster. Laurent grinned.

"Sorry, we had a big run on those this morning. An entire first grade class came in and bought us out."

"Damn. Now I'll have to walk."

York laughed.

"Thanks, Marc," he said.

"I suggest riding on side streets until you get the hang of a single speed. It is an adjustment."

"Will do. I'll see you at the next practice, Coach."

"Coach?" Laurent asked after York departed.

"I'm coaching the Alpha Alpha Omega Little 500 team."

"And here I thought you'd graduated."

"Oh, I did. Long, long ago."

"Not that long."

"True."

"So why are you coaching?"

"Because my frat asked me."

"Do you get paid?"

"No. I'm doing it because I love biking and it's fun to hang out with brothers from AAΩ again."

"Hey, you get to hang out with me at least three days a week," Aaron said.

"True, but I have to pay you."

"You better believe it!"

"Aaron is a frat brother," I explained.

"Oh, so it's like a nepotism thing. You only hire Alpha Alpha Omega boys. It's a good thing I don't need a job," Laurent teased.

"I have four guys working for me. Aaron is the only member of my frat."

"So, no girls huh?"

"Actually, only one applied and she showed up forty minutes late for her interview, not a good move. I have no problem with hiring females unless they are going to come in late."

"I guess they're okay, but they aren't my favorites." Laurent winked.

"What are you in the mood for this evening?" I asked.

"Well, since you asked..."

"I mean what kind of food."

"Do you like Indian?"

"Not so much."

"Good, I hate it."

"Then why did you ask?"

"It was a quiz. Mexican?"

"I love Mexican."

"Good, me too."

"It's nearly closing time. Once we shut down and lock up we'll head to the east side. I feel like eating at Casa Brava. It used to be good. Hopefully that hasn't changed."

"It's yummy, but then I haven't found a Mexican restaurant I don't like," Laurent said.

"Great."

Aaron and I shut down the shop while Laurent waited. I let Aaron out the front, then locked the door and turned the sign to "Closed." I turned off the lights and led Laurent out the back.

"I do like your car," Laurent said as we climbed in the Camaro.

"I'm partial to Camaros myself. It was tough giving up my old one, even though I had no choice. It finally died on me. I have a lot of great memories of that car."

"Especially the back seat I bet."

I smiled.

"Yeah, the back seat and the hood."

Laurent raised an eyebrow as I started up the Camaro and pulled out of my parking spot.

"So, you've been playing with the frat boys, huh? I'm jealous," Laurent said.

"I've been training them. When I'm with them we spend most of our time on our bikes."

"Most? What do you do the rest of the time?"

"I'm sorry, that's a frat secret."

"Oh, I see. Orgy. I've heard about you frat guys."

"You've watched too many movies. How is school going?"

"Great. I like my classes. It's so much better than high school."

"Yeah, that's what I thought too."

"I like the parties too, although I'm not a heavy partier. Don't tell anyone, but I don't much like drinking."

"I didn't either. A little is okay, but I never enjoyed feeling out of control."

"Some of the guys get wasted. I would not want to be them in the morning."

"Have you ever been hung over?"

"Once, in high school. My parents didn't say a word, but Dad made me go to school. It was Hell."

I laughed.

"Have you ever been hung over?"

"No and it's an experience I hope to avoid, along with a burst appendix, falling off a cliff, and other equally fun adventures."

"I haven't experienced the other two, but if they are anything like a hangover I will pass. My only real vice is sex."

I smiled.

We soon reached Eastland Plaza on 3rd Street near College Mall. Casa Brava was directly across from the mall itself. I parked and we walked inside.

Soon, we were seated at a booth in a quiet corner. Our waiter took our drink orders and brought us chips and salsa. I waited to try the chips until he also brought us water in case the salsa was too hot, but it was just right.

When our waiter returned Laurent ordered Enchiladas Verdes and I ordered a steak Burrito Loco.

"There are so many hot guys on campus," Laurent said as we ate chips and salsa.

"Really? I hadn't noticed."

"Sure you didn't. You even told me you and Dorian broke up because there were so many hot guys around."

"Yeah, but I only hooked up with half of them."

Laurent nearly choked on his water.

"If you hooked up with half the hot guys on campus you wouldn't have had time for classes."

"Or sleep."

"Did you hook up with a lot of guys?"

"A fair number, but I don't think I'd call it a lot. I tended to stick with the same few with a new one thrown in now and then."

"That sounds like me. I wouldn't want just a series of one-night stands and I wouldn't mind finding a boyfriend. Yeah, I know you said I should wait, but I want one."

"It depends on who you meet. College is a great time to play the field, but if you meet someone very special then you should date him. I had friends who met someone in high school and are still with them."

"Really? I thought high school romances never worked out."

"I know a handful that have. My friends Brendan & Casper, Ethan & Nathan, and Shawn & Tristan are still together."

Our orders arrived. The unbelievably fast service at Casa Brava obviously hadn't changed since my school years. The food smelled delicious.

"How is it?" Laurent asked after I'd taken a bite.

"It's crazy good."

Laurent paused for a moment.

"Oh, I get it. Burrito Loco," he said.

"Yeah, you have to love the name."

Laurent sighed.

"It's nice to get away from school."

"You can't be tired of it already."

"No, but I spend a lot of time in classes and even more reading. Sometimes I feel as if I do nothing but read. I have papers I need to start and... well, there is too much to do all at once."

"You'll get it down. The beginning of the semester can be tough, but once you get on top of things it's easier. I always worked ahead and got everything out of the way as soon as possible."

"Please don't tell me you were one of those guys who handed in their research papers early."

"Very early."

"Oh, I hated guys like you in high school!"

I laughed.

"I wasn't like that so much in high school, but in college I figured out than since I had to do the work one way or another, I might as well get it done. Not only did I not have to worry about papers when everyone else was frantically trying to finish. I had the pleasure of making them all hate me."

"You're a little bit evil."

"Oh, I'm a horrible person. I never share my chocolate and I go around at Christmas and tell kids there is no Santa Claus."

"I bet you don't."

"Okay, I made the part about Santa Claus up, but I tend to hoard chocolate."

"Who doesn't?"

We continued talking while we ate. I enjoyed Laurent's company. I had looked forward to our time together all day and had even given what I chose to wear special consideration. If I wasn't careful, I could fall for this boy and therein lie danger. In four years he would graduate and most likely leave Bloomington forever.

"You want any dessert?" I asked when we had nearly finished.

"Oh God no."

"Me either. I usually don't make it this far. I take a box home with me most of the time. My idea of cooking is heating the leftovers from the night before."

"I'm actually a good cook, but in my dorm I'm limited to my microwave."

"I can cook, but I don't like to all that much so I usually don't."

We paid our checks and walked back out to the car.

"Let's go to your place," Laurent said.

I had the feeling we would do more than make out if I took Laurent home. I had stopped things before they went too far on our first "date," but I'd thought a lot about the situation since then. I was twelve years older than Laurent, but what did it matter? He was obviously interested in me and he was old enough to make his own decisions. He was also very attractive and he knew how to kiss.

I drove back to my apartment and parked behind the shop. We went inside and up the stairs. I flipped on the lights.

Laurent stepped toward me, pulled me close, and kissed me. I didn't resist as he pulled me toward the couch.

Our lips explored and our tongues entwined, increasing my need and desire for this handsome young man ten-fold. When Laurent's hands began to roam I didn't stop him, but instead ran my hands over his torso. He was so slim I could feel his abdominal muscles even through his shirt.

I began to breathe harder. I pulled Laurent close and ran my hands down to his ass. He pressed against me and moaned slightly, then leaned back and tugged at my shirt. I allowed him to pull it off and then removed his own.

Laurent wasn't muscular, but was slim and defined. I loved the shape of his sexy torso and his small brown nipples. I nibbled on his ears, licked his jawline, and chewed on his neck, making Laurent moan louder. I lowered my lips to his chest and licked and sucked on his nipples. He whimpered with pleasure.

Laurent grabbed my head and pulled my face to his. He kissed me passionately while his hands roamed all over my torso. I groped the bulge in his shorts. He was hard as a rock.

I pulled Laurent to his feet and led him into the bedroom. We undressed each other as we kissed. The moment we were naked, Laurent sank to his knees and pulled me into his mouth. He was young, but he knew what he was doing. Of course, I did too at his age. By eighteen I was quite accomplished.

I gazed down at Laurent as he made me moan. He looked up at me and the sight very nearly made me lose control. I closed my eyes and concentrated on exquisite pleasure. Laurent was a talented boy. I let him keep going until I was near the edge, then I pulled him to his feet, kissed him, and pushed him down on the bed.

I leaned in and had him moaning in seconds. I only traveled up and down his length half a dozen times before he groaned and lost control. I kept going until he finished, then climbed up on the bed with him. He immediately crawled on top of me and put us in a sixty-nine position. He was already up to go again.

For the next several minutes we brought each other pleasure. When I couldn't hold back a moment longer I moaned loudly to warn Laurent and then cut loose. Laurent groaned and experienced his second orgasm of the evening.

Laurent climbed off me and then into my arms. He lay his head on my chest and I wrapped my arms around him.

"That was freaking incredible," he said.

"You're a talented young man."

"Not as talented as you, daddy." Laurent giggled.

"Hey, I'm not *that* much older than you."

"It wouldn't bother me if you were. Age is just a number. Besides, I like older men. They are so much better in bed and so much better period."

"After your performance I think there's something to be said for youth."

"I can go again if you want."

"I'm good for tonight."

"Me too. This is nice."

Laurent cuddled up to me and kissed me.

"Can I stay tonight?"

"I don't see why not."

It was early, but we fell asleep in each other's arms and didn't awaken until the next morning.

***

"I love *Breaking Away*," Cam said as we sat in the Alpha Alpha Omega lounge while waiting on the rest of the guys for a training session.

"I told you it was a great movie."

"I recognized several locations on campus; Franklin Hall, the Back Alley, the Commons, and others. Dave made a great Italian. I loved his accent. Maybe I should try to sing in Italian as you did when you tried out for the team." Cam switched to an Italian accent for the last sentence.

"I wouldn't advise it. I think I was in danger of being beaten when I did it."

Cam laughed.

"Okay, maybe not, but I can see why it is your favorite film. You even look a little like Dave Stoller in the photos on the wall."

"Very little."

The guys slowly gathered until we were all present. We headed outside and began our ride.

As I did at the beginning of each ride, I spent a few minutes trying to get the names of the boys down. I knew most of them now. Soaring Eagle was one of the first names I learned, both because his name was so unusual and because he definitely looked Native American. Kang was similarly easy to remember. Kang was from China, but he spoke English better than I. I learned Cam's name early on. Austin I could remember because he had my old room in the frat house. It was more difficult to match a face and name for York, Sam, Matt, Pierce, Reese, and Baxter, but I experienced only minor confusion at this point.

We had already worked our way up to thirty-five miles and only one of the boys had dropped out. He was on the lacrosse team and decided he could not handle both. I was surprised we had lost only one of our number. Training for the Little 500 is not as easy as it looks to a casual observer.

I took us through the hilly country roads near Griffy Lake. Going downhill was a breeze, but uphill was murder. It was a great workout for the calves.

"I think you're trying to kill us," Sam groaned after an especially steep ascent.

"That's my plan. The four who survive make the team."

"Might as well give up now, Sam," York said.

"Never, I will dance on your grave!"

The scenery was breathtaking. There were trees everywhere and their intertwining limbs often formed a tunnel and provided us with welcome shade. Griffy Lake was not large, but the sun sparkled on the surface and looked especially brilliant as we exited a tunnel of trees. This is not a route used often in my day and I doubted I'd bring the guys this way again, but it switched up our training. I wanted to keep each session fresh and challenging.

The guys were very relieved when we hit more level terrain. I was somewhat relieved as well. My legs ached a little, but years of riding had given me very strong calves that helped me deal with tough ascents.

I led the guys back toward Bloomington and eventually to Armstrong Stadium. The gates were unlocked, so we went inside.

"Since you guys are worn out from that little ride, you can rest while I teach you how to properly perform an exchange. Each team must do a minimum of ten during the race. A bad exchange can cost us a win so those who make the team must have it down.

"Let me walk you through it first. The rider on the bike will come in fast, brake hard, and jump off to his left. The rider taking over will climb on the bike from the right side. The rider rotating in should have his hand on the handlebar the moment the rider coming off removes his hand and be swinging his leg over the bike as the other rider gets off. The bike should never fully stop. The more momentum you can keep, the better."

Some of the guys looked more than uncertain.

"I know it sounds difficult. It is at first, but with practice it flows beautifully. We'll use my bike and I want all of you to give it a few tries. This is tough to master. You may even fall so make sure you have your helmet on. Who wants to go first?"

Matt and York put their hands in the air first.

"Okay, Matt, ride the bike around the track one time, then come in for an exchange between this line and this one. If it's outside that space, it's no good. I want you to come in fast, brake hard, and get off the bike as fast as possible."

Matt climbed on my bike and took off.

"York, don't hesitate when he comes in. Your right hand should replace his on the handlebar almost instantly and your butt should replace his on the seat in less than a second. The moment his foot comes off the right pedal, yours should go on. Don't worry if you screw it up the first time. Go for speed."

Matt soon approached, riding fast. He soared in, slammed on his brakes, and jumped off the bike. He actually fell, but didn't take the bike down with him. York did a good job, but his foot slid off the pedal and he nearly wrecked the bike as he took off. In only a few seconds he was racing around the track.

"You did better than you think, Matt. You fell, but you were out of the way. Your fall did not slow up the exchange. You did a very good job.

"Cam, get ready to go in. We'll rotate through everyone until you've all done it twice."

The following minutes were more a parody of exchanges than anything else. Three more riders fell trying to get off the bike and one fell getting on. Two others nearly wiped out while taking off. By the time each of the boys had attempted two exchanges most of them were grumbling or embarrassed.

"Okay guys. You suck."

Every head snapped up. I laughed.

"You weren't expecting me to say that, were you? It's true, for the most part you suck, but no worse than any rider on any team in the history of the Little 500. Exchanges are difficult and doing them properly takes practice. I brought you out there today to fail so you could get an idea of what to do and what not to do. You need to fail before you can succeed. That said, I witnessed some good techniques. All you need is practice."

"May I ask how you did on your first try?" Baxter asked.

"You may ask... Okay. I'll tell you. I didn't do too badly, except I was a little too aggressive and actually pushed the rider down who was getting off the bike. The timing of my exchange was great, but my execution left much to be desired. I assure you that you will all improve dramatically with practice. Performing an exchange will become so natural that you won't even think about it. Okay, let's head back."

We rode the few blocks to AAΩ and then dismounted.

"Did I do okay?" Cam asked. "My foot slipped off the pedal, which would lose us a second or two in the race, but I'm sure I can keep from doing that the next time."

"You did very well for your first time. I meant what I said; I took you guys onto the track today so you could fail. I purposely didn't warn you about some of the likely problems because you can learn more by making your own mistakes."

"Do you have any more nasty surprises for us?"

"If I told you, it wouldn't be a surprise, but actually no. I want to get you guys on the track and have you ride tightly packed together so you can see what's it like. I know I encourage you to ride close during our training sessions, but it's different on the track, especially on the turns. I will let you guys make your own mistakes before I pass on my experience because as I said, you can learn more by making your own mistakes."

"I can't wait."

Cam's eyes gleamed with enthusiasm. He reminded me of myself my first year.

"Well, I have a test tomorrow so I should study. I'll see you soon?" Cam asked, stepping closer. For a moment I thought he was going to kiss me and my body reacted.

"Yeah, the day after tomorrow," I said, swallowing hard and trying to calm myself.

"Until then."

Cam walked away. He even looked like Alessio from behind. He had such a hot ass. I shook my head to clear it. I should not be thinking of him in that way. I was his coach and I wasn't in college anymore. I climbed on my bike and rode the short distance home.

Bloomington had not changed since my college years. There were sexy boys everywhere. I had four working with me. They surrounded me during Little 500 training sessions and I passed scores of them whenever I walked on campus. I wasn't surprised by their presence, but I was surprised that some of them were interested in me. I had already hooked up with Laurent and I detected interest from Cam. More than a few boys had checked me out on campus. Maybe I hadn't lost quite all my sex appeal.

***

"What are you doing for lunch?"

I looked up from the counter where I was working on invoices and smiled at Laurent

"Probably getting a sandwich from Jimmy John's or Dagwood's."

"No. That's not it. You're taking me to the Tudor Room."

"I am?"

"Yeah. You are."

"I guess we'd better get going then. It's nearly noon now. Aaron, you'll be okay until Jake gets back. Right?"

"I'll be fine. Get out of here."

Laurent and I walked outside.

"I'll pay for my own, but I thought it would be fun to have lunch together somewhere nice."

"No. I'll pay. I remember what it's like being a broke college boy."

Laurent smiled, grabbed my arm, and walked close beside me. I admired his courage, but we only drew a few looks and none of them belligerent. One girl smiled at us. Most of the guys who noticed merely looked a bit surprised.

"I enjoyed the other night. We need to do it again soon," Laurent said.

"Yeah?"

"Yeah. In fact, I want to do it every night!"

I laughed.

"I don't know if I can maintain that pace, but I'll try to accommodate you."

"So do you mind if I stop by this evening?"

"Not at all. I'll give you my number when we reach the Tudor Room."

We walked up the wide brick sidewalk that led between Dunn's Woods and Franklin and Maxwell Halls. The brick was crowded with college students on their way to and from classes or heading out for lunch. August had slipped into September, but Bloomington was still experiencing fine summer weather. It was almost too hot under the noon sun, but the gentle breeze that stirred the leaves of the trees cooled us off nicely.

We followed the path between Maxwell and Owen Halls. A huge ginkgo tree stood on our right. I grinned.

"What?"

"I was remembering one of the first times I walked down this path in the autumn. The ginkgo tree has fruits that smell horrible. It's a beautiful tree with a nasty surprise."

"Maybe I'll take another route come fall."

"You might want to do that. I seriously thought someone had hurled. That's what the fruits smell like when they begin to decompose. It's nasty."

We entered the IMU and walked down the hallway. We passed through the South Lounge where every couch and chair was occupied. I grinned when I heard a boy snoring as he slept on a couch. It was not uncommon for students to sleep in the lounges. As we stepped into the next hallway I paused for a moment to admire a familiar painting.

"Have you ever noticed this?" I asked, indicating the work by T.C. Steele.

"Not really."

"I love the colors. Look at the blue of the sky and the green of the trees. This was painted decades ago, but it looks like it could have been painted yesterday."

"Are you an artist too?"

"No. I have no artistic talent, but I have a couple of friends who are artists. They taught me to appreciate it." I smiled to myself and did not mention the life-size nude statue of me that now sat in the Cincinnati Art Museum. That was a story in itself.

We walked the short distance to the Tudor Room and entered. It had changed little. It will still beautiful and elegant with it's patterned red carpet, linen covered tables, and tapestries and paintings on the walls. I couldn't count the times I had eaten here with my Verona friends. Brendan and Casper especially loved it.

The hostess gave us a small table near a window that looked down over a courtyard. We placed drink orders and hit the buffet. There was a nice selection. I tried tilapia with cranberry sauce, green beans, and mashed potatoes. Laurent returned to our table with creamy asparagus soup, Italian pasta salad, and tilapia.

"This is excellent. I love this place," Laurent said.

"I told you it was great. Aren't you glad you made me invite you?" I grinned.

"Very glad."

"It's probably the best food in Bloomington and I love the atmosphere. It's elegant without being stuffy."

A few of the diners near us were dressed up, but then there were others dressed in sweat shorts and tank tops. Laurent and I both wore cargo shorts and polos. The Tudor Room was very much come-as-you-are and I loved that.

I noticed yet again how very handsome Laurent was as he sat across from me. The more time I spent with him the more I liked him. He was very mature for eighteen and not obsessed with drinking and parties like so many freshmen.

"Oh, did you hear the news? *A Christmas Carol* is coming to the IU Auditorium in December," Laurent said.

"The Broadway production?"

"Yes, starring your ex-boyfriend."

"No. I didn't know that! He didn't tell me."

"It was only added last week."

"I haven't spoken to him in a couple of weeks."

"I have to see it."

"Then I will take you."

"I was hoping you would say that."

Laurent looked at me expectantly.

"Yes, I will introduce you to Dorian."

"Yes! I love you!"

"Oh, I think you're merely using me to get to him."

"Think again, daddy, but the fact that your ex-boyfriend is Dorian Calumet is a nice bonus."

"I'm going to kick his butt for not letting me know he was coming to Bloomington. It will be great to see him again. I haven't seen him since he was home for Christmas last year. I'm glad to get a chance to see *A Christmas Carol* too. I considered flying to NYC to catch it, but I can't get away from my shop for long."

"I can't wait to see him play Scrooge."

I laughed.

"Dorian is as unlike Scrooge as he could possibly be, but he can play any part. When we were dating and he played Dorian Gray in high school I totally believed him when he was up on the stage. It was as if he was a completely different person."

"He must have been fun."

"Dorian is... unique. You never quite know what he's going to do. He also gets excited about everything and I mean everything. He's wonderful and he's intense."

"Maybe the two of you should have stayed together."

"No. We wanted different things in life. Dorian is all about the theatre. He adores NYC. I'm more of a small town guy. I'm far less glamorous and far more sedate. My little bike shop here in Bloomington is my dream."

"You could have opened a bike shop in NYC."

"Perhaps, although I doubt I could have afforded the rent on a retail space there and the cost of living is high. Here, I'm able to buy my own building. It's a small building, but I can afford the payments and when I'm done it's mine. New York is far too big for me. There are too many people and don't even get me started on traffic. I'm convinced most of the cab drivers are insane. Bloomington is more my speed."

"I like Bloomington, but I might want to live somewhere a little larger. I don't think NYC is my style either, but perhaps something in between."

"Life will take you where you belong."

"You think so?"

"Yeah. I groped to find my way when I began college. I seriously considered becoming a newscaster, but then I met Hunter, a rather hunky wrestler with a passion for biking. I began riding with him and before I knew it I had joined his fraternity so I could try out for the Little 500 team. I liked bike riding before I met Hunter, but it wasn't my bliss. Meeting Hunter changed my life."

"Maybe you're my Hunter."

"I doubt it, unless you're beginning to fall in love with biking."

"Not so much."

I grinned.

"It doesn't matter if I'm your Hunter or not because you will find your own or you'll stumble onto the path you need to follow."

"Oh, I hope I have a Hunter, especially if he's a hunky wrestler. Did you guys hook up?"

"Oh yeah. At first we were only biking buddies because I was still dating Dorian, but later we got intense. Then, Alessio came along and I fell for him, but he and Hunter ended up together and I ended up alone. That sounds sad, but alone is exactly where I needed to be then."

"And now?"

I shrugged.

"Alone is still good. I don't know that I have time for a serious relationship. My shop is a lot more work than it seems from the outside. I want to find someone, but it doesn't matter if it's soon or if it takes a long time. I'm happy as I am."

"Well, I like you a lot, Marc."

"I like you too, but you'll be gone in four years."

"That's not a certainty."

"No, but it's likely. That's not to say we can't have fun now."

"I'd like to have some fun *right now*. I want to jump across this table and..."

"That might disturb the other diners and we are having fun. Aren't we?"

"Yeah, but it's not the best kind of fun."

I grinned. "Later, tiger."

"Mmm, yes. You're right. This is fun. I've waited all my life to date a handsome older man, not that we're exclusive. I'm not trying to scare you off. I just mean casual dating."

"I enjoy spending time with you. I was a little reluctant at first because I felt as if I were taking advantage, but then I figured out that was ridiculous."

"Oh, you aren't taking advantage. I want to be with you."

"I think that much is obvious after the other night."

Laurent laughed.

"I hook up with a few guys my age, but they don't have what older guys do. They're good for sex, but not so much for everything else."

"I'm sure some are. It's never wise to generalize."

"I'm sure you're right, but I like older men. I always have."

"That could have been dangerous when you were ten."

"That's not what I meant! I never dreamed of anyone offering me candy to get in their car. I just found older men sexy and mature. When I was ten, I had a major crush on a neighbor who was fifteen. When I was fifteen, I liked a twenty-four-year-old college student. Now, I like you."

"At least you have good taste. I don't know about you, but I'm ready to the dessert table," I said.

"I'm right behind you," Laurent said as I stood, then he whispered in my ear, "so I can check out your hot, hot ass."

I grinned and possibly even blushed slightly.

Laurent and I walked to the front where the best part of the Tudor Room was located. There were so many desserts it was hard to choose. Before us sat pecan pie, lemon pie, petit fours, chocolate mousse, apple pie, peach pie, chocolate cake, cherry cheesecake, as well as cakes and desserts I couldn't name. There were also fresh strawberries, blueberries, and whipped cream. I put the smallest pieces of chocolate cake and pecan pie on a plate, along with a petit four and a few strawberries and blueberries. I made a side trip to the coffee bar for hot tea. Laurent returned to our table with chocolate cake and chocolate mousse with strawberries.

"Back in my college days I made attempts to try all the desserts, but I never succeeded," I said.

"Who could?"

"I think my record was seven and that was counting cookies. I only managed that many by taking the smallest pieces I could find."

"I love desserts. I am a chocoholic."

"It's a good thing you like chocolate. I don't trust anyone who doesn't."

"There is something sinister about those people. Isn't there?"

"Definitely, just like those perverts who like girls. Eww."

"Hey, I have some friends who like girls. They're not so bad," Laurent said.

"I know a few who are okay, two especially."

"I know several. My dad for one."

"So you guys get along well?"

"Yeah. I announced I was gay when I was twelve. My parents didn't think I was old enough to know, but told me they loved me no matter what. My brother's reaction was the best. He just looked at me and said, 'Duh!' I think he knew before I did."

I laughed.

"Is your brother gay?"

"No, Jett is one of those perverts who like girls. For a while, I was dating his girlfriend's older brother."

"That must have been interesting."

"He accidently walked in on us getting it on once."

"Ouch. What did he say?"

"Nothing, but he didn't stick around. I walked in on him and Hailey going all the way about a week later. I didn't stick around either."

I laughed again.

"Jett and I get along well. We fought some growing up, but nothing serious. He didn't have a problem with me being gay."

"I don't have any brothers or sisters. Sometimes, I wish I did. Other times, I feel lucky."

"Are your parents okay with you being gay?"

"Yeah, they've always been supportive. I was lucky. Dorian unsettled them a little at first because he's as stereotypically gay as they come, but it didn't take them long to adjust. He's like another son to them even now. Mom clips out every mention of him in the newspapers and puts it in a scrapbook."

"That's great. Hmm, you didn't ask me the question."

"What question?"

"If my brother and I messed around."

"Well, he's not gay and it's also none of my business."

"Most guys ask."

"I have two friends who are brothers and both gay. They get asked that question a lot. It seems like a lot of people are obsessed with incest. I guess I find it hot in a way, at least in theory, but I'm not into any of my relatives."

"I bet you are and you're just saying that," Laurent teased.

"You wouldn't say that if you knew my relatives. I actually don't have that many. I guess a couple of my cousins are kind of hot, but I don't want to do anything with them. You seem overly interested in this topic. Is there something you want to tell me, Laurent?" I teased.

"Nope. My brother is an attractive guy. He's hotter than me for sure, but I never thought of him like that."

"Well it's a good thing I wasn't hoping for a juicy story."

"Yeah, because I don't have one, at least not an incest story. Now, if you want to hear about me and our high school football team... Oh wait. I'm confusing fantasy and reality again.

Actually, some of the guys on the football team weren't all that attractive."

"I played soccer in high school."

"Oh, any locker room stories?"

"Well, it was a great place for sight-seeing, but I think sex in locker rooms mostly only happens in porn."

"Yeah, but it's a good fantasy. Of course, there is way more to life than sex. Chocolate for one thing. It can be better than sex."

"Are you trying to tell me something?"

"What? No! You're better than any chocolate, Marc."

"Now that is high praise."

We lingered over dessert, talking and laughing. When we departed, Laurent tried to pay for his lunch, but I wouldn't let him.

"Thanks for lunch. I have to get going. My next class is soon. I'll see you tonight," Laurent said, then hugged me. I smiled as I turned away and headed back to the shop.

I walked through the crowded IMU. I almost expected to see Dorian, Brendan, Jon or my other friends. On days like today I felt as if I should still be in school. The fashions may have changed slightly, but otherwise I almost felt like I had stepped back in time. I wondered how long IU would be here and how long students would still fill the IMU. Would the university and the buildings still be here in a thousand years? There were universities in England that had been around for centuries so why not IU?

I walked outside and down the many flights of steps that led to the eastern end of Dunn Meadow. I strolled along slowly, in no particular hurry to get back. I took the time to listen to the running water of the Jordan River and to gaze at the green grass of Dunn Meadow. Of course I did not fail to gaze at the boys lounging on the grass either. I loved this place and to think it was only a block from my home.

"You'd better not let the boss catch you taking such a long lunch," Jake said as I entered the shop.

"Yeah, I hear he's a real bastard."

"Hey, I'm not saying anything. You never know when he might be listening."

"Anything happen while I was gone?"

"Aaron left for lunch about twenty minutes ago. He sold a bike while you were gone. Someone brought in an old Roadmaster for repair and service so I've been working on it since I got back."

"Great. If you need any help with it, let me know, although I doubt you will. I think you're as good at bike repairs as I am."

"That's why I get the big bucks."

I got busy. There was always something for me to do. Taking care of customers was only the beginning. Even with one or two employees to help me most of the time I had my hands full. Quite often, it took both Jake and me to handle the bikes that came in for repair and maintenance. There was a great deal of record keeping as well, plus ordering inventory and keeping track of it all. I was never quite finished with any of it and that was fine by me.

The hours passed quickly. I ate so much at lunch that I only had a banana before heading to Alpha for practice. Only two guys had dropped out so far, so there was still quite a large group of us as we rode through Bloomington and out into the country. Despite my warning, Cam had taken up my old job of singing in fake Italian. The guys groaned, but it also made them laugh. Cam was a much better singer than me so it wasn't as painful for the current crop of Little 500 hopefuls as it was back in my day.

Cam grinned at me mischievously as he sang. He also checked me out a few times. I definitely had another college boy interested in me. I didn't mind, except for the conflict of interest. Then again, there was none. I would make my recommendations based solely on talent, just as Hunter had done years before. When I tried out, I was having sex with the team captain on a regular basis, but I earned my spot. Even if Hunter was willing to play favorites, which he was not, he knew I would have been furious if he favored me because we were involved.

We had a strenuous ride of some forty miles before we returned to the frat. Some of the guys were obviously winded, but most handled the pace well. I constantly watched for potential AAΩ Little 500 material. The problem was that at this point I had too many guys in mind.

"What are you doing tonight?" Cam asked as he parked his bike.

"I have plans. I have someone coming over later."

"Oh." Cam's disappointment was obvious.

"Yeah. Sorry."

"How about tomorrow after practice?"

"I should be free then."

"Good. You want to get something to eat then?"

"Sure."

"Then it is a date," Cam said, giving me a smile that could only be described as seductive.

I hopped on my bike and took off so Cam wouldn't notice the bulge forming in my shorts. You'd think I'd have better control over my dick at my age, but it still had a mind of its own.

I returned to my apartment, showered, dressed in comfortable shorts and a "Peralta's Bike Shop" t-shirt and made myself a baloney, cheese, lettuce, and salad dressing sandwich. Even after the long ride I wasn't especially hungry. Well, I wasn't hungry for food. Laurent and Cam made me hungry for something else. I hoped it wouldn't be long before I heard from Laurent.

I only had an hour to wait for Laurent to call. He arrived a few minutes later. He pulled me straight back to my bedroom and practically attacked me. Young guys were definitely intense. We were naked in moments and were all over each other. We writhed on the bed for two hours, making out, feeling, fondling, and exploring each other's bodies with lips and tongue. I got Laurent off twice with my mouth and then again when I mounted him and gave him what he desired. I even experienced two orgasms and I hadn't done that in quite a long time.

Laurent stayed the night again. I enjoyed feeling him beside me in the night nearly as much as I did the sex. I hadn't slept beside someone on a regular basis since Dorian. I had missed it more than I thought.

I even fixed Laurent breakfast the next morning. I awakened a little early so I slipped out of bed and stirred up pancake batter. I added blueberries and pecans and heated up the skillet. While I flipped pancakes I fried bacon in the microwave. Frying it in a skillet was a messy business and I inevitably got burned when the grease popped so I had long ago switched to cooking it in the microwave. As long as I remembered to cover it with a paper towel the mess was minimal.

Laurent padded into the kitchen area when I was grilling the last of the pancakes. He looked so sexy in nothing but his boxers that I considered ravaging him, but then neither of us had the time.

"You fixed me breakfast? I think I love you."

I laughed.

"There is juice, milk, and tea in the refrigerator. Help yourself then sit down. It's almost ready."

I placed a plate of bacon and a platter full of pancakes on the table and then sat opposite Laurent. His hair was slightly messy, but it only served to make him cuter.

"I usually have Pop Tarts," Laurent said.

"Yeah. That was my usual breakfast in college. It still is quite often. I don't often cook much for breakfast besides maybe toast."

"This is wonderful. Don't worry, I won't get spoiled and expect you to cook breakfast every time I stay over."

"I woke up a little early this morning. Otherwise I wouldn't have had the time."

"Mmm, I love blueberry pancakes. I've never had them with pecans before."

"It's one of my favorites. I also like raspberry and pecan. I'll make them for you sometime."

"I'd like to repay you, but I'm not much of a cook, so I guess I'll have to do it with sex."

I grinned.

"I think I may use you to replace my regular workout. I think you're more strenuous."

Laurent wiggled his eyebrows.

"I'm more fun too and I bet your workouts don't make you moan."

"Don't get me started. We don't have time."

"So no sex on the kitchen table this morning?"

"Don't tempt me."

"Maybe this evening."

"I'm going out with one of my riders this evening."

"Oh, adding a little variety. Huh?"

"It's not a date or a hookup. We share an interest in riding."

"I bet you do."

"I meant riding bikes."

"Of course you did." Laurent stuck out his tongue.

We chatted for the remainder of breakfast. It was nice not to eat alone.

"Can I use your shower?"

"Of course. Everything you need is in the bathroom."

"I won't leave a mess. I promise."

"Good. I'll probably be downstairs by the time you finish."

"I'll come say 'goodbye' before I leave. Thank you so much for breakfast."

Laurent gave me a kiss, then headed to the bathroom. I put the remaining pancakes and bacon on a plate, covered it with plastic wrap, and put it in the refrigerator. It would be lunch today or perhaps supper tomorrow. I cleaned up the mess and then headed downstairs.

I unlocked the door and turned the sign to "Open." Todd arrived soon and we began our day. A customer came in looking for a tube, then another arrived seeking a flashing taillight. Both were gone by the time Laurent came downstairs.

"I'm heading out. Sell lots of bikes today."

"I'll try."

Laurent gave me another kiss. Todd noticed, but paid little attention. I smiled as Laurent departed and walked toward campus.

***

"I'll meet you back here in half an hour," I told Cam as the others headed into the frat house.

"Great. I need a shower. My shirt is sticking to me. That was quite a ride."

"I thought I took it easy on you guys today."

"Ha!" Sam said, looking back over his shoulder.

"Hey, I'm ready to do it all over again," Cam said.

"That makes one of us. I'll see you soon."

I took off on my bike and made quick trip home to shower and change. It was an unseasonably hot day and I had taken the guys on a strenuous ride. Everything I was wearing was soaked with sweat, even my socks.

I stripped and stepped into the shower. The slightly cool water was refreshing and I loved the scent of my strawberry shampoo. When I stepped out of the shower less than ten minutes later I felt much better.

I walked into the bedroom. Laurent had even made the bed before he left that morning. I could say one thing for him. He was neat. The only sign he'd used my shower that morning was his towel and washcloth, both neatly hung over the shower rod to dry. I hoped to see him again soon. I had little doubt I would.

I climbed in the Camaro and drove to the frat to pick up Cam. I appreciated that this car had a working air conditioner. Cam was waiting out front and hopped in when I pulled up. We drove the short distance to Bucceto's on the east side near College Mall and were soon sitting in a booth.

"What would you like?" I asked

"Pizza."

"They have some great specialty pizzas here. Do you trust me?"

"If it doesn't involve anchovies. Yes."

When our waitress returned, I ordered a large campfire pizza.

"Onion marmalade?" Cam asked, reading the ingredients of the pizza as our waitress departed.

"Hey, you said you trusted me."

"We'll see if I still do in a few minutes."

"Have the guys pounded you for singing in Italian yet?" I asked. There had been very vocal complaints during practice earlier.

"No, but I have been threatened. I pretend I think it's a compliment."

I laughed.

"I used to threaten my teammates that I would sing if they gave me trouble."

"Do you think I have a good chance of making the team?" Cam asked.

"Yes, but at this point I wouldn't count anyone out. There are varying levels of ability, but right now there isn't anyone that I think doesn't belong."

"I *really* want to make the team."

"Keep in mind that if you don't this year, chances are excellent you will the next."

"Maybe so, but I want to make it this year. I'm not asking for any special favors, but is there anything I can do to increase my chances. I'll do *anything* to make the team." For a moment, I thought Cam was making me an offer and I wasn't exactly pleased. "What I mean is, will putting in more time in the gym help? Should I put in extra time on speed or endurance? Or maybe I can work on exchanges with one or two of the other guys."

I was immediately relieved.

"All of that will help. Working on the exchanges is probably at the top of the list."

"Am I doing something wrong when I make an exchange?"

"No. That's not what I meant. Exchanges are difficult so it takes a while to get your technique down. A bad exchange is also the fastest way to make yourself look bad during the actual tryouts."

"Oh. You had me worried."

"My advice is to train hard, but don't overdo it. It is possible to over train. Don't go crazy with it."

"Okay, new topic. I don't want you to think I wanted to go out to grill you about tryouts. I really just wanted to spend time with you. It's just that making the Little 500 team is something I want badly, so it's usually on my mind."

"I understand."

"What's it like being out of school? I feel like I've been in school my entire life."

"You have mostly. I have to say it doesn't suck. It's more fun being my age than yours. I don't look as good as I did in college and I'm past my physical peak, but I not only know where I'm going now, I'm mostly there. I can see myself staying in Bloomington for the rest of my life. At your age, so much is uncertain. Much of that uncertainty disappears when you get older. I don't like to think about turning forty or fifty or sixty, but I think it will be okay when I get there. Thirty seemed old to me when I was in high school, but now I feel mostly the same as I did back then."

"I wish I was finished with school."

"Get all you can out of your college years. Don't be in a hurry for them to be over. Once they are there are times you'll wish you could go back. It's more fun being my age, but that doesn't mean being your age isn't also a good time. I had a blast in college."

"Parties?"

"A few, but it was mostly the people I met here and the experiences I had with them."

"Sex?" Cam teased.

"Yeah, sex, but a lot of other things too; biking, taking part in frat activities, watching movies in the IMU, and sometimes even going to classes. The campus is a beautiful place. It's one of the reasons I wanted to come back. I think Bloomington is an ideal location for a bike shop, but there's so much here. The university brings a lot of culture to what would otherwise be just like any other town. There are concerts and plays and all kinds of events. There are museums and so many restaurants. There is more artwork on display in the hallways of the IMU than there is in my entire hometown. Just being here was great back then and is again now.

"This is a special time of your life, Cam. You should make the most of it. I know sometimes it seems like a semester will never end. Hell, I had some class periods I thought would never end, but all too soon it's all over."

Our pizza arrived. Cam tasted it and his eyes widened.

"This is good!"

"I told you."

"I had my doubts. I've never heard of onion marmalade and it didn't sound promising."

"It does sound bizarre. It's like artichoke or spinach dip. Neither sounds good, but both are great."

"It's nice to get off campus. I've been so busy I haven't had the chance lately, except when we ride."

"I know what that's like. I was always busy, especially at the beginning of every semester. I think getting away for a while allows you to work better. Taking small breaks helps too. When I read or studied for classes I worked about fifty minutes and then took off ten. It made a big difference. If I was going at it for a long time, I took a long break. I got out of my room and walked on campus for a while. I think that allowed me to remember more and get more done than I would have if I pushed straight through."

"I might try that. I have trouble stopping when I'm working on something. I want to get it done. I'm very goal orientated."

"There's nothing wrong with that, but it's easy to push yourself too hard."

Cam shrugged.

I enjoyed talking and eating with Cam. I was lucky I had found two young men I could go out with. The fact they were both handsome was a bonus. I was old enough now I appreciated the beauty of youth. Perhaps it's a good thing I didn't recognize that beauty when I was young or I could have been conceited.

There was very little pizza left to box up when we were finished, but I had it boxed and gave it to Cam. I drove him back to Alpha Alpha Omega.

"I'll see you at the next practice," I said.

"Yeah, thanks for dinner and thanks for the leftover pizza."

"You're welcome."

Cam paused.

"Marc?"

"Yeah?"

Cam hesitated, then quickly scooted over, kissed me on the lips, slipped out of the car, and shut the door, leaving me slightly bewildered and breathing a bit harder.

I drove home wondering about the kiss. Cam seemed faintly attracted to me at times, but I was never sure if I was seeing what I thought I was seeing. I guess I didn't need to ponder whether or not he was interested. He kissed me. He was obviously embarrassed about his attraction or perhaps merely shy. Cam didn't strike me as the shy type, but maybe he was when it came to expressing interest in guys.

Was this a good thing or bad? There was a conflict of interest. Cam desperately wanted to make the Little 500 team. I would not be making that decision, but my recommendation could make or break a rider. I was reasonably sure I could remain objective, but could Cam? He was very attractive and reminded me so much of Alessio, but perhaps it wasn't wise to get involved with him, at least not until after the team was set.

That time wasn't far off. Perhaps I could fend him off until then, but how did I do that?

I had unique problems, if they could be called problems. I had two sexy young men interested in me. I guess if I was going to have a problem, it was the best type to have.

Chapter Five

"Why the hell didn't you tell me?" I asked.

"You didn't ask."

"Listen, smart ass..."

Hunter laughed.

"You should be glad we didn't ask you to help us move."

"Hey, I would have helped."

"Sure, you can say that now."

"I still want credit. It is the thought that counts. How long have you guys been living here right under my nose *without bothering to tell me*."

"We've only been here three days. See? We didn't wait that long. It's not like we've lived here a month."

"I would have beaten you both senseless if you lived in Bloomington a month and didn't tell me."

"We didn't, so calm yourself, Marc. You are invited for supper on Friday if that works for you."

"Yeah, that will be great. I don't have practice on Friday."

"Practice?"

"I will tell you about that later so you can stew in your own jealousy."

Hunter laughed.

"What time does your shop close?"

"On Friday I stay open until eight, but I'll let Todd close up.

"How about six then?"

"I'll be there, if you give me the address. Or do you expect me to knock on doors until I find you?"

I wrote down the address as Hunter told me. It was only a few blocks away.

"Okay, got it. I'll see you then." I disconnected and put down my phone. "I can't believe it."

"Can't believe what?" Todd asked.

"Two of my best friends from college moved to Bloomington. I talked to them two weeks ago and they didn't say a word."

"They sound like a sneaky lot."

I laughed.

"You don't mind closing up on Friday. Do you?"

"No problem. I'll just wait until you leave and then close early."

"Todd..."

"Kidding! I'm just kidding."

I grinned.

"I'm so excited. I've missed the old gang. Having Hunter and Alessio in town will be great."

"So, are they a couple?"

"Yeah. They met in college and have been together since."

"Man, maybe guys are better at staying together than girls. The longest I've been with a girlfriend is a few months."

"I think it depends on the individual. You'll likely meet *the* girl someday."

"Why are you single, Marc?"

"You mean at my age?"

"Well..."

"I haven't found the right guy. I've been so busy for the last several years I suppose I haven't even tried."

"You don't seem concerned. Aren't you afraid of ending up alone?"

"I haven't thought of that much either, until now! Thank you so much!"

"Sorry."

"I'm kidding. I have time. I'm not quite ready for the nursing home yet."

"Yeah, you've got a couple of months at least."

"How would you like to work weekends, Todd? *All* the weekends."

"Did I say a couple of months? I meant... uh... uh..."

I laughed.

"Get back to work slacker."

"Yes, boss."

My mind reeled. Hunter and Alessio had moved to Bloomington? It was so out of the blue it didn't seem possible. I thought they were more than happy out in Virginia. To say I was surprised that they quit their jobs and moved here was an understatement.

I hadn't seen Alessio or Hunter since I visited Bloomington for Alessio's graduation. We had meant to visit each other, but we were all too busy and Virginia wasn't exactly close. Now, we could see each other as much as we wanted. Of course, I didn't want to intrude upon their lives. They had been a couple for many years now so I was a third wheel. Still, it would be great to see them now and then. Perhaps we could all ride together once more.

Friday could not come soon enough. I felt like a kid waiting for Christmas. The shop kept me busy and so did training my younger frat brothers. We spent more time working on exchanges. A couple of the guys could not seem to get it, but most were progressing nicely. I was already beginning to make notes on who I thought would be best for the team.

I had Cam to think about too. He was discreet during practices. He hadn't kissed me again, but when others weren't around he gave me a few looks that made me breathe harder and made the front of my shorts tighter. I'm not sure I could have resisted him if he made a move on me.

Laurent kept me busy as well. He also made it easier to keep my hands off Cam. There was no conflict of interest with Laurent and, although young, he knew exactly what he wanted and wasn't afraid to go after it. We ate together at Dagwood's after practice on Thursday and then went to my place for intense, sweaty sex. He stayed the night. He always did now. I didn't get up early enough to fix a serious breakfast, but we shared bagels and cream cheese before he departed for class and I walked downstairs to open the shop. I liked Laurent *a lot.*

Friday evening came at last. I went upstairs a little after six, cleaned up, and grabbed the Yankee Candle I had purchased to give Hunter and Alessio. I drove the short distance in my Camaro and parked near their home, a small Tudor style stone cottage. It looked like the kind of place I wouldn't mind living in myself. It was beautiful and neither too large, nor too small.

I was slightly nervous as I walked up the stone pathway, then the steps, and knocked. Moments later, Alessio opened the door. He grinned, pulled me inside, and hugged me tightly.

"It's so good to see you again, Marc! We've both missed you!"

Alessio was a few years older than the last time I had seen him, but he barely looked it.

Hunter stood as I entered. I smiled at him, but my smile faded slightly. Hunter looked older. Where the years had barely touched Alessio, they had not been so kind to Hunter. He looked more than a decade older and barely half that time had passed since I'd see him last.

We hugged. Hunter had kept in shape. He was still muscular. I was glad he hadn't let himself get fat as so many college athletes do after they graduate. If anything, he was too thin.

"Supper is almost ready. Let me go check on it," Alessio said.

"Anything I can do to help?"

"No. I remember your cooking abilities." Alessio grinned.

"Hey! I'm not that bad! I can cook! Brendan was the one who couldn't toast a Pop-Tart without burning it!"

"Yeah, you were good at Pop-Tarts, but as for anything more..."

Alessio departed before I could retort.

"I am so glad you guys are here! You really should have told me you were coming. I really would have helped you move in."

"I know you would have, but we hired movers for that. We wanted to surprise you."

"I don't know what would have surprised me more. This is a nice house."

"Not quite like our rooms in Alpha. Huh?"

"Um. No."

"How do you like living on top of IU?" Hunter asked.

"I love it. It's great living right over the shop. When I'm done for the day I just walk upstairs."

"We'll come by and check out your shop soon."

"Great. Maybe we can all bike together."

"Maybe." I could hear hesitation in Hunter's voice. "Let's move into the dining room."

I followed Hunter into the next room. There was an actual dining table. The dining room was separated from the kitchen only by an island. Otherwise, the two rooms were one.

"Oh, I like the open floor plan," I said.

"That's what we liked. None of the rooms feel closed in. No one has to hide away in the kitchen to cook. We'll probably spend more time in here than in the living room."

"What smells so good?"

"Lasagna," Alessio said.

"I didn't know you could cook Italian," I said. Alessio arched an eyebrow. He was from Italy.

"My mother taught me to make it. She tried to teach Hunter as well, but the results were... not so good."

"His mother was very diplomatic. She suggested I let Alessio do the cooking in our home."

"How was Italy?"

"Which time? I love it. We gave some thought to living there, but both of us truly want to be in the states."

"My family loves Hunter, especially my mother," Alessio said.

"I love his mom. She reminds me of Sophia on *Golden Girls*. She's a tiny woman, but she orders around her grown sons as if they were kids and they all obey her."

"You do not want to mess with Mama," Alessio said.

"I never tried," Hunter said.

Alessio opened the oven and the scent of Lasagna and oregano filled the air. He carried it to the table and set it on a pad.

"Want me to help?" Hunter asked.

"No. You stay where you are. This will only take a few minutes."

Soon, Alessio brought out cooked apples. I could smell the cinnamon. Then came break sticks oozing with garlic and butter.

"Help yourself," Alessio said.

I took my plate and did just that. I had to wait before I could taste the lasagna because it was still bubbling.

"This is incredible! I love Fazoli's lasagna, but this is a hundred times better."

"That is because it is actual Italian lasagna and not a copy," Alessio said.

"Leave Hunter and marry me!" I said.

Alessio and Hunter both laughed.

I had never tasted anything quite like the lasagna. There was so much cheese it was almost chewy. The spices, some of which I could not identify, were perfectly balanced.

"You could open a restaurant," I said.

"Far too much work. My cousin runs a restaurant back home in Mantua. I love to cook, but that would make it into work."

The cooked apples were the best I'd ever tasted too, even better than my mother's and that was hard to imagine. There was a lot of cinnamon in them, but not too much. The breadsticks were equally as delicious. They were moist with butter.

"So catch us up. What did you mean when you said you had no practice this evening?" Hunter asked.

"I'm coaching the Alpha Alpha Omega Little 500 team."

"No shit?" Hunter asked.

"They had zero returning bikers."

"Not even anyone who had unsuccessfully tried out last year?" Alessio asked.

"No. Jens, the current head of the AAΩ council, doesn't think it has ever happened before. He came and asked if I'd train the team and coach this year."

"There is no one better for the job," Hunter said.

"Not even you?"

"Not even. You were the best there ever was, Marc."

"Wow. Why didn't you tell me that in college?"

"Hey, after Adam carved that statue of you I figured your head was swelled enough."

I laughed.

"We went through Cincinnati just to see your statue again," Alessio said.

"You didn't."

"Yes, we did and we took photos."

"Oh lord."

"You mean you've never made the trip to see yourself immortalized?" Hunter asked.

"Hardly. I only went to look at it once after the unveiling and I picked an afternoon when I thought no one would be around. I even wore a baseball cap and sunglasses so no one would recognize me."

It was Hunter's turn to laugh.

"Sure, it's funny to you, but for weeks after the unveiling I walked around afraid that everyone recognized me."

"It was still an honor. Many would give a great deal to be the subject of a work by Adam Abernathy," Alessio said.

"Who would have thought my insane roommate would turn out to be a great artist? Do you know that one of his sculptures recently sold at Sotheby's for $1.2 million?" I asked.

"You ex-roommate is a world famous artist and your ex-boyfriend is a Broadway star. Why in the hell aren't you famous Marc?" Hunter asked.

"I'm a loser I guess." I grinned.

"Yes, but you are our loser," Alessio teased.

"Thank you so much. I think."

"You've done very well, Marc. You have realized your dream. You always wanted to open a bike shop and you have done so."

"Yes. I'm happy with what I have. I wouldn't trade lives with Adam or Dorian."

"Did you read Anton's latest book?" Hunter asked.

"His latest was a text book for post-graduates and too far above my head," I said.

"I didn't know he'd written a text book. I meant the one that made the best seller list."

"Yes, I did and I almost couldn't understand it, but he does a good job of putting advanced physics into everyday terms."

"See. There's another one of the old gang who is famous."

"Not everyone became famous. Brendan never made it into the NFL. I think he's happy coaching high school football. He told me that even if he had gone into the NFL he would have coached high school ball when he retired from professional sports."

"Yeah and I never won a Olympic gold medal for wrestling, but I'm fine with that. I would probably have had a better chance if I'd actually tried out for the team," Hunter said.

"That would have helped," I said.

"I'm happy here, especially now that you guys have returned. I felt a little lonely when I first came back. The town and university look much the same, but everyone I knew was gone. I've met some people since I moved back, but it's not quite the same."

"It will never be the same, but it can still be wonderful. I liked living in Virginia, but I always wanted to come back here," Hunter said.

"I always had Bloomington in mind for my bike shop. It was never a certainty, but when the time came this is where I came to seek out a retail space and I found one less than a block from the university on Kirkwood."

"Perhaps it was meant to be," Alessio said.

"I'm glad we're all here together again."

We continued talking while we ate. A little later Alessio brought out hot tea and cannoli.

"I've never had cannoli," I said.

"Once you have it, you'll crave it," Hunter said.

"There are many different types. The main ingredients of this version are cream cheese, cinnamon, and pecans," Alessio said.

I tasted mine and moaned.

"Oh wow this is good! I love Italian food."

"Cannoli actually originates in Sicily, but it goes good with Italian," Alessio said. He still retained his sexy Italian accent. If anything, he was even more attractive.

We talked over dessert, but I could tell Hunter was getting tired. He had trouble keeping his eyes open.

"This has been wonderful, but I should get going. I would invite you guys over to my place for supper, but I'm afraid my cooking skills are not equal to yours Alessio. Instead, I'll take you out to eat soon. It won't be as good at this, but I don't have to tell you there are lots of great restaurants in Bloomington."

"That sounds great," Alessio said.

I hugged both of my old friends again and then departed. It was funny I thought of them as my old friends when I had last seen them only a few years ago, but sometimes my college years felt as if they were far behind me. Other times I felt as if I had just graduated.

Hunter was not his old self. He didn't look bad and yet he didn't look good either. I hoped he wasn't one of those unlucky guys who aged rapidly. Perhaps he'd recently been ill or maybe the move had worn him out. It didn't seem to have affected Alessio. He was little changed. I was probably concerned about nothing and yet I was uneasy.

***

I didn't have much time to think about Hunter in the coming days. September was slipping away and it would soon be time to select the Alpha Alpha Omega Little 500 team. I tried to squeeze in as many practices as possible to give each of the brothers who wanted to make the team the best chance possible. Then, there was my shop, which took up most of my day and often part of my evenings and nights. Laurent and I continued to go out and each time he stayed the night. I lived a busy life!

I rode with the brothers to Armstrong Stadium where I had arranged to use the track. Once there, I divided them into three teams for a mock and much shorter, Little 500. Once the teams were set, I assigned the pits and indicated the boundary lines for exchanges.

"This will be a race of fifty laps. That's one quarter of the Little 500, but it will give you an idea of what the race is like. There will also be thirty fewer teams on the track, but this is the best we can do with what we have. I'm going to give you five minutes to decide who leads off for your team. I'm not going to count exchanges, but I want each rider to get out on the track at least twice."

I didn't say anything about pacing or give any advice. I wanted the boys to get a taste of what racing was like and make their own mistakes.

A few minutes later, I lined up the starters and then yelled "Go!" They took off and their teammates cheered them on.

Our mini-race lacked the excitement of the real thing. We were missing thirty teams, a few thousand spectators, and camera crews from sport's networks, but the guys still got into it. When the three teams passed I heard the familiar loud whir of tires and bike chains I had not heard for years. During the actual race, the sound was truly loud, but even this mini-version took me back to my racing days.

The guys were much improved on their exchanges, but there were still mishaps. I thought my boys had progressed well in the short time they had practiced.

The way my little brothers got into the race one would have thought it was the real thing. They cheered each other and raced with focused intensity.

There were a couple of near collisions, but no accidents. The fifty laps passed quickly. Near the end I could tell some riders were getting tired. They were the ones who had not yet learned to pace. I didn't have a flag so I pulled off my shirt as the riders came around the final lap and used it to wave in the winner. The other two teams were not far behind.

I pulled my shirt back on as the final riders came back around the track and waved everyone to the bleachers.

"Good job guys. I saw some good exchanges and some good moves on the track, but also a few mistakes. I purposely sent you out without the benefit of my advice. Did any of you notice anything you did wrong?"

"I made a huge mistake," York said. "I went at it full blast. I was able to pull us well into the lead, but later I ran out of steam. I didn't have anything left. I thought with only riding about a third of the fifty laps that I could ride full-out, but I didn't have enough time to rest between my turns on the bike."

"Perfect. That is one of the main things I wanted you to learn. Pacing is critical and it's difficult. It's easy to get caught up in the race and go all out, but then later you've got nothing. Even with proper pacing every rider is tired by the end. Without it, you may have nothing left to give. This race was only fifty laps. Multiply what you experienced today by four."

"Yes, but aren't there times a rider should go all out?" Kang asked.

"Certainly, especially in the last couple of laps. The first year I rode in the Little 500 our strategy near the end of the race was for two of our riders to give it everything they had for as long as they could endure it. They purposely burned themselves out to better our position. Another rider paced himself and went in when the others were finished. Most of the time, a rider has to be very careful to conserve his energy. It doesn't matter how young and tough you are, this race will drain you."

"I very nearly clipped Sam on our first turn. I didn't realize how difficult it is to ride that close while racing," Baxter said.

"It's very easy to hit another rider. Even experienced riders do it on occasion. I've encouraged you to ride close during our practices, but even that can't truly prepare you for the race. I'm actually amazed we only had near collisions today."

We continued critiquing our performance until we felt we'd covered everything.

"Okay guys, that's it for today. We're going to do the same thing in a few days as a tryout for the team so be ready. Next time, I'll be taking notes. The time for practice is nearly over."

The guys took off in small groups to ride back to the frat, but Cam held back.

"Want to get something to eat?" he asked.

"Yeah, I haven't eaten yet."

"How about... Dagwood's?"

"Sure. Let's ride."

I was struck once again how much Cam reminded me of Alessio, especially now that he took on an Italian accent part of the time to annoy and amuse his biking brothers. I almost felt as if I was back with Alessio again, but Alessio was nearly my age and living right here in Bloomington with Hunter. I felt almost as if I was drifting between the past and present, but Cam was not Alessio. He had his own, unique personality, which I quite liked.

A few minutes later, we parked our bikes near Dagwood's and walked inside. Cam ordered a Hoosier Hoagie, which came with turkey, roast beef, Swiss cheese, and whatever toppings one desired. I thought it sounded good so I ordered one too and saved myself the trouble of deciding.

We took our drink cups and picked a table near the window where we could watch the traffic on Indiana Avenue and pedestrians on the sidewalks.

"I think practices are going very well," Cam said.

"Yeah, the guys have improved a lot in a short time."

"We would be a disaster without you."

"I doubt that, but you would be at a disadvantage. Every other team almost certainly has at least one experienced member. That experience is vital."

"You are our only hope to have even a chance to place. Without you this would be a rebuilding year and nothing more. We might not even earn a spot in the race."

"I won't argue with you since not every team earns a spot. The first year I raced I think there were something like forty-three teams trying out. That meant ten didn't get to race."

"I hope we can at least place, whether or not I make the team."

"You have a good shot, but you have tough competition. There are a couple of the guys that I don't think are ready, but even they have time yet."

"I think I know who you mean."

Our sandwiches were soon ready. Cam hurried to pick them up before I could stand.

"I love the sandwiches here," I said.

"Me too. They're bigger than those at Subway, not that I have anything against Subway."

"Yes. I think Dagwood's and Jimmy John's are both better."

Cam eyed me while we talked and his attention excited me. He reached across the table and took my hand, causing my heart to race. He released it after a few moments, but I was tempted to lean across the table and kiss him. I fought the temptation, but it wasn't easy.

Was it easier for me to fall for guys now that I was older? I was very much taken with Laurent and with Cam. My old feelings for Alessio reignited the moment I saw him again or perhaps those feelings had never gone away. My feelings for Hunter had quickly risen to the surface as well. If things had worked out differently, I could easily have ended up with either Hunter or Alessio.

I tried not to think about any of that and instead enjoyed my time with Cam. It was what it was and it made me feel alive.

We finished our sandwiches too soon. I don't think either of us wanted to part just yet.

"Would you show me your place? I'm curious. Aaron says you live over your shop."

"Sure. Why not?"

We tossed our trash and walked back out to our bikes. We climbed on and then rode for a total of perhaps a block before we reached the back of my shop. We wheeled the bikes inside and I led Cam upstairs.

"It's fairly simple. All my money goes into the shop and paying for the building."

"I love the view," Cam said after he walked to the window and looked down at Kirkwood Avenue. You can see both campus and KOK, depending on which way you look."

"Yeah, the view is nice, but the location is better."

"True. You're close to everything."

"I could easily get by without a car and just rent one when I really needed it, but I love my Camaro too much to give it up."

"It must be nice to have a place to yourself."

"It is, but it's too quiet sometimes. There is something to be said for living in a frat house."

"You sound like you miss it."

"I do. Those were fun years. I miss a lot of different periods in my life, but now is as good, only different. Two of my old frat brothers have even moved back to Bloomington and I'm directly involved with Alpha again. I have the best of both worlds."

"I admire how you have your life together," Cam said, drawing a little closer.

We stood silent for a few moments, then Cam leaned in. I did so as well, but did not kiss him because I wasn't entirely sure it's what he wanted and I had reservations. I didn't have time to ponder the situation, for Cam tentatively kissed me. He pulled back for a moment and then kissed me more deeply.

"I want you," he whispered into my ear.

We made out while Cam's hands roamed. Any reservations I had were pushed to the side by sexual desire. He reminded me so much of Alessio and yet had his own appeal. My own hands began to roam. Cam's body was hard and firm. Touching him drove me insane with need.

Cam sank to his knees, unbuttoned and unzipped my shorts, then pulled them down and leaned in. I moaned as he went to work.

Cam wasn't experienced, but the sight of him on his knees more than made up for his inexperience. He had me moaning in moments.

I didn't think things would go this far with Cam. I was content to eat out and spend time with him, but Cam obviously had other ideas and I must admit I wanted him.

"I'm getting close," I warned after a very few minutes. Cam kept going until the last moment and then pulled back as I lost control. Pleasure flooded my body.

Cam stood. I guided him to the couch and leaned down in front of him. It was time to return the favor. He was so aroused I had difficulty removing his shorts. Once I did I leaned in and made him moan.

"Oh my God. No one has ever..."

That's as far as Cam got before he exploded in my mouth. He groaned with ecstasy.

Cam quickly zipped up the moment I pulled away. His face reddened slightly. I stood then sat beside him.

"Are you okay?" I asked.

"Yeah. I'm fine."

He didn't seem fine, but some guys were like that, especially if they weren't entirely at ease with sex with another guy. Of course, by college boy thinking, we hadn't had sex. We had merely fooled around.

"I should get going. I have a ton of studying to do," Cam said.

"I remember those days too well. I had a great time."

Cam smiled shyly.

"Me too."

I walked Cam downstairs and held the door open for him while he pulled his bike out.

"I'll see you at practice," I said.

He nodded and then departed.

I walked back upstairs. Now that it was over, I wondered if I had done the right thing. There wasn't anything exactly wrong with hooking up with one of the riders, but I wasn't completely at ease with the idea either. I reminded myself that Cam made the first move. I even held back to make sure, but *he* had kissed *me*. There was no doubt he wanted what had happened, even if he experienced a little guilt about it once it was over. That was to be expected since he was obviously not experienced with guys.

I put it out of my mind. Cam was an adult. He was free and capable of making his own decisions. The only possible conflict was the fact I had much to say about who made the team and I would not let our relationship affect my decision. Hunter didn't all those years ago and we were far more heavily involved. I earned my spot back then. If Cam made the team it would be because he earned it.

Chapter Six

I talked and laughed with Laurent as we sat in The Commons near the Burger King enjoying our Whoppers and fries. He asked me to meet him for lunch and it sounded like fun. Once again, I felt as if I was in college.

The Commons was crowded, which was not surprising considering it was nearly one. Almost every table was filled and the noise level was high, but not so loud Laurent and I couldn't talk.

I gazed down the length of The Commons to the Back Alley for a moment. Part of *Breaking Away* was filmed right here and in the bowling alley beyond the glass doors and just in front of the doors. I had bowled in the Back Alley with my Verona friends and my frat brothers. I grinned when I thought of how badly Brendan bowled.

"What?"

"I was reminiscing. When I was in school, one of my friends was the quarterback of the football team."

"Yeah? Was he hot?"

"Very, but that's not the point. Brendan was extremely athletic, but a group of us went bowling and Brendan couldn't bowl worth a damn. I mean he truly sucked. It was hilarious. It made him seem more human. Brendan was gorgeous and good at just about everything concerned with sports, except bowling."

Laurent laughed

"Did you guys hook up?"

"No. Brendan is gay, but he had a boyfriend. They're still together."

"I was hoping for a juicy story."

"You are a bad boy, Laurent."

Laurent grinned. He took my hand across the table and leaned in close.

"Aren't you glad I am?"

I smiled then looked up and caught Cam staring at me as he walked past. He did not look pleased. Could he possibly be jealous? I dismissed the thought as unlikely, but he was not happy. I turned my attention back to Laurent.

"I'm glad you wanted to meet for lunch today. It's good to get out of the shop."

"You should go out for lunch every day."

"I don't feel like I have time. There is always work to be done. I'm not complaining. I love it, but it's difficult to get away."

"Maybe I'll make you get away more often then. I have power over you."

"Oh do you?"

"Yes, I do." Laurent leaned in close and whispered in my ear. What he said made my shorts bulge. It was a good thing I was sitting down.

"Okay, you have power over me but I have power over you too."

"Oh, yes daddy."

A girl passing looked at us for a moment. Laurent burst out laughing. I enjoyed spending time with this boy, whether we were dressed or naked.

Laurent's time was limited and soon he had to rush off to class. I needed to get back to the shop, but I took a moment to walk to the other part of The Commons near the Pizza Hut to gaze at the Little 500 trophy that was on display in the window of the bookstore. This was *the* trophy. Smaller, but still quite large trophies were given to the winners, but this was the enormous cup that was presented each year. I had held it twice. It was a memory I would never forget.

I walked to the exit and then on the path that led past Dunn Meadow. Once again I realized how truly lucky I was to be back in a place I loved. There were so many good memories here and the present wasn't bad either.

I was back in the shop in less than five minutes. Jake was busy repairing a bike. Three college boys entered moments after I did and a couple more not long after them. I was soon busy talking about bikes. Yeah, the present was good.

**

I rode into the AAΩ parking lot with the boys. We had just completed a strenuous ride. I was a little sweaty, but not too much since the weather had turned cool.

"This is a familiar sight."

I looked up and grinned. Hunter and Alessio stood on the sidewalk.

"What are you guys doing here?"

"Well we are members of Alpha Alpha Omega. We dropped in to look around our old home," Hunter said.

"It hasn't changed much. Has it?"

"Very little."

"Hey, are you guys hungry? I owe you supper. Let me take you out."

"Sounds good to me," Alessio said. Hunter nodded.

"Hey, Marc. Want to get something to eat?" Cam asked as he walked toward us.

"Hey, Cam. I want you to meet a couple of my friends from college. They're both Alpha brothers. This is Hunter and Alessio."

The guys shook hands.

"Did you guys race?"

"Hunter was the captain of the Little 500 team," I said.

"And Alessio raced for three years," Hunter added.

"Awesome! I'd love to hear about your experiences."

"Why don't you join us? We're going out to eat," I said.

"I don't want to intrude."

"You aren't. Besides, Hunter would love telling you about how great he was." I grinned.

"Hey!"

"Okay, cool. I would love to, but I'm a little sweaty. Can I clean up real quick?"

"Actually, I need to clean up a little too."

"Come on. I'll loan you a washcloth and towel," Cam said.

"Do you guys mind waiting in the lounge? We won't be long. I promise," I said.

"Not at all. It will give us a chance to talk to some of the boys," Hunter said. Alessio nodded his agreement. I wondered if Alessio noticed Cam's resemblance to himself.

"Come up to my room," Cam said.

I followed Cam inside and up the stairs. He pulled off his shirt as we entered his room. Cam had a nice body, but I didn't more than glance, especially because his roommate was in.

"Want to borrow some clothes?" Cam asked.

"No. I'm just need to clean up. We aren't going anywhere fancy. I'm thinking Casa Brava."

"Sounds good."

"Here's a towel and washcloth. I'll pass the soap and shampoo over the partition."

"I was going to clean up in the sink, but that sounds better."

Cam stripped. Since I now had a towel, so did I. I stole a glance of Cam's naked body, but only a glance because I didn't want to get excited.

We wrapped our towels around our waists and headed down the hallway to the bathroom. I knew the way well. Cam's room was only a couple of doors down from the room I once shared with Adam.

We hung our towels on hooks and took stalls next to each other. I turned on the hot water and enjoyed the massage of the powerful spray.

"Here you go," Cam said.

I reached up and took the shampoo. I squirted out a little and handed it back. I worked the mint-scented shampoo into my hair. I felt better already.

Soon, Cam loaned me his soap. I lathered up. Showering always made me a little horny and I fantasized for a few moments about Cam entering my stall and ravishing me as the hot water pounded down upon us. I gave up the fantasy quickly because I was becoming noticeably excited.

I rinsed and exited the shower, then grabbed my towel and dried off. Cam came out soon after. Since we were alone, I used the opportunity to check out the rest of him. Damn, he had a hot ass! Now I could finally see all those qualities that I could only feel through his clothing while we made out and I sucked him off.

.

We returned to Cam's room and dressed. My biking attire wasn't ideal for dining out, but it was good enough.

"Thanks for loaning me a towel and washcloth. I'm buying this evening."

"You don't have to pay for supper because I loaned you a towel and washcloth," Cam said.

"I owe Alessio and Hunter for having me over for supper. I'm paying for theirs so I might as well pay for yours too. No arguing. I'm very stubborn."

"Okay. Okay. I'm a poor college kid so I won't argue."

Cam's roommate was busy studying and completely ignored us, except when I entered the first time, when he looked up from his book, smiled and nodded, and went right back to work.

We walked downstairs where Hunter and Alessio were talking to some of the brothers, including a couple of my riders.

"Are you two spreading rumors about me?"

"That's why we're here," Alessio said.

"The things they've told us. I can't believe you did things like that in college!" Baxter said.

"Like what?"

"Uh. Uh."

"Yeah, that's what I thought."

"Baxter has never been that good with thinking," Matt said.

"Shut it."

I laughed.

"Okay. We're ready. I rode my bike so you guys get to drive," I said.

"Good, I don't think I'd want to ride in your decrepit Camaro anyway," Hunter said.

"Sadly, the old Camaro is no more, but I have a newer one."

"I hope it doesn't require duct tape to keep it going," Alessio said.

"No, this one is duct tape free. All the doors and windows even open."

"That's quite a step up."

"It sure is. Not only does it have air conditioning, it also starts even when the engine is hot."

"You are moving up in the world, Marc," Hunter said and grinned.

We walked outside. Cam and I followed Hunter and Alessio to a recent model blue Mustang convertible.

"Why am I not surprised?" I asked.

"Well, you didn't think I was going to drive a station wagon or a mini van did you?" Hunter asked.

"I hoped you hadn't fallen that far, although my nightmare was that you two bought an old people car."

Alessio laughed and climbed into the driver's side. Cam and I got I the back.

"Where to?" Alessio asked.

"Casa Brava. Remember where it is? Unless you two aren't in the mood for Mexican?"

"I remember and it sounds great," Alessio said.

"I love Mexican, although I prefer Italian," Hunter said, winking at Alessio.

Hunter turned in his seat so he could face Cam.

"So what do you think of Marc as a trainer and coach?"

"He's awesome. He's taught us a lot."

"You can tell me what you really think later when Marc isn't around," Hunter teased.

"Hey!" I said.

"That is what I really think."

"Well, he should be good. I taught him everything he knows about biking."

"I would argue with that, but it's basically true. My interest in biking and racing is all Hunter's fault."

"But if he pretends to be Italian, it is not my fault!" Alessio said. I still loved his accent.

"Are you kidding? Cam sings in mock Italian during rides to annoy everyone," I said.

"You should stay away from Marc. He is a corrupting influence," Alessio said, then grinned at me in the rearview mirror.

Alessio parked near Casa Brava and we walked inside. The scent of Mexican food made me even hungrier than I was when I entered. We placed our drink orders, then browsed the menus.

"I had the Burrito Loco the last time I was here. It was great. I'm going to try the Burrito Pancho Villa this time. The grilled chicken, bacon, and melted cheese sounds great," I said.

"Oh, they still have Tacos Adobo. I ordered those sometimes back in college. I loved the Mexican sausage," Alessio said.

After much discussion, Hunter decided on a Chimichanga Casa Brava and Cam a Burrito Chipotle. We ordered and then munched on chips and salsa.

"Tryouts should be coming up soon. Right?" Hunter asked.

"Very, very soon. Next week in fact. The council is going to have a tough time deciding because there are a lot of good riders. I'll provide them with a list of each riders strengths and weaknesses as well as my top picks, but I'm glad I don't have to make the final decision."

"You have now entered my old world," Hunter said.

Hunter looked thinner and slightly pale. I noticed that his movements were a little slower getting in and out of the car, as if he was weak. Hunter noticed me looking at him. I thought about asking if he'd been ill, but then thought better of it.

"I guess you didn't have it as easy as I thought," I said.

"So, tell me about riding in the Little 500," Cam said, gazing at Hunter and Alessio expectantly.

"It was a dream come true, but I was so nervous my first year I almost got sick before the race," Alessio said. "Once I was on the bike, it was exciting and a little scary."

"Scary? How so?"

"There was so much riding on my performance. I did not want to let my brothers down. There were also so many bikes so very close to together. I feared I would cause a pileup."

"It's nerve racking at first, but you quickly grow accustomed to it. Soon, the mass of riders feels like fighter jets flying in formation. Everyone is intent on winning, but no one wants to collide with anyone else. There is a camaraderie between riders, a little like there is between frat brothers," Hunter said.

"That is a great feeling. I joined Alpha because of its reputation of producing great Little 500 teams, but I found that belonging to the frat meant even more to me. I have remained in touch with most of my brothers," Alessio said.

"My greatest fear is screwing up an exchange," Cam said.

"Hunter is an expert at screwing up exchanges," I said.

"Funny Marc."

"What?" Cam asked.

"During Qualifications the first year my shoe came untied and a lace caught in the chain as I jumped off the bike for an exchange. I went down and the bike would have too if the next rider wasn't already getting on. I managed to break the lace after jerking my foot hard a few times, but the delay dropped us down to 30th place."

"What did you guys do?"

"We made a second attempt for a better place. We ended up with 3rd after I taught Hunter how to tie his shoes," I said. Hunter gave me a fake glare.

Our food arrived soon. The service was very quick at Casa Brava.

"This is delicious," Cam said.

"I am a great cook. Aren't I?" I asked.

"Humor him. Marc thinks he's cooked if he orders something in a restaurant," Hunter said.

"Hey, I can cook. I merely choose not to do so. I'm not Brendan."

"Oh man. Remember the time he tried to make toasted cheese?" Hunter asked. I laughed

"What?" asked Cam.

"He set the toaster oven on fire. I still can't figure out how he did it. How is Brendan anyway?" Hunter asked.

"He's great. If anything he's in better shape," I said.

"Bastard," Hunter said. "I miss him."

We realized we were largely leaving Cam out of the conversation, so we went back to talking about racing. We kept talking all through supper and even after.

I noticed that Hunter tired as we sat there. I also noticed Alessio watching him. It was Alessio who suggested that we head back shortly after we finished eating. He drove Cam and me back to the frat.

"Thanks for supper, Marc. You are a great cook," Alessio said.

"You're welcome. I'll see you soon."

Alessio and Hunter departed.

"Want to come in for a while?" Cam asked.

"I should get home."

"Please, just for a while. My roommate will be out most of the night. We'll have the room to ourselves."

Cam drew closer and gazed into my eyes. My resistance dissolved.

"Okay."

I followed Cam inside, but had second thoughts as we neared his room. I hesitated as he unlocked and opened the door.

"I don't know if I should," I said.

"You should. Now get in here," Cam said and practically dragged me into the room.

He closed and locked the door, then pressed himself against me and kissed me deeply.

Rational thought went out the window as we made out. Cam tugged at my shirt and I let him pull it over my head. I pulled his off as well. We continued to make out and undress as we made our way to his narrow bed. Cam sat, pulled me toward him, shoved down my shorts, and then pulled me in his mouth.

He still wasn't very good at giving head, but that didn't mean I didn't enjoy it. The mere sight of him doing it was hot.

Cam didn't continue long before he stopped and looked up at me.

"I want you inside me."

My breath came harder than ever.

"Have condoms?"

"In the drawer."

I walked to his dresser and opened the drawer. There I found lubricated condoms as well as a small bottle of lube. I put the condom on and then a liberal layer of lube.

"I've never done this before," Cam admitted.

"I'll go easy."

I guided Cam unto his back and pulled his legs up over my shoulders. He looked scared.

"We don't have to do this if you don't want," I said.

"I want it."

I was as gentle as possible, but Cam still grimaced and cried out slightly as I entered him. I held perfectly still.

"Breathe, Cam. If you want to stop, just tell me."

I was patient and Cam did not tell me to stop. It took several long moments before I was completely in. I held perfectly still for several more moments before I pulled back out and ever so slowly began to thrust.

Cam began to relax and I could tell the pain was turning to pleasure. It wasn't long before he began to moan. He wasn't the only one. Cam was a very hot young man and his resemblance to Alessio only served to make him more alluring.

It had been a long time since I'd had a virgin. That too, added to the intensity of the situation. I feared I would not be able to maintain control as long as usual, but I had no need to worry for Cam lost control within a few minutes. He groaned loudly and went off like a geyser. The sight sent me over the edge as I moaned as we both climaxed together.

Cam didn't want to remain in bed after we finished like Laurent. He quickly stood and wrapped a towel around his waist. I took that as my cue to dress and leave.

"I'll see you at practice tomorrow," Cam said as we both exited his room.

"Have a good night."

I walked outside and then walked my bike home. My sexual encounter with Cam was hot and yet it lacked the passion I felt with Laurent and the passion I'd once felt with Hunter, Alessio, and Dorian. Cam was a very attractive young man, but something was missing when we were together. I understood his hesitancy. He made the moves tonight to be sure, but he seemed reluctant to go through with what he'd started, almost as if he'd changed his mind. That's why I asked him if he wanted to continue. Some guys took on more than they could handle. It's hard to think straight when worked up.

Perhaps I'd made a mistake. I did not mean to get involved with Cam. I probably should not have, but I hadn't been strong enough to resist when he came onto me. The fact that he came onto me made me feel less guilty, but I still felt as if I had not made the right choice.

There was no need to dwell on it. I would see how Cam acted around me tomorrow.

Luckily, this was not a night Laurent was over. I could have handled going at it again, but once was enough for one night. I didn't have an endless supply of boys so I preferred to pace myself.

***

"This is it guys. This is your last chance to prove yourself. I'll submit my recommendations to the fraternity council after we're finished and then it's in their hands. You need to show me what you've got today, but keep in mind that I've been observing you since the beginning and what you've done before counts as well, especially those things you've done right.

"For tryouts, we're going to run another practice race of fifty laps with three teams."

I divided the guys into teams, gave them five minutes to decide on their riding order and strategy, and then started the race.

The truth was I had mostly made up my mind about who to recommend by this point, but I watched closely. What the boys did today did count. It was a final chance for those I found lacking to improve my opinion of their skills. It was the last chance for the others to show me they were more talented than their peers. I had no favorites. I wished they could all make the team, but the truth was that a very small number of them weren't ready yet. My job was to pick the best of the best.

I wished once again I had not slept with Cam. Nothing much had changed between us since I took his virginity and yet I sensed something beneath the surface. Perhaps I was only imagining it or perhaps Cam thought he'd made a mistake too. My main problem is that I'd put myself in a bad position. I had worried that others might think I was playing favorites if I recommended Cam, but I was faced with an entirely different problem. Cam was not among my top choices. I would recommend him as I would most of the others, but he was not in the top four. He wasn't even in the top six. I hoped he didn't feel slighted.

I was proud of my younger frat brothers. They had improved much in a very short time. I had no doubt I could build a great team with those who made the cut. Hopefully some of those who didn't make the team this year would try again next year because that would make next year's team all the stronger. I doubted I would be directly involved after this year, but I wanted to do all I could to help my frat brothers.

Some of the exchanges needed work, but no one fell down. Some exchanges were things of beauty. There were no wrecks on the course and no major screw-ups. I was glad to see the guys finishing strong.

I waved my jacket as the winning team crossed the finish line. The others were not far behind. I directed everyone to the bleachers after the race.

"Good job guys. I truly mean that. You have all improved in the short time we've been practicing. Only four of you make the team, but you've all done a great job. I want to encourage those of you who don't make the team to try again next year. Most don't make the team on their first try."

"Did you make the team your first year?" Baxter asked.

"Actually, I did."

Some of the guys groaned.

"Yes, I was one of *those*, but I practiced for over a year to get there, both on my own and with team members from the previous year so don't hate me.

"I also want to encourage those who don't make the team to come and practice with the team anyway. It's a great way to improve your performance for next year.

"So, that's it guys. I'll submit my recommendations this evening and then your fate lies in the hands of the council. I'm glad I've had the opportunity to ride with all of you and I hope all of you will return for the next practice."

The guys slowly departed. I knew that some of them would not keep practicing if they didn't make the team, but hopefully at least a few would. Now came the tough part, making my final decisions.

I rode back to the frat with some of the guys, then sat alone in the lounge. I considered each rider one final time and wrote out my recommendations. When I finished, I walked upstairs and knocked on the door to Jen's room. He was senior, so he had a single.

"Here it is. It's up to you now."

"Yes, but when the council is finished it's all up to you again."

"No, then it's up to me and the team and mostly the team. I'm only the coach."

"The best coach we could possibly have. Thanks for doing this, Marc."

"Thanks for asking me. I love being involved with Alpha and the Little 500 once again."

I headed out. Now, all I had to do was wait. I was interested to see who the council picked. I was glad I didn't have to experience the anxiety of the riders. When I tried out, waiting those final hours to learn if I had made the team was Hell.

I entered my empty apartment and turned on the lights. Part of me wished I still lived at the frat, but I had my time living there and now it was done.

The apartment felt empty. I needed to adopt a dog or cat. A cat would be far less trouble, but I could walk a dog on campus. The problem was, I would have to walk a dog whether I wanted to or not, in all types of weather. Maybe I'd be better off with a fish, but then fish weren't great company. I would give it some thought.

I hadn't taken the time to eat earlier so I fixed myself a bowl of cereal. It didn't make much sense to cook for one. Eating cereal alone in my apartment might sound pathetic, but I happen to like cereal. I could have gone out if I wished, but I didn't feel like it. This was one of those nights I wanted to stay in.

I allowed myself some rare time to do nothing after supper. I forgot about all the work that needed to be done and watched TV instead. I didn't always have to be productive.

My cell rang just before 9 p.m.

"Hey, it's Jens. We've made our decision and already posted it."

"That was fast."

"Yes, we went with your recommendations and picked your top four. Everyone agreed. Those four are some of the best brothers in AAΩ."

"Great."

"I should warn you. Cameron is pissed. I think he expected to make the team."

"He is good, but... well, you saw the list and my comments."

"Yes. He stormed out cussing."

"I hate that he's taking it so hard. He's good, but not as good as the riders we picked."

"I just wanted to let you know. You'll have your dream team."

"Great. Thanks Jens."

"Good night."

I smiled. I was glad the council went with my top four. I knew my input had weight, but it was not a foregone conclusion that my recommendations would rule.

I knew Cam wouldn't be pleased if he didn't get a spot. Part of me hoped the fraternity council would give him one. There were certainly worse choices, but I couldn't in good conscience put him in the top four. He was seventh out of the group in fact. He was an excellent rider, but wasn't ready to be part of a team. He was somewhat lacking in his exchange skills. He had a promising start, but went downhill instead of up. Hopefully, I could convince him to try again next year. All he truly needed was more practice.

My mind began racing with plans for upcoming practices. The AAΩ team had true potential. I had a few months to get them in shape, including a very few weeks when we could still ride outside.

Chapter Seven

I walked into the Alpha Alpha Omega lounge to meet with the team and those who wished to continue practicing with us. I noticed Cam was not present.

"Let's get started," I said to quiet everyone down. "First, I want to congratulate those who made the team. You four are the best of the best."

The three riders who had not made the team clapped for Baxter, Austin, Soaring Eagle, and Kang.

"Matt, Pierce, and Reece, I hope you're here because you plan to train with the team. I can't promise you'll make the team next year, but each of you will have an excellent shot. The decision about who to pick for the team wasn't easy and I'm not saying that to make you feel better. I mean it."

The guys smiled.

"I have a copy of the Official Little 500 Handbook for all of you. Those of you on the team need to be familiar with all the rules and it won't hurt the rest of you to read it either. We do not want to lose the Little 500 on a technicality," I said as I handed out the handbooks.

"There will not be a test, but I will expect you to know the rules so you'd damned well better study the handbook.

"Now that the team has been selected, it's time to get serious with training. We have a very few weeks left for outside training and we want to take advantage of that. During the cold months, you'll train on stationary bikes in the SRSC. You will also do some weight training, especially on your legs. We will get back outside as soon as the weather permits, but by then the race will be on top of us.

"Everyone put your handbooks in your room and get ready to ride. We're doing fifty miles today."

The boys departed for their rooms and I headed out of the lounge. Cam and I passed in the hallway. He glared and me and didn't speak. I considered trying to talk to him, but thought it best to wait.

The boys gathered at the bike racks and soon we set out. We rode through town first and then out into the country on one of our now-familiar routes. The weather was cool and great for riding. We were at the very end of September and October would soon be upon us. I hoped for a warm fall and mild winter so we could continue riding outside as long as possible.

"The next eight miles is a flat stretch, so let's pick up the pace and I want you to ride as close together as possible. That's how it will be a good deal of the time in the race."

The boys picked up speed and closed in. A collision was a very real danger, but better now than during the race in the spring.

My younger brothers did well. There were some close calls, but no one went down. We all rode with helmets and gloves, but those didn't protect everything and hitting the pavement hurt. All riders learned that sooner or later. Every rider either has gone down on the pavement, will go down, or even more likely, both.

The fifty miles went by quickly. I could tell the guys were tired when we once more returned to the frat, but no one was panting and no one looked ready to drop. A few weeks training had made a world of difference. I bid the boys goodbye and pedaled home. I needed to shower and change before I headed to Hunter and Alessio's house for supper.

I arrived at the Gonzaga-Overmyer home with only the scent of Mitchum and Burberry Brit cologne clinging to me. I smelled much better than I did at the end of my fifty miles with the team. I wore khaki slacks and a hunter green polo.

"Why does it always smell so good here?" I asked as Hunter let me in.

"Because you always come when it's time to eat," Hunter said.

"Hey, if you don't want me here you shouldn't invite me. You know I'll show up if there's food."

"Alessio said it's almost ready so let's go sit at the table."

Hunter moved slowly and sat down with effort. Our eyes met. I very nearly asked him what was wrong, but Alessio entered just then.

"I made rosemary cream chicken. I remember how you used to order it at Bucceto's sometimes."

"I'm sure yours is even better. You should open a restaurant. I would eat there daily."

"Serve yourself. I will be right back with garlic bread."

There was already a large salad bowl on the table so I started with that. The salad had large olives as well as red onions and fresh Parmesan cheese. I tried some before getting any pasta. I couldn't identify the dressing, but it was wonderful.

"This is great," I said, then dished some rosemary cream chicken onto my plate.

Alessio returned with bread. Hunter began to rise to fill his plate.

"Let me get it," Alessio said.

I almost said something about Hunter training Alessio as a servant, but I felt uneasy. Something was wrong.

"How is the team?" Hunter asked.

"They are coming along nicely. Three who didn't make the team are training with us. When this is all over I think I'll be able to leave AAΩ in great shape for next year."

"You definitely pulled their ass out of the fire," Hunter said.

"Without someone experienced this would have been only a rebuilding year. Even if we don't place this year, AAΩ will be in a good position for next year."

"I envy you, Marc," Hunter said.

"Hey, if you had moved back a little sooner the frat might have asked you to coach."

"You're a better choice," Hunter said.

"I don't know about that."

"I do. I'm good, but you're better."

"Alessio, this is incredible," I said.

"I am relieved to hear you say that. I've never made rosemary cream chicken before."

"Seriously?"

Alessio nodded.

"Damn, how do you guys keep from getting fat?"

"Lots of sex," Hunter said, then grinned.

"That is the most fun way to exercise."

We had a very pleasant meal. Bucceto's was my favorite Italian restaurant, but Alessio's cooking was even better. I guess the chefs at Bucceto's did not have an Italian mother to teach them.

"I made cheesecake for dessert. I'll be right back," Alessio said as we finished our pasta.

"Can I borrow Alessio to cook for me a couple evenings a week?" I asked. Hunter smiled.

"Sorry, you know how selfish I am. I don't share."

"I don't blame you. I wouldn't share him either."

Alessio returned with a raspberry cheesecake.

"Oh man that looks good," I said.

Alessio cut me a big piece.

"I don't think I want any right now," Hunter said.

"You're eating a little piece. I have hot tea almost ready too."

"Yes, Alessio," Hunter said. Alessio smacked him playfully.

I noticed that Hunter had not eaten much. That was not like him. He was no longer a wrestler or bike racer, but he didn't eat enough for a small child.

"Oh. My. God. This is the best thing ever," I said after I tasted the cheesecake. Alessio returned just then with hot tea for all of us.

"Come on, Marc. Don't hold back with the compliments. Tell me how much you really like it."

I laughed.

"I have one problem with the team. Well, not actually the team, but with one of the riders who tried out. Cam didn't make the cut and he is pissed."

"He'll get over it. Not making the team is a blow," Hunter said.

"Jens warned me that he was plenty pissed and if looks could kill I'd be dead. I think he expected to be chosen. We even, uh..."

"You slept with him," Hunter said with a slight grin.

"Yeah, against my better judgment. He came onto me. I should have had more sense but my dick was thinking for me. I wonder now about his motives. Maybe he only hooked up with me to get a spot on the team."

"Don't put yourself down, Marc. You're still very attractive," Alessio said. Hunter nodded.

"Maybe, but I'm also thirty. I'm sure most college boys think of that as old."

"If that was his motivation, then he doesn't belong on the team," Alessio said.

I shrugged.

"He wasn't one of my top choices because others were better. When things started with him I worried that I wouldn't be able to be objective. If he made the team I'd probably be second guessing myself."

"I wouldn't worry about him. If he doesn't come around it's his loss."

"Yeah, but it's also the fraternity's loss. If he trained with the team he'd likely be a great rider by next year."

"There's not much you can do about it," Alessio said.

"True, although once he cools off I may try to talk him into training with us. Training with the team did me a world of good."

After we finished our tea and dessert, we moved into the living room. Walking the short distance was an obvious effort for Hunter. He wasn't well. He and Alessio shared a look. I had the feeling I wouldn't have to ask what was wrong.

Hunter and Alessio sat close together on the couch. Alessio held Hunter's hand. I smiled to see them happy together, but they weren't truly happy. They were happy with each other, but something was amiss.

"I know you've noticed I'm not particularly healthy," Hunter said.

I nodded.

"I don't know how to tell you this Marc, so I'll just tell you. I have cancer."

"Oh, Hunter."

"I've gone through chemotherapy twice. The second session seemed to work, which is why we went ahead with our move here, but... it's back and... well, I'm out of options."

Tears began to well up in my eyes.

"You can try the chemotherapy again, right? The IU Medical Center is..."

Hunter shook his head.

"We discussed it with my doctor back home and my new doctor here. The cancer is not responding to treatment."

"But you can't just give up!" I said more loudly than I intended. I bit my lower lip to keep it from trembling.

"If I thought it would work, I would go through it again, but the cancer is not only back. It's spread. I might have a little more time if I went through the treatments again, but I want to enjoy the time I have left. I don't want to spend my last weeks ill from chemotherapy."

Tears rolled down my cheeks. This was far worse than I'd feared. I looked back and forth between two of the great loves of my life, silently imploring them to make everything okay, but it wasn't going to okay. I began to cry. Alessio moved to the arm of my chair and hugged me. I calmed myself down in a few moments.

"Why didn't you tell me about this sooner? I would have come to Virginia and..."

"That's why," Hunter said. "I didn't want you to put your life on hold for me. We managed just fine."

"There's nothing that can be done?"

Hunter shook his head.

"How long?"

"Six months at most. Maybe three. Maybe not quite that."

The color drained from my face.

"I don't know what to say."

"You don't have to say anything," Hunter said. "I just want to spend time with you while I can."

"You can have all the time with me you want, although I don't think time with me is such a great prize."

Hunter smiled. Alessio hugged me, then moved back to his place by Hunter. There were times in the past I wished I had ended up with Alessio instead of Hunter, as selfish as that thought was, but now I was glad Alessio was at Hunter's side all these years.

"I don't expect you to put your life on hold and I do still have a life of my own. I just want the three of us to be together now and then."

"I'd like that. I'm already thrilled you two moved back here and not just because of Alessio's cooking."

"He didn't want to tell you at all, but we knew we couldn't hide it for long," Alessio said.

"Yeah, I'm not an idiot."

"Eh-eh," Hunter said.

"Hey, just because you're sick doesn't mean I won't hurt you."

"Sure, pick on me when I'm weak. You wouldn't have dared when I was a wrestler stud."

"I dared plenty of times."

"Yeah and you always got your butt kicked."

"It's the perfect time for revenge."

"Oh that is low," Hunter said, but grinned.

It felt good to joke around, but my heart wasn't really in it. We grew silent.

"If there is anything I can do..." I trailed off.

"What I want you to do is treat me as you always have. I want to enjoy what the three of us have together. Despite what is happening to me. I'm happy, Marc."

"That's all I ever wanted for you."

"I know."

"I should get going. I can tell you're tired and I'm sure you two would like some time alone," I said.

"Oh, we still like our alone time. We like it most every night," Hunter said. Alessio punched him lightly in the arm.

Hunter stood. I walked to him and hugged him close.

"I love you," I said.

"I know. I love you too."

I hugged Alessio next.

"I love you too."

"And I you."

I stepped back.

"I'll see you soon. I'll take you out for supper next time, or I can get takeout if you prefer."

"Sounds good," Hunter said.

I bid my friends goodbye and stepped outside. The smile immediately disappeared from my face. I walked to the car feeling dead inside, then drove home.

I didn't go into my apartment when I arrived. Instead, I walked the short distance to campus and followed the path that led between Dunn Meadow and the Jordan River.

It felt... unreal, as if I had stepped into a reality that could not exist. In my mind, Hunter was still the boy I met when I attended IU. He was strong, beautiful, and immortal; we all were back then. We were older now, but not yet old. Hunter, Alessio, and I should have had many, many years left together.

Hunter couldn't be dying. He couldn't. I remembered watching him wrestle for IU. I could still see him on the mat wearing his tight singlet, his bulging muscles enough to intimidate an opponent. How could he go from that young god to a sickly man who had six months to live?

I didn't think I could handle what was to come. I didn't think I could bear to watch Hunter weaken and die. But what was the alternative? Throw away the remaining time I had with him? I could never and would never do that. And what about Alessio? This had to be harder for him than for me. I needed to be there for him and for Hunter. I truly had no choice. I had to be strong and endure what was soon to come. My friends needed me. I had very little time with Hunter left and I didn't want to miss a minute of it.

I breathed in the cool evening air and realized only then I was standing by the Showalter Fountain in front of the auditorium. The sound of falling water filled the air. The mist caught the moonlight. I had sat here with Hunter when we were younger. We could have easily become a couple and yet that's not what either of us wanted at the time. Then, Alessio came along. I fell for him, but he was already falling for Hunter. There was something between them that was not there with Hunter and me. I was jealous certainly, but I never let that jealousy grow into anger. I guess I could have hated Alessio, Hunter, or both, but they were my friends and I loved them. I was glad I did not allow myself to grow bitter. Instead, I was happy for them. I was happy they both found someone, even though that someone was not me.

This shouldn't have happened. They should have grown old together. We should all have grown old together. Now, Hunter's time was almost up and there was nothing I could do about it.

"Hey."

I looked up.

"Laurent. What are you doing here?"

"I like to walk at night. What are you doing here?"

"I..." Tears welled up in my eyes and I began to cry. Laurent quickly sat down beside me and hugged me close. He kept on holding me as the pain inside came out.

"I'm sorry," I said when the tears stopped.

"Don't be sorry. What happened?"

I told him about Hunter, and about Hunter, Alessio, and me in our college years. I probably told him more than he wanted to know and yet Laurent seemed interested in it all. When I finished, I patted his hand.

"Thanks. I guess I needed someone to talk to."

"Maybe that's why I'm here. Come on, I'll take you home. Can I spend the night?"

"I don't feel up to sex tonight Laurent."

"Not to have sex. I just want to sleep with you. I don't think you should be alone right now."

"Thank you, Laurent. That would be wonderful."

Laurent held my hand as we walked through campus toward my apartment. We didn't speak as we walked in the moonlight. It was enough just to be together.

I made a pot of hot tea when we arrived at my apartment and pulled out a box of Scottish shortbread cookies. We sat at the table and had a snack.

"I know what you're feeling. I had a brother who died of cancer," Laurent said.

"I thought your brother was going to IU?"

"Jett is going to IU, but Dustin was the oldest. He was three years older than me. He died when I was fifteen."

"I'm sorry."

"He was a senior in high school. It happened very quickly. My parents took him to the doctor because he was getting really weak and two weeks later he was dead."

"That must have been difficult to handle when you were fifteen."

"It's tough to lose someone you love at any age. It didn't seem real when I found out he was sick. It didn't seem possible. Dustin was the most athletic of us. He was on the football team. He was playing one week and then next he was too weak to walk to the bathroom. I was so angry when he got sick. It was completely wrong and unfair. I wasn't angry at anyone or anything in particular, just angry."

"What did you do?"

"I sucked it up. I decided I didn't have time to be angry. I wanted to be with Dustin while I could and I needed to be strong for my family, especially my mom.

"I know what it's like for you. I wish I could tell you everything will be okay, but it will never be okay again. It does get easier. At first, I didn't feel like I could go on, but I did. Now, I'm glad I did and I'm glad I spent time with Dustin while I could. I'll never forget him and I'll always miss him, but I know he wouldn't want me to stop living because he did. I know that for sure because that's exactly what he told me before he died. He said, 'Laurent, don't waste a fucking second being sorry when I'm gone. I have no choice. I'm going to die. You do have a choice. I want you to live your life and enjoy it. Do the things I'll never get to do.' That's what he said to me. That's what you have to do too, Marc."

"Yeah. I know. I've already decided I want to enjoy what time I have left with Hunter. Alessio will need me too. This will be even harder for him."

"Being there for someone else makes it easier. I was so focused on helping Mom that I didn't have much time for my own pain."

We talked for a while more, then Laurent took me by the hand and led me into the bedroom. We undressed and climbed under the covers. Laurent kissed me once and then we held each other until we fell asleep.

***

"I need you to come to the frat house. We've got trouble." That's all Jens said on the phone.

I wondered what was up as I drove to Alpha Alpha Omega. Had one of my riders hurt himself? It could be almost anything.

I parked, then walked inside and up to Jens' room.

"Come in. Have a seat."

"What's this about?"

"There has been an accusation against you. Cameron claims that you raped him."

"What?"

"He says you came into his room on the pretext of talking to him about the team. He says you offered him a spot if he'd have sex with you and when he refused you raped him."

"That's bullshit!"

"For what it's worth I find it highly unlikely, but he's threatening to go to the police unless you're removed as the coach."

"Shit."

"I don't know what to do. We need you, but…"

"Fuck that little bastard. We did have sex and maybe it wasn't a smart move on my part, but he came onto me. In hindsight I'm sure he thought I'd give him a spot on the team because he slept with me. That's why he was pissed off when he didn't get a spot. I didn't recommend him because others were better. I didn't rape him and I'm not letting him bully me."

"What do you want to do?"

"I want the AAΩ council to convene and hold a formal hearing."

"What if he goes to the police?"

"Then he does and I'll deal with it. If he wants to claim I raped him then I'll make him prove it. I know he can't because it didn't happen."

"I don't think we can keep you as coach until this is cleared up."

"Then we'd better clear it up quickly."

Jens smiled.

"I'll set it up. I'll notify Cam. If he wants to proceed I'll have to get a formal deposition from him. I'll try to do that as quickly as possible, but all this will take some time."

I left Jens' room stunned. I knew Cam was pissed about not making the team, but I didn't think he was low enough to go this far. I considered confronting him, but that would be a bad idea. Instead, I asked one of the brothers passing in the hall where I could find Austin's room.

I knocked on the door.

"Hey Coach."

"I'm glad you're here. I need you to take over practice this evening."

"Uh, why me and why?"

"You are the strongest team member and have the best grasp of what needs to be done. I may need you to run practice for a few days, perhaps even permanently."

"What? You're not leaving us? We need you."

"It wasn't my choice. I've been accused of something rather heinous. I've asked for a formal council hearing, but until it happens you are in charge."

"It's Cam. Isn't it?"

"How did you know?"

"He's been fuming ever since he didn't make the team. I even overheard him say he'd make you pay."

"You're sure?"

"I'm sure."

"I hope you're willing to tell the council that."

"I am."

"Good."

"What did he accuse you of doing?"

"Raping him."

"That's bullshit! You wouldn't do something like that!"

"I appreciate your confidence. I didn't."

"I should get the guys together and fuck him up."

"No. Don't. I'm going to take him on in the council meeting."

"The team will be behind you."

"Thanks, Austin."

I departed knowing that the team was in good hands for now. I couldn't believe Cam had actually accused me of raping him. How could he be so vindictive? I wondered now if anything between us was real or if it was all a calculated manipulation by Cam to get what he wanted. I felt used.

First, Hunter. Now, this. I should have known disaster was on the horizon. Everything was going too well. I had my shop at last and Hunter, Alessio, and I were back together again. I hoped the council didn't believe Cam. I was certain he could not prove anything in a court of law, but he didn't need to prove anything to the council. All he had to do is convince them I was guilty and I would be kicked out of Alpha Alpha Omega. College was over, but membership in my fraternity meant a great deal to me. I didn't want to lose that.

***

"I'll rip his fucking head off!" Hunter said.

"Hunter, calm down. Have a seat," Alessio said.

We were sitting in Hunter and Alessio's living room, waiting on the take out I had ordered. I had just told them about the charges against me.

"Everything will be okay, Hunter. I didn't do it so he can't prove I did it."

"You could still be kicked out."

"I know."

"This makes me so God-damned angry!" Hunter said. He hit the sofa table, causing everyone on it to bounce.

"I'm not so pleased myself. For what it's worth, Jens doesn't believe him and Austin said he overheard Cam say he was going to make me pay."

"Yeah?"

"Yes. Austin wanted to get the team together and kick the shit out of Cam."

"If they do I want in."

"We're not going that route, Hunter, but thanks."

"This burns my ass."

"It will be over in a few days. Austin has taken over training the team for now. He can replace me if need be. Maybe I shouldn't have told you."

"No. You should have. We're your friends. We're here for you."

"Yes, but my problem is nothing compared to yours."

"That doesn't matter."

I smiled

"You haven't changed."

"No, but is that a compliment or insult?" Hunter asked.

"Hmm, let me think..." I said rubbing my chin.

"Jerk."

The doorbell rang. I answered it with Alessio so I could pay for our orders from the China Buffet. Hunter wasn't doing especially well today. He wasn't up to going to our old haunt, so I had it brought to him.

I managed to get Hunter's mind off Cam's accusation by reminiscing about old times, particularly the cookouts at Brendan & Casper's apartment. The food helped as well. The General Tso's chicken and other items we had ordered from the China Buffet was just as good as they were in our college years. I only wished that Hunter would eat more.

We had an enjoyable evening. Hunter and Alessio showed me photos from their visits to Italy. Alessio had some hot male relatives, but then that should have come as no surprise. I had always found Alessio extremely attractive.

I left early because Hunter was tired, but the evening was a good distraction for me. I didn't like Cam's accusation hanging over my head and I didn't like missing practices either. I knew Austin could handle them, but I wanted to be there.

***

I received a call from Jens only three days after Cam made his accusation. He said I should be at the frat house at 7 p.m. I closed up the shop as usual at 6, then went upstairs and fixed myself a peanut butter, jelly, and marshmallow sandwich.

A little before 7 p.m. I drove to the frat. The lounge had been rearranged so that it looked much like a courtroom, except instead of a judge's bench there was a long table. The fraternity council was seated behind it with Jen's sitting in the middle. Two chairs stood spaced about ten feet apart out in front of all the others. Jen's motioned to the one on the left. I took a seat.

Several brothers were already seated, including the entire team and all those who had tried out, except for Cam. He arrived a couple of minutes later. He looked around confused. When he spotted me he glared.

"What's this about?" Cam asked.

"You have made a serious charge against a brother, so the council has convened for a formal hearing. I thought you understood this would occur when I took your deposition," Jens said.

"Hearing? He's not a brother! He's a former brother who doesn't belong here at all!"

"Once a brother, always a brother, unless removed for a serious infraction. You should know that, Cameron. You have made a charge of such a serious infraction. Take a seat," Jens said, pointing to the other chair.

"This council is now in session. Brother Cameron Raycraft has accused Brother Marc Peralta of rape."

The room was filled with murmurs, although I had no doubt many of those present already knew about the accusation, especially the team. Jens smacked a gavel on the table to quiet the room.

"Marc, how do you plead?"

I stood.

"Not guilty."

"Of course he's not guilty," Austin said loudly. Jens banged his gavel again.

"You're all against me!" Cam snarled.

"We are your brothers. We are not against you, but you have made a charge against another brother. We are here to determine if there is a basis for that charge. If found guilty Marc will be stripped of his membership in Alpha Alpha Omega."

Cam said nothing further.

"Please tell us about the alleged incident."

Cam stood.

"The very real incident took place the evening before the Little 500 tryouts. Marc came to my room and offered me a spot on the team if I would have sex with him."

One of the brothers coughed "bullshit" behind me. Jens smacked his gavel again.

"Of course, I refused. I'm straight and I wouldn't have had sex with him to get a position if I was gay. Marc grew angry. He grabbed me and then... raped me."

Cam was a good actor. He actually sounded like he was going to cry near the end. Jens turned to me.

"Tell us about the alleged incident from your point of view, Marc."

"I just told you what he did! There is no other point of view!" Cam shouted. Jens smacked the gavel hard.

"You have made your statement. Now the accused will make his."

I stood.

"Cam invited me into his room that evening. I told him I needed to be getting home. He insisted. In fact, he physically pulled me into the room. Once there, he kissed me."

"You fucking liar!" Cam shouted.

Jens smacked his gavel down on the table hard.

"One more outburst and you will be removed until your turn to speak comes again."

Cam glared at me and sat back down.

"Please continue, Marc."

"Cam pulled my shirt over my head, then went down on me."

Cam began to stand, but then sat back down when Jens stared at him.

"Soon after, Cam asked me to have sex with him."

Cam nearly stood again, but controlled himself, which I'm sure wasn't easy because the brothers were whispering among themselves and I heard some quiet laughter.

"Define sex," Jens said.

"He wanted me to fuck him."

"Slut," one of the brothers coughed into his fist.

Jens smacked his gavel down again.

"Did you?"

"Yes."

"Did he ask you to stop?" Jens asked.

"No. I even asked if he wanted me to stop since it was his first time. He never once asked me to stop. The longer I did it, the more he enjoyed it."

I looked to the side. Cam had turned completely red. I saw Baxter stuff his fist into his mouth to keep from laughing.

Jens turned to Cam.

"Do you have any proof of your allegations? Did anyone witness what went on in your room that evening?"

"Of course not! Do you think he would rape me in front of a witness! I see where this is going. It will be my word against his and he'll get off with no punishment."

"I bet they both got off," someone whispered behind me. The comment received a laugh. I don't think the council was able to hear.

"You have no proof," Jens said.

"Fuck this! I'll go to the cops!"

"You are free to do so, but the police will want proof as well."

Jens turned to me.

"Do you have any witnesses that can prove your innocence?"

"No," I said.

"See?" Cam said.

"Yes he does." Cam and I looked back. Reece stood.

"Please come forward and tell the council what you witnessed," Jens said.

As Reese walked forward I vaguely remembered someone in the hallway when I entered Cam's room and perhaps when I departed as well, but I wasn't sure. I didn't know about the particulars of the accusation until I heard them only moments before. My main hope rested in the fact that Austin overheard Cam say he was going to make me pay.

"I was in the hallway when Cam asked Marc into his room. Marc said something like, 'I don't think I should' and Cameron said something like, 'Yes, you should so get in here.' Then, he pulled Marc into his room."

"Liar!" Cam snarled.

Jens hit his gavel on the desk again. "Shut up, Cameron!" Jens looked back at Reese. "Did you see or hear anything else?"

"Not then, but later. I saw Marc leaving Cam's room. Cameron said, "I'll see you at practice tomorrow' or something similar and Marc told him to have a good night."

"Anything else?"

"No. Marc departed."

Jens looked out at the brothers.

"Does anyone else have evidence to provide?"

"I do," Austin said, standing. "It's not evidence about that evening, but I think it's important."

"Proceed."

"I overheard Cameron tell Michael that he was going to make Marc pay for not getting him a spot on the team."

"That's a lie!" Cam shouted.

"No. It's the truth," Michael said.

"Anything else? Anyone?" Jens asked.

No one spoke.

Jens looked at the other council members.

"We will recess while the council confers in private. We will return in one hour." He hit the gavel on the table.

Cam stormed out of the room as the council departed.

"What a fucking asshole," Reece said.

Some of the brothers made cracks about Cam, others laughed. He was not a popular guy at the moment. I almost felt sorry for him.

My team approached me as did the others who had tried out.

"We know this is bullshit, Marc," Soaring Eagle said. "We've been around you long enough to know you would never do something like that."

"Part of it is my fault. I didn't use good judgment. I..."

"Let your cock do your thinking? Been there. Done that," Pierce said.

"Are we talking about that skank you fucked last year?" York asked.

"Shut it, York. You'll stick your dick into anything that moves."

"Maybe he can try Cam," Sam said, then paled. "Sorry Marc, I didn't mean..."

"It's okay. I doubt any of you are into guys so..."

"No. I'm sorry. That's not how you treat a brother."

"But Cam? Seriously coach?" Matt teased.

"Hey, Cameron is attractive, at least on the outside."

"I never liked the bitch," Baxter said. "No offense, Marc, but I bet he bent over for you to get a spot on the team."

"I didn't realize it at the time, but I think that's exactly what he did," I said.

"Well, we're behind you. No matter what happens, although I wouldn't worry. Jens and the council didn't look happy with Cam."

"Yeah, when they looked at Cam they looked like they'd just tasted something nasty," Kang said.

I talked with my guys and some of the other brothers while we waited. No one was hostile toward me. It was no secret that I was gay, although I don't know how many knew before the hearing. They certainly did now. I wasn't pleased that everyone knew my private business, but Cam left me no choice.

The hour was nearly up before Cam returned. He sat in his chair and refused to look at anyone. The rest of us returned to our seats when the council came back into the room. Jens banged his gavel.

"This hearing is now back in session. After weighing the testimony, the council finds Marc Peralta innocent of the charge against him."

Cam swore, but I couldn't tell what he said.

"Cameron Raycraft, please stand."

Cam looked uncomfortable as he did so.

"The council also finds that you made a false accusation against a brother. Due to the seriousness of the false accusation, the council strips you of your membership in Alpha Alpha Omega. You have twenty-four hours to vacate your room."

Cam's mouth dropped open and all the color drained from his face. The room grew deathly quiet. Cam looked around at the faces of those seated. Some of the brothers glared at him, some shook their heads, and others refused to look at him at all. Cam looked at me. He was clearly devastated.

"Does he have to be kicked out of the fraternity?" I asked.

Jens gazed at me.

"Yes, he has violated the very foundation of all fraternities. Instead of standing by a brother, he sought to have you removed as coach and as a brother by lying."

I sighed. He was right. I knew it, but I couldn't find it within myself to wish Cam's punishment on anyone.

"Fuck you guys!" Cam said and hurried out of the room.

My team slapped me on the back, but I couldn't help but feel bad for Cameron. He had done something terrible, but I didn't like seeing him kicked out.

"Good riddance," Reece said.

"Thanks, Reece."

"Hey, I only told what I saw. The more I listened to Cam, the more I knew what he was saying was bullshit. You can't rape the willing or the eager."

Some of the guys laughed. They quieted as Jens approached me.

"I'm very sorry about all of this Marc. You should not have been put through this ordeal."

"I'm the one who requested a hearing. I knew what would come out when I did. I'd rather not have everyone know what went on between Cam and me, but my only true regret is that I was stupid enough to put myself in a bad position. You'd think I would be old enough to know better."

"You didn't do anything wrong. We've all put ourselves in bad positions."

"Yeah, but I have less of an excuse. I'm sorry Cam had to be kicked out."

"It was very noble of you to speak up for him after what he did."

"I saw the expression on his face and I know how I would feel if I was kicked out of the fraternity. Being a part of Alpha means a great deal to me."

"It is a shame, but we can't have someone like Cam as a brother."

Jens nodded to me and departed.

"Well, guys, I can't say it's been fun, but thanks for your support. I'm heading out."

"Need some company tonight coach?" Matt asked. Baxter punched him in the arm. "Too soon?"

"Much too soon, idiot."

I grinned.

"Thank God you'll be coaching us again. Austin is a disaster," Soaring Eagle said.

"Hey!" Austin said.

Soaring Eagle smiled.

"No one is happier to have you back than me," Austin said.

"I'll see you guys at the next practice."

I walked out feeling slightly humiliated, but even more vindicated. I doubted Cameron would make further trouble, but there was nothing good about the whole mess.

Chapter Eight

The golden leaves of Dunn Woods surrounded Hunter, Alessio, and me. This had always been one of my favorite spots on campus and I wasn't alone. I think everyone loved this bit of wilderness in the midst of the university.

I gazed down at Hunter as he sat in his wheelchair. He smiled at me. Alessio stood behind him, pushing the chair. Hunter was capable of walking, but he tired so easily we knew he could not make it through the IMU to the Tudor Room, where we were having Sunday Brunch. Since he wasn't exerting himself we took the scenic route.

"Its like being inside the flame of a candle," Hunter said.

"I never thought of that, but I see what you mean," Alessio said as he looked around at the golden leaves illuminated by bright sunlight.

"It's nice to know this place will never change, at least not for a very long time," Hunter said.

"Yeah, Herman Wells and the Dunn family saw to that."

When the Dunn family turned over the property to the university more than a century before it was with the stipulation that this section of woods would never be developed. Herman Wells, the most famous president of Indiana University, was a great lover of trees. Thanks to him, no tree on campus could be felled without going through a lengthy process. As a result, IU was one of the most beautiful campuses in the U.S.

"I wonder what this place will look like in a thousand years," Hunter said.

"Kirkwood Hall and many of the other limestone buildings may still be here," I said.

"I hope so."

We strolled through the heart of the woods to its eastern boundary and then followed the brick path that ran along the edge of the woods and toward the IMU. Ahead and to our right were the great old limestone or brick buildings of IU: Lindley, Kirkwood, Wiley, Owen, and Maxwell Halls. Most of the structures, perhaps all, were over a hundred years old.

The autumn weather was brilliant and warm. It would be a perfect day for riding later, but the morning was reserved to spend time with Hunter and Alessio.

Nearly all of IU was accessible to wheelchairs, but it still took extra time to get around. I had never before realized it, but even something so simple as walking into the IMU took longer when one had travel up the long ramps instead of dashing up the short flights of steps. It gave me a new understanding of those who couldn't get along as easily as I could.

I held open the doors to the south entrance of the IMU as Alessio pushed Hunter inside. To our left was Alumni Hall where many events were held, but we turned to the right and soon entered the South Lounge.

The lounge was empty now, but on weekdays it was packed with students. I gazed at the limestone fireplace as we passed. The gas flames licked artificial logs and looked quite real. I had sat beside that fireplace and studied many times during my college years. There was something comfy about a fire.

We exited the lounge and entering another hallway, passing my favorite T.C. Steele painting. The Tudor Room was just ahead to the left. I could already hear the music of the piano.

We stepped into the elegant Tudor Room and walked up to the hostess stand. We were escorted to our table and then headed for the buffet.

Hunter ditched his wheelchair so that he could get his own food and sit in a real chair. He was lucky he could do so, but then I would not call Hunter lucky. Merely going out for brunch was likely to wear him out.

I pushed that thought aside. Hunter did not need to see me sad. I had plenty to be happy about. I was with Hunter and Alessio and that was reason enough.

I returned to the table with an omelet, French toast, bacon, Tudor Room casserole and eggs Benedict. I made a trip to the tea and coffee bar for hot tea. By the time I returned our waitress had returned with the cranberry juice I had ordered.

"Now this is what I call breakfast," Hunter said.

Hunter had not been eating well and the food on his plate was nothing compared to what he would have devoured in his college years, but it was a good deal more than I'd see him eat recently. Alessio seemed pleased to see he had an appetite as well.

"You know who I miss? Anton," Hunter said.

"You miss pretending you thought he was twelve," I said.

"Hey, that was mostly Brandon and Jon, although he did look like he should have been in middle school."

"Did you see the picture of him on the cover of his latest book? He still looks like he should be in high school," Alessio said.

"I wonder how many degrees he has," Hunter said.

"I'm not sure. I know he has at least a couple from IU and a couple more from Cambridge. He is a genius," I said.

"Remember when we used to quiz him?" Hunter asked.

"And no matter what we asked, he knew the answer," I said. "I miss Anton too, but I miss Brandon and Jon even more. What do you want to bet they still go off on each other?"

"Yeah, they just do it by email and text now," Alessio said.

We all laughed. It was so good to see Hunter laugh, but then he was in the best spirits of any of us. I wondered if it was easier for him to know he was soon to die than it was for us.

"At least the three of us are all here. Before you guys moved to Bloomington it was just me," I said.

"You and how many college boys?"

"Hey, I've only been involved with two."

"You're a dirty old man, molesting those innocent boys," Hunter teased.

"Hey, they were both legal and I'm thirty. I'm not old yet."

"Two ha! I bet you've hooked up with twenty," Hunter said.

"I didn't even get around that much in college," I said.

"That's not what I heard," Alessio teased.

"Uh huh. I had my share, now Dorian... That's another matter. I promise, I have only hooked up with two since I came back and that was one too many."

"I'm glad they tossed that creep out of the frat," Hunter said.

"I was sorry to see it happen, even after the stunt he pulled, but the council was right."

"You could have him prosecuted for what he did," Hunter said.

"Yeah, but I don't think there is any need. He's been punished enough. I never dreamed the council would kick him out."

"He got what he deserved," Alessio said.

"Maybe so, but it's still a shame. Being a member of Alpha Alpha Omega has always meant a great deal to me."

"You're welcome," Hunter said. I grinned.

We had a wonderful brunch. Alessio and I went back for more food, then dessert. Hunter only returned to the buffet for a piece of chocolate cake. I had the same cake, plus pieces of pecan and key lime pie.

We talked over tea and coffee even after we finished dessert, but only for a short time. Hunter was quite obviously tired. He would likely take a long nap once he was home. I was a little sleepy myself, but only because I was stuffed.

Hunter sat back down in his wheelchair and Alessio pushed him out.

"I can take a turn if you get tired," I said to Alessio.

"Oh no. You'd shove me down a steep hill!" Hunter said.

"Would *I* do something like that?"

"No comment," Hunter said, then grinned.

We said our goodbyes at the car and then I walked home. It made no sense for me to drive since I lived so very close.

I enjoyed the short stroll home. The fall day could not have been more beautiful and I was glad I was able to share a part of it with my friends.

The afternoon was nearly as enjoyable. I spent part of it in my shop then rode to AAΩ to train my team. We had a long ride then practiced exchanges. The boys largely had them down now, but further practice was still valuable. The exchange was one of the most critical parts of the race and the part where the most could go wrong. By race day I wanted my team to be so skilled at exchanges that they became natural. There would be no opportunity to practice them in the winter, but we would hit it again come spring.

I headed straight back to my shop after practice. I spent hours there most every day, but I never grew tired of it. My shop was my dream come true. There was little I liked more than riding bikes, talking about bikes, and helping customers pick out just the right bike. We were selling a lot of the AMF Roadmasters to Little 500 team members. I had advertised in the *Indiana Daily Student*. The ad mentioned that we kept them in stock. There wasn't much demand for them outside of the Little 500 crowd so no big stores like Target carried them. There were only two other bike shops in town and they usually didn't keep them in stock.

My shop was doing well and I was pleased to call Bloomington my hometown. If Hunter weren't ill all would have been well.

***

The team and I neared the end of our ride in the crisp November air. The fifty-mile ride was strenuous, but the cool temperatures kept us from working up too much of a sweat. We sailed into the Alpha Alpha Omega parking lot and stopped at the bike racks.

"Okay guys, you have one hour to clean up and change and then I'll meet you back here," I said.

The boys headed inside. I pulled out my cell and called Alessio to give him an update on our time of arrival then headed home to shower and change.

An hour later was I back at the frat. Sometimes I felt I spent as much time there as I did in my college days. The team and those who regularly rode with us assembled in the lounge and then walked outside to our bikes.

We set out on another ride, but this one was only a few blocks. Minutes later, Hunter and Alessio's driveway was filled with bikes.

I knocked on the door. Hunter opened it and smiled.

"Hey, Marc. Come in everyone."

The lot of us stepped into the living room. Alessio came out of the kitchen for a moment and I made introductions.

"This is Hunter and Alessio, both are Alpha brothers and both rode on winning teams in the Little 500. Hunter was my team captain and coach.

"This is Matt, Pierce, Reece, Baxter, Austin, Soaring Eagle, and Kang."

"It's wonderful to meet you all, but I have to get back to the kitchen," Alessio said and disappeared.

"Let's all move into the dining room. Supper is nearly ready," Hunter said.

We all moved into the next room and found a seat at the dining table.

"I recognize you from the team photo in the lounge. What's it like to win?" Soaring Eagle asked Hunter.

"It doesn't suck. It's rather like being a hero and celebrity for a day, but I'll tell you, merely racing is a rush. Winning is more fun, but I enjoyed racing even when I was on a team that didn't place."

I knew the boys had plenty of questions for Hunter, so I slipped into the kitchen.

"Damn, it smells good in here. Need any help?"

"Yeah, you can help me carry things out in a moment. Since there are so many of us I'm going to set everything out on the sideboard."

"What did you make?"

"I've kept it simple. I made spaghetti and meatballs, mozzarella and Italian sausage calzones, cooked apples, and breadsticks. For dessert I made chocolate cake."

"Holy crap those are huge meatballs," I said, drawing near the range.

"There are pitchers of iced tea and Coke in the refrigerator. You can take them out first."

I began making trips. The guys offered to help, but I told them I'd handle it. Alessio soon joined me in moving the feast into the dining room. Each time I entered the guys were listening intently to Hunter or laughing at something he said.

"He's enjoying himself," Alessio said when we were in the kitchen together between trips.

"How has he been doing?"

"Not bad. He tires easily and doesn't eat enough, but he mostly feels good."

"This was a great idea."

"I thought Hunter would enjoy it. I know he'd rather be out there with you guys, but since he isn't able I thought we could bring the team to him."

We made a few more trips and soon everything was ready.

"Okay guys, help yourself. There is plenty and more in the kitchen. There is both marinara and Alfredo sauce for the spaghetti."

The guys lined up and filled their plates while thanking Alessio of all his work. Soon, we were all seated at the table.

"This is the best thing ever," Baxter said after tasting his spaghetti.

"Alessio is from Italy," I said.

The guys couldn't stop complimenting Alessio's cooking and I knew why quite well. I had opted for Alfredo sauce on my spaghetti instead of the traditional marinara and it was incredible.

"You can cook and ride. If only I could find a girl like you," Pierce said.

I grinned. His compliment came out a bit odd, but I knew he meant it sincerely.

"That's how I reeled in Hunter. I needed an advantage, half the girls and guys were after him," Alessio said.

"How did you wrestle and train for the Little 500?" Kang asked Hunter. Hunter's wrestling had already come up in conversation.

"It wasn't easy, but when you love something you make time for it. Of course, I barely had time to breathe during wrestling season."

"Hunter almost made the U.S. Olympic Team," I said.

"Really?" Soaring Eagle asked.

"Yes. That's a nice way of saying I didn't make the team."

"Even getting a tryout is incredible. You must have been good."

"Let's just say I didn't lose often."

"Have any embarrassing stories about our coach?" Austin asked mischievously.

"I don't have any stories, but..." Hunter said, standing and walking over to a drawer in the sideboard.

"You wouldn't," I said.

Hunter grinned at me. He pulled out a large photo.

"Have any of you visited the Cincinnati Art Museum?"

"Oh lord," I said.

The guys shook their heads.

"If you do, make sure to check out the Adam Abernathy statue."

Hunter turned the photo around and showed it to the guys. They didn't get it at first, but then looked at the photo, then at the statue.

"It's you!" Austin said, laughing. I could feel myself blush.

"You posed nude?" Matt asked.

"Actually, no. Adam was my roommate. I knew nothing about the statue until he unveiled it in the IU Art Museum."

"Whoa!" Soaring Eagle said.

"After that, everyone on campus knew what I looked like naked."

"So you really looked like that? You were hot back then," Baxter said.

"He's not so bad now either," Hunter said.

"For that, I will almost forgive you for showing them that photo," I said.

"Remember, I had nothing to do with it," Alessio said.

"He's lying. It was his idea," Hunter said.

Alessio shook his head. He looked innocent, but I wasn't sure.

"Having a statue carved of you by a famous artist is a big deal. Why didn't you tell us?" Reese asked.

"You didn't ask. It's not a big secret. Some of our brothers know. I hired four of them to help me move in this summer. We were talking about roommates so I told them about sharing a room with Adam Abernathy and the statue."

"I should have a statue carved of me while I'm still hot," Matt said.

"Who says you're hot now?" Baxter asked.

"All the babes on campus."

"Uh huh."

"I would love to tell you embarrassing stories about Hunter in college, but I already related the shoe lace incident."

"You had to tell them about that, didn't you?" Hunter asked.

"Only to prove the importance of exchanges."

"Yeah, right."

"What was coach like in college?" Kang asked.

Hunter grinned.

"He was wild, out all night, every night. He was drunk most of the time and the biggest slut on campus. He went through guys like you wouldn't believe," Hunter said.

"You are so full of shit," I said.

"Why does everyone keep saying that? Actually, Marc pretty much had it together during his college days. I'm sure it was the influence of his big brother in the frat."

I rolled my eyes.

We ate until everyone was stuffed, but we all still had room for chocolate cake. The boys remained and talked a good while after dessert and then gushed with praise and gratitude over the meal that Alessio had prepared.

I remained after the guys departed.

"I would say that was a successful evening," I said.

"It was wonderful, but I'm really tired," Hunter said.

"Why don't you turn in? I'll help Alessio clean up."

"Yes, father."

I crossed my arms and glared, Hunter laughed. He gave me a hug and Alessio a hug and kiss, then headed to bed.

"He had a wonderful time. This was good for him," Alessio said.

"He was the life of the party."

"It was good for me too. There were long stretches when I didn't even think about the fact that I don't have much time left with Hunter. I don't know what I'm going to do without him Marc."

I hugged Alessio.

"My shoulder will be available to cry on at all hours of the day and night."

Alessio hugged me back, then released me.

"Okay, let's get this mess cleaned up," I said.

***

The snow flew outside the windows of Peralta's Bike Shop. December had come and ended any chance to train my team outside. The guys largely trained on their own now, since training was limited to riding stationary bikes and lifting weights in the SRSC. I enjoyed the free time, but I missed riding through the countryside.

I looked at my watch. Dorian was due to arrive soon. He had flown into Indy and was taking the Bloomington Shuttle the rest of the way. I offered to pick him up at the airport, but he wouldn't hear of it. With all the snow I was glad I didn't have to make the trip.

"I'm heading out. I'll probably be gone at least a couple of hours, maybe more. Call me if you need me," I said.

"I think we can manage. I doubt many people will be coming in for bikes today," Aaron said.

"Quite true."

"It's a blizzard outside," Todd said.

"You know what we called weather like this where I lived in northern Indiana?" I asked.

"What?"

"Spring."

The guys laughed. It was true. Winter often came early and stayed late in Verona. I loved the warmer climate of Bloomington, but today was not one of its warmer days.

I headed upstairs and dressed for the winter weather in my hooded grey coat, then put on my gloves and walked outside to clear the snow off my car. It looked like a good two inches had accumulated.

After my task was completed. I hopped in the car and drove the short distance to the Biddle Hotel entrance to the IMU and parked in a temporary parking space. In less than ten minutes the Bloomington shuttle arrived. I got out and waited for my ex-boyfriend as the passengers disembarked.

Dorian stepped out wearing a fashionable sweater and coat that practically screamed New York City. He grinned and immediately hugged me.

"Marc!"

"I'm so glad you're here, Dorian. Let's grab your bags."

Dorian had four large bags and two smaller ones. Each was stuffed to the bursting point.

"I wasn't aware you were packing for the entire theatre company," I said.

"Are you kidding? I'm traveling light!"

"Light for you maybe."

When the last bag was in the trunk and backseat of my Camaro we climbed in.

"Are you sure you want me to stay with you? There are hotels in Bloomington," Dorian said.

"I'm sure. This way I get to see you more. I've missed you so much."

"I have missed you."

We were at my place in approximately two minutes. It took that long only because I drove more slowly due to the slick streets. Dorian and I lugged his bags up the stairs, then took off our shoes and coats. We hugged once more, longer this time, and then Dorian kissed me on the lips.

"I like it," he said, gazing around my apartment.

"It's not fancy, but the location alone makes me love it, plus it's mine as soon as I pay off the building."

"In New York City an apartment this size can easily go for $2,000 a month."

"Holy shit."

Dorian walked to the window and gazed out. The snow continued to fall heavily.

"I love the view."

"Would you like some hot tea?"

"Yes please."

I put on the kettle.

"How is Hunter doing?"

151

"He's weak, but he's not doing too bad considering. Alessio insists we come over for dinner soon."

"Oh, I'd like that. How is Alessio?"

"Physically he's fine, but this is rough on him."

"How could it not be?"

"Yes and it's going to get rougher."

"I'm sure you'll be there for him."

"Yes, but I can't take the pain away of what's coming, for either of us."

"Do you think Hunter will be up to coming to see the show?"

"Yeah, we can drive him right up to the side entrance. He tires easily. He uses a wheelchair for longer distances, but he can walk if it isn't too far."

"Good, I have seats reserved for the three of you and that boy you told me about."

"Laurent?"

"Just how many boys are you involved with Marc?"

"Oh, only the freshman and sophomore classes. I haven't worked my way up to the juniors and seniors yet, or the graduate students."

"I'm sure you will."

"Hey!"

Dorian laughed.

"My God you look good. Seriously Dorian, you look twenty."

"It's a curse. You look great yourself, Marc. No one would guess you're an old man of thirty."

I steeped the teapot and poured our tea.

"Is it okay if we go out to eat later or are you too tired? I promised Laurent he could meet you. He's a huge fan."

"I'm not tired and I'd love to meet him."

"He will be thrilled. He loves you."

"You must be terribly fond of him as much as you talk about him in your emails."

"Yeah, I like him a lot."

"Enough to get serious?"

"He's eighteen, Dorian."

"So?"

"So he's at a different point in his life and he will likely leave Bloomington after he graduates."

"He might not. He might want to stay with you."

"Well, we're keeping things casual."

"Oh, so lots of sex. Huh?"

"He is eighteen, but we do other things. We go out to eat, we watch movies here, and just hang out."

"I'm glad you have someone."

"Oh, I'd better call him and make sure he isn't busy this evening, although when he finds out he's going to meet you I'm sure he'll cancel anything he has planned."

I made my call. Laurent wasn't busy, although he did scream with excitement.

"He's not busy."

"I heard." Dorian smiled.

"Want to see my shop?"

"I would love to see it."

We walked downstairs. Dorian took in the shop and grinned.

"It's great, Marc! It looked smaller in the photos you sent. Oh, there's your Little 500 bike."

"Yeah, it's back on the wall for now. When spring arrives I'll be riding it with my team again. Oh, I'd like you to meet a couple of the guys who work for me. This is Aaron and Todd. Guys, this is Dorian Calumet."

"Wait. I saw you on Broadway. My parents took me to see Peter Pan when we visited NYC," Todd said.

"Yeah, Dorian is a Broadway star," I said.

"I wouldn't go that far," Dorian said.

"I would. It's true. Dorian is being modest, which is quite unlike him."

"Thanks so much, Marc!"

"It's very nice to meet you," Todd said.

"Aaron is a member of Alpha Alpha Omega," I said.

"Oh, so he's one of your frat brothers, the younger generation," Dorian said shaking his hand.

"I'm afraid I haven't seen you on Broadway."

"You're forgiven. Not everyone can come to New York City."

"Dorian is appearing in *A Christmas Carol* in the IU Auditorium," I said.

"I already have a ticket," Todd said.

"I'll come to see you then," Aaron said.

"I'll get you guys better tickets," Dorian said. "Make sure to remind me, Marc."

"Thanks!" I could tell Todd was especially pleased.

After Dorian met the guys I gave him a tour of shop. It didn't take long, but I was proud of my place.

"This is a great location. I almost couldn't believe you found a space right on Kirkwood when you told me."

"Yeah. I couldn't have found a better location. We're doing very well."

Dorian and I returned upstairs where we sat on the couch and talked. We had endless things to talk about, from his adventures in NYC to memories of our days back in Verona. No time at all seemed to pass before the hour arrived to pick up Laurent.

"Where would you like to eat?" I asked Dorian as we climbed in my Camaro. The snow had slowed considerably, but was still coming down.

"Is Bobby's Colorado Steakhouse still open?"

"Yes, a lot of places aren't, but Bobby's is still there."

"Let's go there then, if you don't mind."

"Of course I don't mind. You'll only be a here a few days so you get to choose."

"Where does Laurent live?"

"In our old dorm."

"Briscoe?"

"It's the only dorm we both lived in."

"I guess that's right."

I turned right onto 7th Street from Indiana Avenue and drove past Dunn Meadow. I turned left on Woodburn so we would go past Dorian's other old dorm. I had plenty of time to see the sights, but Dorian did not.

"Living in Edmonton Hall was great," Dorian said as I drove by it slowly.

"You're just saying that because Tim was such good eye candy."

"He did look good without a shirt. In the warm months he rarely wore one."

"If I had a body like that I wouldn't either."

"You have a great body Marc."

"Yeah, but I've never had Tim's bulging muscles or abs and I never will."

"That makes two of us." Dorian laughed.

I turned right on 10th and then left on Fee.

"Remember when nearly all of us Verona boys attended IU? Remember when Brandon, Jon, Nathan, you, and I lived in these three dorms," Dorian said as we passed Foster and McNutt and headed down the hill to Briscoe.

"Yeah, I miss those days."

I entered the circular drive in front of Briscoe and parked in a fifteen-minute pickup space. Dorian and I got out and walked inside the lobby. It was as far as we could go since we didn't have student IDs.

We didn't have to wait long before the elevator doors opened and Laurent appeared. He swallowed hard when he spotted Dorian.

"Dorian, this is Laurent," I said.

Laurent reached out to shake Dorian's hand, but Dorian hugged him.

"It's so nice to meet you. Marc has told me a lot about you. He's right, you are extremely handsome."

Laurent blushed.

"I can't believe you're you," Laurent said.

I couldn't help but laugh. Dorian smiled.

"I've been me for a long time so I'm pretty sure I'm me."

"I mean... oh... I can't believe I'm meeting you."

"Believe me Laurent, it's not that big of a deal," I teased.

"It is to me. I thought Marc was putting me on when he said he knew you."

"Oh he knows me."

"Yeah, and I know embarrassing stories."

"Which he won't dare to tell," Dorian said.

"We'll see."

A high-pitched scream made me jump. Two girls rushed toward Dorian.

"You're Dorian Calumet!"

"Is he wearing a name tag?" I asked, but no one was paying attention to me.

"We saw you in *Wicked*. You were incredible! Is it true you're doing a movie with Meryl Streep?"

"If I am this is the first I've heard about it. I've never done film."

"Yes, but I heard you were going to start soon."

"It's a possibility, but I have no plans to do that in the immediate future."

"You should! Can we have your autograph?"

I stood in mild disbelief as Dorian signed autographs for the girls; he was a well-known Broadway star, but he wasn't a famous movie or TV actor or a rock star. I was surprised anyone recognized him.

Dorian signed autographs and talked to the girls. Several others gazed at Dorian, wondering who he was. It was a few minutes before we could make it back to the car.

"Let's get in the back. Marc can be our chauffeur," Dorian said.

"I forgot to tell you, Dorian has a huge ego," I said.

Dorian giggled.

"Let's go driver! Onward! Onward!" Dorian smacked on the back of the seat.

"Grrr!"

"It's so hard to find good help these days."

"Do you get recognized like that all the time?" Laurent asked.

"No. I'm recognized very rarely, except in the theatre district in New York and there no one really cares. I was surprised those girls noticed me and a little scared when they screamed," Dorian grinned.

Bobby's Steakhouse was not very far. In less than ten minutes we were seated in a booth gazing at menus.

"I am buying tonight," Dorian said.

"Oh, I couldn't..." Laurent began.

"No arguing and don't pick out anything cheap or I'll order for you."

"Dorian believes in belligerent generosity. You had best do as he says. He looks sweet, but he's vicious," I said.

"Rawr," Dorian said. "Actually, I spent a few years barely getting by in New York. Now, I have money and the best part of it is being able to make others happy. That makes me happy so really I'm almost being selfish."

"Interesting logic there Dorian," I said.

When our waitress returned Laurent ordered an 8 ounce New York Strip, then Dorian told the waitress to bring him the 14 ounce instead. I ordered a ribeye. Dorian ordered rainbow trout.

"What's acting in front of a big crowd like?" Laurent asked.

"It's a blast, but it can also be tiring. We often do two or even three shows a day. It can sometimes be painful."

"Painful?"

"When I played Peter Pan there were a lot of flying scenes. The rigging is not comfortable and actually hurts sometimes. Practicing was the hardest because I was in a rig for such a long period of time. It took quite a while to learn how to balance."

"I would be frightened."

"It's scary at first, but those handling the wires are professionals. Still, the first time I shot up twenty feet in the air I felt like screaming."

I laughed.

"Did you feel like screaming or did you actually scream?" I asked.

"Well, I might have screamed a little. I don't remember. It was too terrifying."

"Does it ever get boring doing the same scenes over and over?"

"No. They're never exactly the same. Each production evolves. In a way, it's new every time. I never feel like I'm acting while I'm on the stage. I am the character."

"It must be wonderful."

"Are you interested in acting Laurent?"

"Oh, I don't have the talent. I find it fascinating and I love theatre, but I am best suited to sit in the audience."

"Hey, me too," I said. "I could have had a brilliant acting career. I was only lacking one thing. Talent."

Dorian grinned.

"You have talent. I could never win the Little 500."

"Well, it does require sweating."

"Eww! Never!" Dorian squealed.

Laurent laughed.

Dorian regaled us with stories of rehearsals and shows while we waited on our orders. Laurent continued to ask him questions even while we ate. I was largely invisible, but I didn't mind. I would have Dorian to myself often in the coming days.

"You are amazingly attractive. Marc said you were beautiful, but you're more than beautiful," Laurent said. The boy was star stuck, but he was also correct. Dorian had always been beautiful and that had not changed.

"You're very attractive yourself, Laurent."

"If you two would like to get a room," I said.

I caught the expression on Laurent's face. He would have liked that very much. I was certain of it. Dorian smiled.

"On to dessert," Dorian said.

"Oh, I don't know…" Laurent began, but then made a show of snapping his mouth shut when Dorian glared at him. The sight made me laugh.

We all ordered hot fudge brownie pie, which was a chocolate brownie topped with ice cream and fudge. When our desserts arrived a few minutes later, they looked almost too good to eat. Almost.

I drove Laurent back to Briscoe in the once again swirling snow. Dorian got out and gave him a hug, then climbed in the front with me.

"He would have come home with you if you asked him," I said.

"Yes, but tonight I want you to myself."

I liked the sound of that.

We were soon back in my warm apartment. We changed into more comfortable clothes and then snuggled on the couch. It felt so good to be with Dorian again.

We didn't have sex that night. We hugged and kissed, but that was enough for us. I was almost certain we would do more in the future, but it didn't matter. I enjoyed all my time with Dorian. I slept better that night because I could feel him at my side.

Chapter Nine

Dorian had rehearsals for *A Christmas Carol*, but not many because it was all well-established show. Dorian told me the rehearsals were mainly to work out any kinks in performing in a new auditorium.

Opening night in Bloomington was on Friday. On Wednesday, Dorian and I picked out a tree at a lot operated by the Boy Scouts, tied it on top of my car, and drove it to Hunter and Alessio's house.

Alessio helped us pull it inside and then Alessio and I sat it up while Dorian sat and talked with Hunter. Dorian had never been very good with manual labor.

"Is it straight?" I asked when we had the Scotch pine in position in front of the large window that looked out upon the street.

"Well, I certainly hope not! I prefer gay trees!" Dorian said.

"You know what I mean."

"It looks great. Thanks for doing this for us," Hunter said.

"Oh, it's no trouble," Dorian said airily.

"It's certainly no trouble for you," I said, grinning.

"Hey. I picked out the tree, did I not? I even helped tie it on top of the car."

"You did?" Hunter asked.

"Hey, I'm not totally inept when it comes to such things. Almost, but not totally."

"Let's eat before we decorate the tree," Alessio said.

"I hope you didn't go to much trouble," I said.

"We're having spaghetti. It's one of the easiest things to prepare. Dorian, if you'll help Hunter, Marc and I can bring out the food. I only have to put on the finishing touches."

I remembered Alessio's spaghetti well and couldn't wait to eat. The kitchen smelled heavenly. It was filled with the scents of oregano and rosemary, with a touch of garlic. I carried bowls of steaming cooked apples and sauce while Alessio finished the actual spaghetti as well as garlic bread.

"This doesn't look simple to me," I said as I grabbed up Parmesan cheese.

"That's only because you think adding extra cheese to macaroni & cheese makes it a gourmet meal," Alessio said.

"It doesn't?"

Soon, we were all seated at the table. Hunter looked wan and pale, but he was in good spirits. It was hard not to be happy around Dorian.

"Oh my God! This is better than the best Italian in New York City!" Dorian said, when he tasted Alessio's spaghetti.

"Really Dorian, it's so hard to pry a compliment out of you," I said.

"Did you grab Alessio for his looks or his cooking skills?" Dorian asked Hunter.

"Well, I didn't know he could cook, so I'll have to say his looks, although the real reason is because I was always happy when he was near."

I smiled. I knew how Hunter felt.

Alessio took Hunter's hand for a moment and they smiled at each other. I wished they could have long, happy years together, but I feared it was a wish that could not be granted.

"So is this show going to be worth my time?" Hunter teased.

Dorian glared, although the effect wasn't threatening.

"You're playing Tiny Tim. Right?"

"I'm a little tall for the part. I'm playing Scrooge as you know well, Hunter Overmyer.

"Uh oh. He used your last name. You're skating on the thin ice now Hunter, " I said.

"That is going to take some serious acting. You're about as un-Scrooge-like as they come."

"Thank you. It was a challenge at first. I very nearly didn't audition, but it's a classic and I love a challenge."

"I'm sure you'll be incredible, Dorian," Alessio said.

"You know, I think I like you the best. How did you get involved with these guys, Alessio?"

"I'm afraid it was necessary to get into Alpha Alpha Omega and then I just felt sorry for them."

"Hey!" Hunter and I said.

"Well, I'm glad someone took pity on them."

"Hunter and I don't have to sit here and listen to this. We can go anywhere and be insulted," I said.

"That's right," agreed Hunter.

Dorian smiled.

"I have missed all you guys," he said.

"Sure you have. Going to fancy parties, hanging out with celebrities, and signing autographs at the stage door must be a tough life," Hunter said.

"It's hell, but I'm willing to make the sacrifice. Actually, I don't go to that many parties. I like some alone time and I spend a lot of time preparing for performances."

"I had lunch with Laurent today. You are all he could talk about. You definitely have an admirer," I said.

"I like him and he's so handsome. You're lucky to have found him Marc."

"Actually, he found me."

"I'm not surprised. You're wonderful!"

"Oh please stop. That's enough nice things said about Marc," Hunter said, then smiled.

We kept up our conversation all through supper. It was good to be with three old friends. I met Hunter and Alessio in college, but Dorian and I went all the way back to high school.

Alessio made hot cocoa and bought out Christmas cookies he had baked earlier. Hunter put on an Andy Williams Christmas CD and we began to decorate the tree. We put on the multi-colored lights first, then the tinsel. Hunter "supervised" as he called it, but joined us as we began to place ornaments. He tired before we were finished and sat down again, but I was glad he could join in. I tried not to think about the fact that this was Hunter's last Christmas.

It took us over two hours to decorate the tree. Alessio and Hunter had a lot of ornaments, but what consumed the most time was our frequent breaks for hot cocoa and Christmas cookies. If we had not eaten supper just before it could well have taken us three hours.

We stood back and admired our work once we finished. The tree was truly beautiful.

"Hey, what's your tree look like Marc?" Alessio said once we were all seated again.

"I don't actually have one."

"Maybe he should have played Scrooge," Hunter said.

"I have one in the shop, just not upstairs!"

"Something must be done about that," Alessio said.

"Well, I did think of getting a small one for the top of a table."

"Oh, that would be lovely!" Dorian said. "We can do a snow scene underneath with a little Christmas village."

"That does sound nice. We could have Laurent over to help."

"That will be fun," Dorian said.

"You're just saying that because you're hot for Laurent."

"No, I'm saying it because it's true, but he is hot."

"Aren't these older men who pursue young boys pathetic?" Alessio said to Hunter.

"Hey, like I said *he* pursued *me*. He rather likes Dorian too. You should have seen the expression of bliss on his features when Dorian hugged him."

We talked a bit longer, but Hunter yawned. He was obviously tired, so Dorian and I said our goodbyes and headed home. I didn't see Dorian much over the next two days because he was busy giving interviews to promote the show and he was preparing for opening night.

***

Alessio and I helped Hunter to his seat. Dorian arranged for Alessio to park right outside the emergency exit so Hunter didn't need his wheelchair. We had front row center seats. Knowing the star of the show had its perks.

Laurent was so excited he couldn't sit still. He reminded me of Dorian just then. Dorian could never remain still for long and he was always excited about everything. Perhaps that resemblance is one reason I liked Laurent so much. If only he were older we might have become serious.

The show began. I did not recognize Dorian at all when he first appeared as Scrooge. I was quite prepared for him to make me believe he was Scrooge, just as he'd made me believe he was other characters before, but for a few moments I worried that something had happened to Dorian and an understudy had taken over. It was a few minutes before I was sure it was my ex-boyfriend up on the stage. Dorian was that talented.

Like most everyone, I was so well acquainted with the story of *A Christmas Carol* I knew what was going to happen and yet I didn't. This production offered subtle differences and little surprises. There was nothing even a Dickens purist could complain about and yet the old story was made fresh and new. I found myself quite drawn into it and was nearly in tears with concern over Tiny Tim.

It wasn't until the play ended that I came to myself.

"Holy shit!" Laurent said, gazing at me.

I laughed.

"Dorian is the best actor *ever*."

"He invited us backstage to meet the rest of the cast," I said.

"Awesome!"

"I think we'll head home," Alessio said. I gazed at Hunter. He was obviously quite tired.

"I'll help you guys out. I'll be right back, Laurent."

Alessio and I supported Hunter as he walked to the near exit. The ushers held the doors open for us. We helped Hunter into the passenger seat.

"Tell Dorian he was incredible and tell him thank you for tonight. I had a wonderful time," Hunter said.

"Yes, he was magnificent!" Alessio said.

"I'll see you guys later."

My smile faded as I turned away. I was worried about Hunter. He tired ever more quickly as time passed. I was glad he was still able to get out and do things. I wished he could make it until the Little 500 next year, but I knew it would not happen.

Please God, let him make it at least until New Years.

Laurent took my hand and held it for a few moments when I returned. He knew I was worried. We waited until most of the crowd had disappeared to go backstage.

We found Dorian in his dressing room, cleaning off makeup. He was still in costume, but he largely looked like Dorian again.

"You are incredible!" Laurent said.

"Thank you."

"Hunter and Alessio said to tell you that you were wonderful and thank you for tonight. Hunter was tired so they went home."

"Is he okay?"

I shrugged. Dorian took my hand for a moment and squeezed it.

Dorian worked for a few moments more and then looked at himself in the mirror.

"There. I'm always glad to get the makeup off. I don't even know it's there while I'm onstage, but once we're done I want it off my face!"

I laughed.

Dorian began to change out of his costume. I noticed Laurent stealing looks.

"I didn't think your acting could improve Dorian, but tonight was phenomenal. I wasn't at all sure it was you on the stage for quite a while," I said.

Dorian laughed.

Dorian's body was as slim and defined as I remembered it. I swear he looked the same as he did in high school. He pulled on slacks, a white turtleneck and a cream sweater. He was so handsome he almost didn't look real. Laurent could barely stop gazing at him.

"Come on, I'll introduce you to the cast. The boy who plays Tiny Tim is a little hellion, but he's hilarious. You'll love the actor who plays Bob Cratchit too. He's so much like his character we accuse him of not having to act at all."

Dorian introduced us to everyone. I enjoyed meeting the cast, but I had more fun watching Dorian. His eyes sparkled. He was truly happy here. The theatre was his world. It didn't matter what theatre or whether it was large or small. Dorian was happiest surrounded by curtains, backdrops, and stage lights.

Dorian was right about the boy who played Tiny Tim. He had a foul mouth for a kid and his eyes shined with mischievousness. I was glad I didn't have put up with him for I doubted I could do so for more than a few minutes.

Laurent was thrilled to meet all the actors. He was also interested in how the lights and backdrops worked. Dorian took us on a tour. He obviously knew everything there was to know. He knew as much about the theatre as I did about bikes.

"I love being back here. Each theatre has its own personality. Coming back is like visiting an old friend," Dorian said as we stood upon the stage.

"By now you must have plenty of friends."

"Oh yes. I like the old theatres the best, but the IU Auditorium holds special memories for me.

"Hey, I have to run over a few things with our director, but I'll see you later," Dorian said.

"If you need a ride, call me," I said.

"I should be good."

"Thank you so much Dorian. This was a dream come true!" Laurent said.

"Oh boy, there will be no living with Dorian now!" I said.

Dorian giggled, hugged us both goodbye, and gave us both a peck on the lips. I thought Laurent was going to swoon.

Laurent and I walked through the empty auditorium, into the lobby, and out into the night. Snow covered the ground and was even now falling lightly, but the street and sidewalks were mostly clear. We could have caught a campus shuttle to the parking garage near my shop, but we had remained too long. No matter, the walk wasn't far and I didn't mind a walk in the moonlight with Laurent.

I took Laurent's hand and we walked through the familiar landscape of campus. I realized then that the IMU, Dunn Meadow, the Jordan River, and so many other places and locations here were the backdrops for the play that was my life. I felt as familiar with these places as Dorian did with the stage.

"Tonight was incredible! That was even better than when I saw Dorian on Broadway and I can't believe our seats!"

I laughed.

"It was so fun meeting the cast and getting a backstage tour. It makes me wish I had the talent to be an actor."

"You must be more of an extrovert than I thought," I said.

"Sometimes I'm an extrovert, but mostly not. I'm probably not cut out to be an actor, but since I can't act it doesn't matter."

"True."

"You never wanted to be a part of all that?"

"Not really. I find it interesting and I love to watch live theatre, but I wouldn't want to make it my life."

"It's obviously where Dorian belongs," Laurent said.

"Oh there is no question of that. He's always performing whether or not he's on a stage. To Dorian life is one big theatre production. That's one of the many reasons I love him."

"I could go for dating him, but I don't think that would work out very well since I'm here and he's either on the road or in New York City."

"Yeah, you would rarely get to see him. I think Dorian's only boyfriend is the theatre."

"Well, it's been incredible getting to meet him and hang out with him."

"It makes meeting me worthwhile, huh?"

"You were already worthwhile. Making out with you alone accomplished that. I love going out with you and just spending time with you. I have all the benefits of a boyfriend, but none of the obligations. Not that I wouldn't date you if you were interested..."

"Dating would not be a good idea. You'll graduate in four years and who knows where you'll end up. Besides, you do not want to commit yourself to an older man when there are all these college hunks around. This is your time to have fun. When you're my age, most of them won't want you anymore."

"You're still plenty hot!"

"Maybe, but it doesn't matter. Most guys your age would not consider a guy my age, no matter how hot he is."

"It's their loss."

"The nice thing about that lack of interest is that by the time you're my age, sex isn't as big of a deal."

"You're obviously still interested. The last time we hooked up... mmm."

"Yeah, I'm thirty, not dead. I mean that I've had a lot of experiences. I've already been there and done that. Much of the excitement is gone. Sex can still be incredible, like when a college freshman seduces me."

"Anyone I know?"

"Intimately."

Dunn Meadow was a field of white. Someone had built a snow man and a snow dog. All was quiet, except for our footsteps on the sidewalk and our voices.

I was glad to get back inside. Laurent and I pulled off our coats and I made us some hot chocolate to warm us up. We sat on the couch with our mugs in front of a crackling fire on my TV. I could almost swear it gave out warmth.

After we finished our cocoa, we cuddled, then kissed. I would have led him into my bedroom, but Dorian would return soon, so instead I drove him back to his dorm. It was a wonderful night.

***

I turned the sign to "Closed," shut off the lights, and walked upstairs to get ready to depart for a small Christmas celebration with Hunter and Alessio. It was December 23rd and Hunter was still hanging in there, which meant he would almost certainly get to experience one last Christmas.

Dorian's theatre company had moved on nearly two weeks ago. Laurent and nearly everyone else at IU had gone home for winter break soon after. Half the town was gone and tomorrow I would head to Verona to spend Christmas with my parents and hopefully see a few friends.

Most stores were open on Christmas Eve, but I doubted I would miss many last minute sales. It was more important to be home with my parents. They wouldn't be around forever either. I wasn't the only one growing older.

I pulled the party tray I'd purchased the day before at Kroger out of my refrigerator. There was dip surrounded by a selection of cheeses and meats. It would only be the three of us tonight, but I wanted to contribute. I was quite sure Alessio had prepared something wonderful.

I buttoned up a red cardigan, pulled on my coat, and carried the tray on top of a couple of gifts to my car. Snow covered the ground, but the streets were clear. The weather forecast for my trip the next day was good. I hoped it remained that way. Northern Indiana winter weather could be fierce.

I drove a few blocks and soon knocked on Hunter and Alessio's door. Both were handsomely dressed in cream cable knit sweaters.

"I spent all day preparing this," I said as I handed the tray to Alessio.

"Then why does it have a plastic dome and a tag that says 'Kroger'?" Hunter asked.

"Making those was the hardest part! Doesn't it look as if it came from Kroger? I think I did a great job."

"You sure did." Hunter grinned, then hugged me.

The tree Dorian and I helped decorate looked beautiful. I walked closer to admire it and place my gifts under it.

"Hey, you added gingerbread men."

"Yes, there were more, but some have gone missing. Hunter claims that elves eat them during the night but I'm not buying it," Alessio said.

Hunter and Alessio had a real fireplace and a crackling fire was burning away. I must admit it was better than the one on my TV provided by Netflix. Hunter and I sat by the fire while Alessio finished up in the kitchen.

"Heading out tomorrow?" Hunter asked.

"Yeah."

"Tell everyone I know 'Merry Christmas'."

"I will. What are you and Alessio doing?"

"Tomorrow we are spending a quiet day at home. My family is coming the next day."

"I hope that's good news and not bad."

"Hunter laughed. It's mostly good. It's just my parents, not the whole extended family."

"What's that smell?"

"Goose."

"Really? I've never eaten a goose before."

"Alessio is baking a ham for Christmas so he wanted to do something different for the three of us."

"He shouldn't go to such trouble."

"He loves cooking."

"I love eating his cooking, but that requires no work."

We talked until Alessio called us into the dining room. Hunter moved slowly, but required no help. I was glad he was doing fairly well.

A red tablecloth covered the dining room table. Two tall tapers burned on either side of a beautiful centerpiece of white carnations and pine boughs.

"This is beautiful."

"Yeah. Martha Stewart has nothing on Alessio."

Bowls of dressing, mashed potatoes, and green beans already sat on the table. Alessio carried in a roast goose and then a basket of hot yeast rolls.

"This looks and smells incredible," I said. Alessio smiled.

"Now let's eat it all," Hunter said.

Despite his words, Hunter took fairly small portions, but I was glad to see he was still eating. I knew that when he stopped the end would be near. I put that out of my mind and enjoyed Christmas dinner with my friends.

"Are you enjoying your break from training?" Hunter asked.

"There hasn't been much to it since the weather turned cold. I meet with those who can make it at the SRSC once a week, but mostly I expect them to train on their own. The real work will begin again once the weather gets warm enough to ride outside."

"I bet you can't wait," Hunter said.

"I can't. Thank you so much for getting me into biking. It changed my life."

"You are welcome."

"I wonder sometimes where I would be and what I would be doing if I had never met you."

"Maybe you would have gone into news casting. You might have been a local celebrity or maybe you would have even gone national."

"Or maybe he would be one of those crazy weather men," Alessio said.

"That does seem more likely."

"Hey! No ganging up on me."

"You might have even found your way into biking without me."

"I doubt that. Before I met you, my bike was a way to get to classes quickly because there is never good parking available on campus."

"I'm sure you'll take the AAΩ team far."

"I'll try. It's tough with an entirely new team, but they are dedicated. I'm sure they will do their best to win. I'm not getting my hopes up. I look at this as a rebuilding year. We earned a spot and the boys will have the experience of race if nothing else. That will put them in a much better position to win next year."

"You did fine without race experience," Hunter said.

"That's because I had you to train me."

"Yes, and they have you."

I smiled.

"I am great. Aren't I? I guess that's why Adam carved that statue of me."

"Boo!" Hunter said. I laughed.

"What about your family, Alessio? Do you ever see them at Christmas?"

"Oh yes. Hunter and I traveled to Mantua last Christmas"

"He has a big family," Hunter said.

"They all love Hunter, especially my mama."

"The first time I met her she pinched my cheeks as if I was ten."

"So they don't have a problem with you two being together?"

"No. Any problems were resolved long before I met Hunter. My grandmamma told me he was quite a catch."

"One of his aunts pinched my butt."

"Yes and my cousin Alonzo drooled over him. I did not even know he was gay."

"So, how many times have you been to Italy, Hunter?"

"Four."

"Wow. So do you speak Italian now?"

"About as well as you sang Italian in college."

"That bad?"

Alessio nodded.

"I have tried to teach him, but he is..."

"Hopeless," Hunter said.

"I was trying to find a kinder way to put it," Alessio said.

"Thanks, but it's true. I gave up trying after I accidentally asked his uncle if he enjoys sex with chickens."

I laughed.

"How did that happen?"

"I'm not sure what I was trying to say, but I definitely got it wrong. I still remember his uncle's face. I thought I was in major trouble, but then everyone started laughing. When Alessio told me what I'd said I was so embarrassed."

"He turned completely red," Alessio said.

"That's really cool that you visited Italy."

"Especially with my own personal guide. Did you know that Alessio's family ran Mantua at one time?"

"Ran it?"

"Yes, I guess you would call a city-state. They were like the Medici in Florence. There have even been books written about the Gonzaga of Mantua."

"That is pretty incredible."

"It was a long time ago," Alessio said.

"It still must be wonderful to know your family history like that. I don't know much about the Peraltas."

"The Gonzaga were the royalty of Mantua," Hunter pointed out.

"Yes, but that is like being the King of Bloomington," Alessio said.

"It's more impressive than that," Hunter said. "Alessio is just modest."

"Well, it is not like I had anything to do with it. I was not around all those centuries ago."

We kept talking. As if the excellent meal wasn't enough, Alessio disappeared into the kitchen and returned shortly with cherries jubilee.

We laughed and talked as we ate. Hunter was in good spirits and that helped me to push aside thoughts of his death. I knew there wasn't much time left and I wanted to enjoy every moment I had with Hunter, not just to make his life more pleasant, but for myself as well.

We moved into the living room after dessert. Alessio put a log on the fire and we sat in comfy chairs near the tree. I pulled out the gift I had brought for Alessio first. It was wrapped in red paper with little snowmen on it. I had taken special care with wrapping the gifts so they looked rather nice.

Alessio tore through the paper and opened the box to reveal a long, hand-knitted red scarf and matching toboggan.

"These are beautiful."

"They should be warm too. That's wool. I specially ordered them from an artisan in town. I was going to claim I knitted them, but I knew you'd never believe me."

Alessio grinned.

"Thank you so much Marc."

I handed Hunter his gift next. It was wrapped in green paper with Christmas bells all over it. He tore it open to reveal a green hand-knitted sweater.

"Oh wow. Marc, this is too much. You made this yourself, didn't you?" he teased.

"Yeah. Not only did I knit it, I raised the sheep, sheared them, and spun the wool into yarn. Does that sound convincing?"

Hunter and Alessio shook their heads.

"It was made by the same lady. She does spin her own wool."

"Thank you. I have trouble keeping warm enough."

Alessio and I exchanged a look. He had told me about that. It was his suggestion that Hunter's gift be something to keep him warm.

Alessio pulled a gift for me from under the tree. It was wrapped in beautiful red and green plaid paper with a matching bow. I opened it to reveal a framed and matted photo of Hunter, Conner, Jonah, and me holding the Little 500 trophy we won during my first year of racing. It was similar to the one hanging in Alpha Alpha, Omega, but not the same. Everyone in the photo had signed it.

"We had a hell of a time tracking down Conner and Jonah. Attached to the back is an envelope with their email and home addresses. They would both love to hear from you," Hunter said.

"I love it. I can't believe you went to all that trouble!" I said, gazing at it. I moved around so Hunter and Alessio could admire it with me. "We were something back then, weren't we?"

"You are something now," Alessio said, giving us both a kiss on the cheek. I couldn't help but shed a tear. We all hugged for a moment. I wished I could keep hugging them forever.

Chapter Ten

I reluctantly left Bloomington the next morning. I was eager to see my friends and family, but I did not like leaving Hunter and Alessio behind. If the truth be known, I just plain didn't like leaving Bloomington either.

I focused on my destination. The roads were clear so the trip to Verona was only three hours or so. It wasn't a bad drive and I made it shorter by playing Christmas CDs. I wondered what friends would be back in town for Christmas. I knew Dorian would not be there, but we'd had plenty of time together earlier in the month. Laurent was still going on about it when he departed for Christmas break and treasured the memories and the photo Dorian signed for him.

I was looking forward to Christmas with my parents and also the big Selby Christmas party held on the farm each year. It was probably a good idea for me to get away from my shop for a while too. I loved it, but it did consume most of my time and I was never really off since there was always work waiting on me. My time in Verona would be a forced vacation.

The rolling, snow covered hills of southern Indiana slowly gave way to the flat plains of northern Indiana. I could almost imagine the enormous glacier that had flattened the countryside like an impossibly large bulldozer during the last ice age. One could also see where the glacier stopped. It was easy sometimes to forget that Indiana had an ancient history. We had no great castles like Europe or pyramids like Egypt and Central America. At most, there were mounds and the vast majority of those had been flattened by erosion or farming. There had been Native American mounds on the Selby Farm centuries ago, but only bare traces of them remained. Indiana had far deeper history too. Dinosaurs had walked here and the entire state was once a shallow sea. I pondered such thoughts at times when I drove alone.

The snow in the fields grew deeper as I headed north, but only a trace of it blew across the highways. There were a good six inches on the ground as I neared Verona, which did not surprise me. Winter kept a firm grip on Verona at this time of the year.

Mom grabbed me and hugged me the moment I walked in the door. Dad was next. I had the feeling that no matter my age, I would always be their little boy.

"I'm so glad you're home. I fixed up the guest room for you."

"Thanks Mom. Let me get my bags from the car."

I walked out to the Camaro and retrieved my two bags as well as a box of gifts. I would have stayed in my old place in the loft of the barn, but since all my furniture was in Bloomington, the loft was nearly empty. Besides, I would be out and about quite a bit while I was here so I doubted the closeness would become too much.

I put my bags in my room and then placed the few gifts I'd brought under the tree.

"I thought we told you not to buy us anything this year. We didn't get you much," Mom said.

"You know I never listen. Besides, these are just small gifts. I wanted to get you something."

My words seemed to put Mom at ease. She hugged me again when I stood.

"All we really want for Christmas is for you to be here."

"Well, I will be here this evening and all day tomorrow. The day after Christmas I'm going to the Selby Christmas party, but you two are invited as well."

"I don't like parties," Dad said.

"Then you can stay home and pretend to be Scrooge while Mom goes." I grinned. My dad was far from a Scrooge, although he did not care much for crowds.

"I'm sure your mother will force me to go."

Dad didn't look like it would take too much force to get him there. He was probably remembering the desserts of previous years.

"I'm preparing a larger supper so we're having a light lunch. I hope you're hungry."

"I am."

"Come to the kitchen then. I made bologna salad this morning."

"Yes!"

I loved Mom's bologna salad. It was like ham salad, but better. We each fixed ourselves a sandwich and sat down at the old kitchen table. We had potato chips with our sandwiches and that was plenty, especially since I spotted some Christmas sugar cookies with icing on the counter.

"I have a ham in the oven for supper and I'm preparing baked beans, mashed potatoes, and yeast rolls to go with it," Mom said.

"I thought I smelled ham."

"It's so good to have you here," Mom said as she reached over and squeezed my hand for a moment. "How is Hunter?"

I spoke with my parents frequently on the phone. They didn't know our entire story, but they knew Hunter and I were friends and frat brothers.

"He's weak, but he stills feels pretty good. He tires more easily than he did."

"It's such a pity about him. He should not have to die so young. Death should be reserved for us old people."

"Your not that old Mom."

"She's been thirty-nine for years now. In a few more years you will be older than your mother," Dad teased.

"Oh, Dorian said to wish you a Merry Christmas. I can't remember if I told you that before.

"Is he still on tour?"

"Their last performance is tonight, then he's heading back to New York."

"He's not going to visit Verona for Christmas?"

"He said he planned to come later instead of Christmas. I'm sure he's exhausted."

"Well you tell him that when he does come home he has to visit us."

"He always does Mom."

"How is the shop doing?" Dad asked.

"Great, although it's slower in winter. Bike stores don't get the big boost from Christmas that most stores do, but then we don't depend on Christmas sales like other stores either. Bike shops do best in spring and summer. I did sell a few bikes for Christmas gifts as well as accessories and gift certificates."

"Great. I'm glad that's working out," Dad said.

We talked through lunch, then Mom made coffee and I made tea. We moved into the living room so we could look at the tree. A large sugar cookie decorated as a snowman accompanied me.

"How much time did you spend baking cookies?" I asked Mom.

177

"A couple of hours. I didn't make that many."

"I helped cut down on the work load," Dad said.

"Yes, by eating some before I could decorate them."

"It saved you time didn't it?"

I grinned.

"The tree looks beautiful."

"Did you put one up?"

"Yes. I wasn't going to, but I eventually decided to put up a small one on a tabletop. Also, Dorian and I helped Hunter and Alessio put up their tree when he was in town.

"Oh, I forgot to tell you that I went to the holiday market. It's in the same location as the farmer's market. It's held on the Saturday after Thanksgiving every year. There were Christmas trees and wreaths for sale, as well as baked goods and all kinds of hand-made items for gifts. The market has a great atmosphere. There are carolers singing, chestnuts roasting, and even reindeer to pet."

"That sounds wonderful, Marc."

"I bought some cupcakes, cookies, and buckeyes from a couple of girls who baked them. They were delicious."

Mom caught me up on news of relatives, many of whom I didn't know all that well, and she talked about goings on in Verona. I told her about the holidays in Bloomington. Dad mostly listened. He didn't often talk much. He once said it was because he was waiting his turn and it never seemed to come.

We talked a good long while, then Mom went into the kitchen to work on supper. Dad wanted to catch part of a football game, so I bundled up for a stroll around town.

My boyhood home was on the edge of town, but still not far from anything. Verona wasn't that big. It was downright small compared to Bloomington, which was not one of the largest cities in Indiana. I walked through the snowy landscape to the downtown area. There I spotted all the old familiar places; Café Moffatt, Parrot's Pizza, the Green Dragon, and more. I looked up at the apartment above Café Moffatt where Shawn and Tim once lived. The years had passed too quickly.

The windows of the shops were decorated for the season. There were no large retail stores in Verona, but there was a clothing store, an antique store, a hardware store, and a few other businesses. The antique store had toys and dolls from bygone days on display near a beautifully decorated Christmas tree. The clothing store had a painted scene of the Peanuts characters around Charlie Brown's little Christmas tree. Even Café Moffatt had Santa and his reindeer riding over the name of the restaurant and an old home decked out in lights below. Verona was a beautiful place at Christmas. I reminded me of a Norman Rockwell painting.

I walked a few more blocks to Verona's other business area. The Paramount Theatre, the Park's Edge, and Ofarim's were all decorated for the season. The box office of The Paramount was outlined with garland and lights and I could see a large Christmas tree in the lobby. The windows of the Park's Edge were outlined with lights and a wreath suspended by a wide red ribbon hung in each window. The windows of Ofarim's were outlined with lights and a 1950's Christmas scene complete with a '57 Chevy and carolers was painted on the windows.

Across the street, nature had decorated the park with a thick blanket of snow. Lights were strung on the branches of some of the live pine trees and glowed through the snow that had covered the branches. A few kids worked at building a snowman and others made snow angels.

Verona had changed little and yet it felt changed because so many of those I knew when I was a boy had moved on. Even I had departed, but Verona would always be home to me, as it would be to us all. We might only return for holidays or a rare visit, but everyone always came back to this place; even Dorian, who was more at home in the fast paced world of New York City.

I walked to Verona High School and visited the soccer fields. Like most everything else they were covered with snow, but that didn't stop me from remembering all the soccer games I had once played there. Unlike Brandon and Jon, I didn't pursue soccer in college, but I loved playing back in my earlier school days. Both Brandon and Jon were now soccer coaches. I guess we had all found our niche.

I turned toward home, but didn't hurry. I took in the sights and sounds of the holidays in Verona. There was nothing quite like a small town at Christmas.

Later that evening, Mom, Dad, and I sat down at the table for a wonderful supper of ham, baked beans, mashed potatoes, and freshly baked yeast rolls.

We talked as we ate and then talked more over blackberry cobbler. Mom did most of the talking. It had always been that way and that's the way Dad and I liked it.

We had a rather enjoyable evening. When my parents went to bed I moved to the guest room. I would have been tempted to check on orders for the shop, but Mom and Dad didn't have an Internet connection. At least this way I didn't have to feel guilty for not working.

I slept in the next day. As a kid, I could never sleep on Christmas morning. I was too excited. I didn't have that problem now. Christmas could wait until I was ready to get up.

I heard sounds downstairs as I was getting ready. I could smell Mom's French toast as I descended the stairs. Soon, the scent of bacon reached me. By the time I reached the kitchen I was hungry.

"I heard you moving around so I started breakfast," Mom said.

"It all smells so good! Is there anything I can do to help?"

"Set out the plates and silverware. Everything will be ready soon."

Dad entered the kitchen before we had to call him. He poured himself a cup of coffee and sat at the table.

"Breakfast should be like this everyday," he announced.

"If you want breakfast like this everyday, you'll have to fix it yourself," Mom said.

"It was worth a try," he said winking at me.

In a few minutes we sat down to a breakfast of French toast, scrambled eggs, and bacon. Mom had made cranberry topping for the French toast. I covered mine with the topping, syrup, and real butter. It was wonderful.

The bacon was thick and hickory smoked and the eggs were accented with just a little rosemary. Mom was a great cook.

I had both hot and iced tea with my breakfast. Hot tea with breakfast is something I had picked up from my grandmother. When I was quite little, she babysat for me sometimes and if I was there for breakfast she usually made buttered toast and hot tea. Whenever I had the same breakfast, I thought of her. She had been gone for quite a while now, but I would never forget her.

After breakfast, we moved into the living room to open presents. The tree looked beautiful all decked out in treasured family ornaments and blinking lights.

"I didn't put any tags on the gifts. Except for those you brought, everything is for you," Mom said.

"Then you bought too much. You need to cut down and spend your money on yourself."

"We would have never heard you say that as a kid," Dad said and smiled.

"Open the one with green pine cone covered paper," Mom said.

I ripped the package open.

"Clothes!" I faked whined. My parents laughed. "I love this."

I held up a cream, cable-knit shawl collar sweater. I would not have appreciated it when I was a boy. Dorian was the only person I knew who got excited about clothes when he was a kid. I didn't know him back then, but his mom had told me stories.

A package wrapped in blue paper decorated with teddy bears revealed a black cardigan. A gift wrapped in red and white striped paper concealed a hunter green cable-knit sweater. I was beginning to detect a theme.

"I thought you could wear them in your shop," Mom said.

"I will and elsewhere too."

I handed Mom a heavy large box covered with shiny gold paper and decorated by a large red bow. She opened it and looked up at me.

"Marc, this is too much."

"It didn't cost that much. You've always wanted a red microwave, but you never buy one."

"Well, the old one is still good."

"Give it to someone who needs one then and use that one."

It was extremely hard to find anything for my dad. He had no real interests outside of sports. He didn't collect anything. He didn't particularly like to read, except for the paper. There was one thing he liked very much that was only available at Christmas. I pushed a very large box wrapped in green and red tartan paper toward him. He opened it and smiled.

"What did he buy you?" Mom asked.

Dad pretended to hide his gift.

"It's nothing that concerns you."

"What is it?"

Dad held up a box of cordial cherries. I had purchased him an entire case.

"Okay, I might share *one* box with you."

"How many boxes are in there?"

"Thirty-six," I answered.

"Oh good lord."

"You know, I bought one box right after Thanksgiving and haven't found any since," Dad said.

"They tend to sell out before Christmas. I bought these at the beginning of December."

"Thanks. I will put these to good use."

I unwrapped a nice pair of driving gloves and some comfy house shoes as well as a couple of polo shirts. Dad unwrapped a can of cashews, a Whitman's sampler, and a big jar of honey roasted peanuts. I gave Mom some white chocolate turtles from a chocolate shop in Bloomington as well as a big jug of honey I purchased at the last farmer's market of the season. If she knew what it cost she would have died.

When the gifts were unwrapped we sat back and talked. I knew that is what my parents, and especially Mom, wanted from me. Mom loved to talk. Dad merely liked having me there. I knew they missed me and this day was for them.

Relatives dropped by in the afternoon. I didn't know most of them all that well. Mom tended to keep in touch with family members. Dad was just the opposite. I had never even met most of Dad's family.

I would rather have gone out in search of my friends, but I knew Mom was eager for me to see her relatives. I spent the day eating too much divinity and too many Christmas cookies so it wasn't a complete loss.

I headed for the Selby Farm the next afternoon. My parents were coming later, but I was eager to get there. I knew Ethan wouldn't mind if I arrived early. I was sure he could use the help setting up.

I found Ethan and Nathan in the barn, putting tables into place.

"Need some help?"

Ethan looked up and grinned. He hugged me. Nathan was next.

"We're just getting ready to begin bringing everything out. How's Bloomington?" Ethan asked.

"Great. Mostly."

I didn't say more. I had not told any of my Verona friends about Hunter, except Dorian.

"You may be sorry you came early enough to help," Nathan said.

"I notice Brandon and Jon haven't arrived yet."

"They have a true talent for avoiding any kind of work," Nathan said.

"They have had years of practice, but let's not bad-mouth them now."

"Yeah, we want them to hear all this," Nathan agreed.

I followed them into the farmhouse where the table and nearly every available surface was covered with bowls, plates, and platters of food.

"Get this stuff over here first so I can have room to work. How are you, Marc?" said Ardelene.

"I'm good. I ate very little for breakfast so that I can try more goodies!"

Ardelene smiled.

I picked up a large platter heaped with decorated Christmas cookies and followed Ethan out the door. It was the first of many trips. We carried out chocolate, peanut butter, and maple fudge, Mexican wedding cookies, homemade Chex Mix, ribbon candy, a large Christmas cake decorated with a North Pole scene, and more desserts than any one person could possibly sample. There was a cheese tray, a meat tray, cheese balls, tiny wieners swimming in barbeque sauce and lots more.

The three of us weren't the only ones working. I soon spotted Brendan and Casper carrying in seating, Jack setting up heaters and Nathan's younger brother, Dave toting bags of ice.

Guests began to arrive before we finished, but it wasn't until we made the very last trip that Brandon showed up.

"I'm here to help!" he said.

"Yeah, after everything has been done," Ethan said.

"What a bitter disappointment."

I coughed "bull shit" into my fist. Brandon laughed.

Brandon was not alone. He had his wife with him and their five-month old son, Mark, who was named for Brandon's best friend whom he had lost long ago.

Jon showed up not five minutes later with his family.

"Deerfield, you slacker. We just finished settling everything up," Brandon said and grinned.

"Did he actually do anything?" Jon asked us. I shook my head while mouthing "no."

"Shut it, Peralta," Brandon said. I smiled. I had missed these guys.

Jon was married and had two sons, Josh, who was nearly two years old and Jared, who was the same age as Brandon's son. I had seen pictures, but it was still odd seeing my old friends with kids of their own.

"Your boys are so handsome," Brendan said as he walked up. "Luckily they take after their mother."

"You think you're funny Brewer?" Jon asked.

"Well, it wasn't very original, but it's a start."

"So, I heard your football team lost every game this season?" Jon asked.

"Make that won and you'll be correct."

"So, did your team win any games?" I asked Jon.

"Of course! How could they not with such an awesome coach?"

"New assistant?" Brandon asked.

"I don't know why I missed you!" Jon said.

"They will never change," I said.

"Why mess with perfection?" Brandon asked. He and Jon exchanged a high-five. Casper rolled his eyes.

We moved into the barn, which was pleasantly warm if one wore a sweater or light jacket. More and more guests arrived including Shawn, Tristan, Tim, Dane, Scotty, and others from my high school days. There were plenty of others, too, including my parents and Brendan's mom.

Nearly everyone I missed was present. The Selby Christmas party was an annual tradition and was as much reunion as Christmas party. I wished I could take everyone home with me to Bloomington, but our lives had taken us to different places. Jon lived in North Dakota, the poor bastard. Shawn and Tristan lived in Oklahoma. Brandon lived in Florida. Most of the rest of us were also spread out. Only Ethan, Nathan, Brendan, and Casper still lived in Verona. I was glad I lived only a few hours away.

The nice thing about friends is that they are friends whether or not they were present or even near. Nathan and Anton kept in touch and Anton lived on the other side of the Atlantic Ocean.

I paced myself with the finger-foods and desserts. I preferred to try a little of numerous things instead of consuming a lot of a few. That was easier said than done because everything was so good!

In between desserts, I had a few barbeque wieners and other non-sweet items. Brandon saw me with a wiener and raised his eyebrow. He didn't have to say a word to make me laugh.

The crowd thinned as evening came on, but I knew my friends would remain. Brandon and Jon's wives took their kids into the house for a nap. I gazed uneasily at my friends as I nibbled on a frosted sugar cookie that was shaped like a candy cane. I had been putting it off, but I needed to tell the guys about Hunter soon.

"Are you okay Marc?" Casper asked.

"I am, but I have some bad news."

My words drew everyone's attention. Brendan, Casper, Ethan, Nathan, Shawn, Tim, Tristan, Scotty, and Dane all gazed at me.

"Hunter isn't well. He has cancer." Tears rimmed my eyes, but I willed them away. "There is nothing more than can be done. He has weeks to live, at best."

The color drained from the faces of my friends. Casper hugged me.

"Is there anything we can do for him?" Brendan asked.

"I'm afraid not. I hate to give you this news now, but I don't want his death to come as a shock later."

"Is there anything we can do for you?" Nathan asked.

I smiled.

"No, but seeing you all again helps and knowing you're all a part of my life."

"Most of us know what it's like to lose a friend," Brandon said. "We're all only a call away if you need to talk."

"Thanks. Listen, I didn't want to bring everyone down, but I thought you should know. Hunter is still doing okay, although he tires very easily. I visit Hunter and Alessio at least once a week and we go out together too. Hunter is making the most of the time he has left."

Everyone gathered in for a group hug with me in the center. I could not remember us doing a group hug before, but it made me feel like everything would be okay, no matter what happened. I knew these guys would always be my friends and that I could always count on them.

"You know what?" Brandon asked after we released each other. We all looked at him. "I think we should all drive to Cincinnati and check out Marc's statue."

"Oh no," I said.

"You just want to see him naked," Jon said.

"The whole world has seen him naked. Busloads of school kids see him nude daily I bet. That's kind of perverted, Marc," Brandon said.

"Grrr." I smiled. Brandon and Jon could always make me feel better.

The party continued. My news dampened it, but nothing could take away the pleasure of being together. We shared memories and talked about old times until the hour began to get late.

"I should probably get Mark back to Mom and Dad's," Brandon said.

"Yeah, I'm sure my kids are wiped out. I should get going too," Jon said.

"Listen to them. They know it's nearly time to clean up and they're using their kids to get out work," Tim said.

"Using your kids to get out of work is pretty low," Shawn said.

"Hey!" Brandon and Jon said.

"Don't be so hard on them guys. Brandon and Jon have always been slackers," I said.

"I don't recall anyone asking for your input Peralta," Jon said.

"Okay. Okay. We'll help clean up before we go," Brandon said.

"Who said you could volunteer me?" Jon asked.

"I did. The best looking guy gets to decide."

"Ha! Then the decision is not up to you Hanson!" Jon said.

The guys laughed and we began carting leftovers inside. With so many helping we made short work of the task. Ardelene packed up goody bags for everyone. We were stuffed now, but later those Christmas cookies and candies would be most welcome.

We hugged goodbye and then departed. I drove back to my parent's place and let myself in with my key. Mom was still up and sitting in the kitchen with a cup of tea browsing a Country Living magazine.

"You didn't have to wait up. I'm thirty, not thirteen."

"If you came in this late when you were thirteen you would have been in big trouble."

I laughed.

I sat at the kitchen table and had a cup of tea with Mom. I talked about getting to see my old friends. I was tired, but time with those I loved was precious. I never knew when it might end. Even if we were all immortal, I would have wanted to spend time with my parents, but knowing my time with them was limited was a reminder not to take them for granted and not to put things off. One never knew when someone would disappear from their life.

I had breakfast with Mom and Dad the next morning, then packed up the car. We hugged and said 'goodbye' and I headed home. I enjoyed my time in Verona with my family and friends, but I was eager to return to Bloomington. Verona would always be home, but Bloomington was as well. I was pleased life had taken me there.

Chapter Eleven

I spent New Year's Eve with Hunter and Alessio. Hunter napped in the evening so he could stay up until midnight. Hunter and Alessio kissed as 1996 began and then each of them kissed me. I was truly lucky to have shared so much with these two men that I loved with all my heart.

I went home to my empty apartment soon after midnight and climbed into bed. I had to be up in time to open up the shop at ten the next morning, although I didn't anticipate many customers on New Year's Day, but I had bikes to repair and Jake, who often handled repairs, was on winter break. I didn't mind. Business was slow at this time of year so it was nice to have something to do. Working on a bike reminded me of the summer months when I could ride in the warm sunshine. It's too bad I couldn't save up summer days to spend in the winter. How I would have loved to experience a hot August day in cold January! At least Bloomington was nearly ten degrees warmer than Verona on most days and sometimes much warmer. I did not miss northern Indiana winters!

I smiled as I worked in my shop because I was content. I was exactly where I wanted to be. I was living the dream I had dreamed as a student at IU. All the boring business classes, all the saving and planning had led to this. My life wasn't prefect, but then anyone who expected perfection was destined for disappointment. Often, it was the imperfections that made life interesting.

One day flowed into another and the New Year began to slowly slip away. Soon, the students returned from break and Bloomington truly came alive again. I was glad to have the students back and not only because they made up most of my customers. I had missed the boys who worked for me, the frat brothers I trained, and the hustle and bustle of living in a college town. Now, if it would only get warm enough to ride. Training in the SRSC was fine, but I wanted to get out with my team and actually ride. The Little 500 was still weeks away, but I knew those weeks would pass before I knew it.

***

My phone rang. I checked the time. It was 11:36 p.m. I had only been in bed a few minutes. My heart pounded. Calls in the night were never good.

"Hello."

"Marc, it's Alessio. If you want to say goodbye to Hunter you'd better come now." I could hear Alessio's voice crack.

"I'll be right there."

I hopped up, quickly dressed, and rushed to the home Hunter and Alessio shared. The hospice nurse let me in and directed me to the bedroom. Alessio was sitting on the edge of Hunter's bed. I sat down beside him.

"You came," Hunter said very weakly.

"Of course I came. I love you."

I tried not to cry. I really did, but tears slipped down my cheeks. Alessio's eyes were red, but he wasn't crying just now. Hunter closed his eyes and I was afraid that was it. I didn't want to let him go. Alessio leaned over and kissed him on the lips. I did so as well.

Hunter's eyes reopened. He seemed to want to speak, but couldn't so he smiled instead. Alessio and I sat on either side of him now. Hunter motioned us close. He took one of our hands in each of his and then placed them together.

"Take care of each other," he whispered, then closed his eyes and stopped breathing. Alessio and I sat holding hands, crying. Hunter was gone.

We sat for a long time. When we stood I took Alessio in my arms and held him tight. When I released him, I led him into the living room and nodded to the hospice nurse.

I took Alessio into the kitchen and made us a pot of tea. We didn't speak for a long time. Instead, we sat, sipped our tea, and tried to deal with what had just happened. I looked at the clock and then the calendar. It was barely still February 18th.

"I'm glad you were here, Marc. I'm glad you *are* here. I was afraid I would be alone. I knew a hospice nurse would be here, but it's not the same."

"I'll stay as long as you want. Nothing is more important to me than you."

Alessio smiled at me for a moment.

"I hoped we'd have more time, but I'm also glad it's over. Sometimes, in the night, I couldn't stop myself from listening to him breathe. Any time there was a pause, I thought he was gone, but then he'd take another breath. I wish I'd died instead."

I reached out and squeezed Alessio's hand.

"Of course you do. It's easier to die than it is to lose someone you love. We both loved Hunter. We both still do. My life would be completely different if I had never met him and I don't think it would have been better. Losing him is hard, but we are lucky we had the opportunity to know and love him. If I could erase the pain I'm feeling now by going back and never meeting him, I wouldn't. Pain is the price we pay for love."

Alessio nodded.

"I don't know how I can get through these next few days," Alessio said.

"With me at your side. We will get through it together."

"I should call Hunter's parents and break the news. I started to call them right after I called you, but they live much too far away and Hunter didn't want them here. He only wanted you and me when the time came."

I thought about that while Alessio went into the other room and made his phone call. Hunter got on well enough with his parents and they were okay with his relationship with Alessio. It touched me to know that he wanted Alessio and me with him at the end instead of his biological family.

I knew the hospice nurse would handle what had to be done next. Hunter and Alessio had made all his burial arrangements in advance, although Hunter was to be cremated instead of buried. Right now, all I had to deal with was Alessio. I wished I could take his pain away, but I couldn't. Nothing would ever completely erase it, just as nothing would ever eradicate the pain I now felt. Hunter was gone and he was never coming back.

Later, I led Alessio to the guest bedroom. I gave him a sleeping pill and put him in bed. I took off my shoes and lay beside him. He hugged me close and we lay there with our arms around each other.

After a long while I could tell by his breathing that Alessio was asleep. I remained awake for a good while longer until I finally nodded off as well. Neither of us awakened until the next morning.

Nothing had changed when we did. Hunter was still dead. It didn't seem right that the sun was shining. Alessio insisted on making me breakfast. I didn't protest because anything that would keep him busy would help. Alessio prepared wonderful scrambled eggs with lots of melted cheese and herbs I couldn't identify.

While Alessio was showering I spoke with the nurse and she told me that Hunter's body would be picked up at ten. She would remain until that last task was completed.

I called Casper and told him Hunter had died. He offered to give the other Verona boys the news and I gratefully accepted. It wasn't easy for me to say the words and right now I needed to concentrate on Alessio, not phone calls.

I thought it best to get Alessio out of the house, so I convinced him to come with me so I could clean up, change clothes, and open up the shop. Jake and Travis were scheduled to work today. They could handle it from there.

After I opened up the shop, Alessio and I stepped outside and walked to campus. There we strolled around, sharing memories of Hunter linked with various locations. Each of us brought back memories the other had forgotten.

We walked around for hours as the students went about their business. Only a few years had passed since we were students ourselves, but it was comforting to know that in a hundred years from now students would likely still be hurrying to class or studying and talking on the benches.

We ended up at Alpha Alpha Omega. We walked into the lounge and gazed at Hunter in the pictures on the wall. He was so young, alive, and strong in those photos. I almost couldn't believe he was gone. He should have lived forever.

"He was beautiful, wasn't he?" I asked.

"Yes, inside and out."

"Why don't you come and stay with me a few days? Your place will be so quiet."

"Thank you, but I need to get used to that. Besides, Hunter left some things for his family and they will probably want to come and pick them up."

"I can stay with you if you like."

"Stay tonight, but then I think it's best if I don't coddle myself. Hunter isn't going to be there anymore. The sooner I face it, the better off I will be."

"Whatever you want, but you know I'll come any time you need me."

"I know."

Alessio turned to me, smiled, and squeezed my hand.

We walked to Alessio's place. Hunter's body was gone and so was the nurse. The house was too quiet. Alessio sat on the couch and stared out into space.

"I feel like he should still be here," Alessio said.

"He should be. He should have been with you for many more years, but I know what you mean. I can't help but expect him to walk in from the kitchen or the bedroom. It's like that when someone is suddenly gone."

"Have you lost anyone you were close to before?" Alessio asked.

"No, but Brandon and Ethan used to talk to me about losing their friend Mark in high school. They both told me how his death didn't feel real for a long time. They kept expecting him to sit down at their table in the cafeteria or wave to them in the hallway. Maybe when we lose someone we don't want to accept it and so a part of us doesn't. A part of us pretends they are still here or maybe we're just so accustomed to having someone around it feels like they still are even after they're gone."

Alessio pulled out a photo album and we sat on the couch and looked at photos of Alessio and Hunter's life together. The first pictures were from their years in college. I had even taken a few of them, but I had never seen most of them.

"Is that your mother?" I asked, pointing to a photo of Hunter with his arm around a small woman.

"Yes. Hunter charmed her completely. My family loved him. I think he was overwhelmed by how they pulled him in and treated him like family. Oh! I forgot to call them."

"It's not too late, is it? It's only a little past noon here."

"It will be a little after 8 p.m. there then. I need to call, but I don't want to give my mother the news."

"I can make the call."

Alessio smiled.

"Thank you Marc, but I should do it. Excuse me."

Alessio went into the bedroom. I continued looking at the photos. Alessio's brothers were very handsome, but then they looked a lot like Alessio. I laughed for a moment when I looked at photo of Hunter with Alessio and his brothers. Hunter was considerably larger than any of them. He was taller and more muscular. He definitely stood out.

I wondered if Hunter and I would have gotten together if Alessio hadn't come along. At the time, neither of us were looking for a relationship, but that could have changed. Perhaps I had missed out on a life with Hunter, but then he had always been a part of my life and Alessio had too. I guess there was no reason to think about the 'what ifs' for things were as they were and they weren't going to change.

Each page of the photo album gave me a glimpse into the life Hunter and Alessio had shared. There were photos of Alessio cooking, Hunter mowing, and the two of them posed in front of the Coliseum in Rome. There were photos of Hunter watering a garden with a hose, Alessio smelling roses, and the two of them standing in front of their old home. I felt a sense of loneliness as I looked at the pictures because I realized that could have been me... with either of them. Things could have easily worked out differently and I could have been with one or the other, for I loved them both. I was about to stray into 'what if' territory again so I veered away. Besides, I would not have deprived them of their life together. Hunter was gone, but at least he'd had those years with Alessio. Alessio was in pain, but at least he'd experienced a life with Hunter.

Alessio returned a few minutes later. His face was anguished.

"It was so hard not to cry when I told mama, especially when she cried. She knew it was coming, but it's still hard for her."

I took Alessio's hand and held it as he sat down again.

"I'm sure she's worried about you."

"I told her you were here. Hunter and I have both told her a lot about you."

"Only the good stuff, I hope."

"There's bad stuff?" Alessio asked.

"No one is perfect."

Alessio and I went out for lunch. Neither of us much felt like eating so we went to College Mall and shared an Italian B.M.T.

from Subway and ate at a table in the food court. People whose lives had not been recently touched by tragedy surrounded us, but I knew that everyone's life was marred by tragedy sooner or later and often more than once.

We walked through the mall next. I spotted several attractive college boys. Alessio noticed me looking.

"Is it just me or do they look younger than when we were in school?" he asked.

"Oh, it's just you."

Alessio smiled for a moment and elbowed me.

"They look younger because we're older. When we were their age we didn't think we looked young. Mom has some photos of me taken when I was in high school. I look like a child. I guess it's a matter of perspective."

We purposely spent a long time in the mall. Both of us picked up a few necessities at Target. We were looking for a way to fill the empty hours. My heart ached and yet I enjoyed being with Alessio. I had never stopped loving him.

When we finished at the mall, we dropped by my shop to make sure all was well and then spent some time in my apartment. We talked a lot, often about Hunter. No matter the topic, we always came back to him. Sometimes we laughed, sometimes we cried, but it felt good to share memories of someone we both loved.

We eventually returned to Alessio's place. We had been there an hour when my cell phone rang.

"What do you and Alessio like on your pizza?" Nathan asked.

"Uh... is this a random quiz?"

"No. We didn't think you should be alone, so Brendan, Casper, and I drove down. We're at Bucceto's on the east side. So what do you like on your pizza?"

"What do you like on pizza Alessio?"

"Italian sausage, green peppers, and smoked gouda. Why?"

"We're about to have company."

I repeated the toppings to Nathan and then told him mine.

"Okay, what's the address? We'll be there in half an hour or so."

I gave Nathan the address and simple directions. Several minutes later there was a knock on the door. Brendan, Casper,

195

and Nathan entered, each carrying a large pizza and a bag from Kroger. They deposited it all in the kitchen and then hugged Alessio and me. They didn't say any of things one usually says when there has been a death; instead, they let us know they cared by being here.

The guys had brought not only pizzas, but also Cokes, ice, bags of Doritos, and a large chocolate cake. We set it all up in the dining room and then everyone sat down to eat.

"This reminds me of impromptu pizza parties in my dorm room," Nathan said.

"You had pizza parties and I wasn't invited?" I said.

"Hey, I said they were impromptu and often in the middle of the night. They were usually Anton's idea."

"We had a lot of pizza parties at the frat," I said.

"Probably orgies too," Brendan teased.

"Oh yeah, every night!"

Alessio smiled.

"I don't remember it that way."

"That was the year you were pledging."

"Sure it was."

"Hunter and I used to order pizza a lot from a little place near where we lived. It was what he called his turn to cook," Alessio said.

I laughed.

"Hey, I know what it's like to lack cooking skills, although I'm merely out of practice. Now Brendan..." I said.

"Hey! So I had a few mishaps in the kitchen."

"Wasn't the fire department involved in those?" Nathan asked.

"No! Why does everyone always have to bring up my lack of skills in the kitchen?"

"We could talk about bowling," Casper said.

"Has he improved?" I asked

Casper shook his head.

"I can't be good at everything," Brendan said.

"Okay, I'll give you that."

"Hunter was good at everything athletic. Me, not so much," Alessio said.

"You were an incredible rider."

"I know how to ride, but I'm not good at much else. Hunter tried to teach me to wrestle, but the results were... sad. I could never beat him."

"Well, Hunter could easily bench 250 and probably 300. I wouldn't feel bad about it," I said.

Alessio looked around the table.

"Thank you all for coming. Today has not been a good day," Alessio said.

"We thought we could provide a distraction. That's the best you can do at a time like this; pull your thoughts away for a while," Casper said.

"Yes, Marc has been helping me do that all day. It does help, but it will not bring Hunter back."

"He was a great guy. I admired him," Brendan said. "Even Brandon and Jon did, but of course they would never admit that to him."

We all smiled when Brandon and Jon were mentioned.

"Did I ever tell you guys about the time Hunter caused a wreck?" I asked.

Alessio smiled, but the others shook their heads.

"We were out riding in town. Hunter wasn't wearing a shirt and he had on skimpy shorts. An older woman was so distracted by him she rear-ended the car in front of her."

The guys laughed.

We shared more memories of Hunter, interspersed with other memories of our college years. It was almost like Hunter was there with us.

After pizza and Doritos, we moved on to the chocolate cake. Brendan, Casper, and Nathan caught Alessio up on some of the events of their lives. Alessio seemed to enjoy himself, although he still looked sad most of the time. That was to be expected. While I had fun talking with my friends, my thoughts kept returning to the fact that I would never see Hunter again.

"We should head back," Brendan said some four hours after they had arrived.

"You are welcome to stay the night," Alessio said.

"No, we didn't come to create work for you. Besides, I have school tomorrow," Brendan said.

"Well, you are always welcome here."

Our three friends hugged both of us tightly.

"If you need anything, just call," Casper said to us both.

"Thank you guys so much for coming," Alessio said. "This was a wonderful surprise."

After the guys departed Alessio and I put away the leftover pizza and then sat together on the couch.

"Thank you for being with me today, Marc. It has been easier because of you."

"You're welcome, but I'm helping myself too."

"Oh, I didn't mean to say you didn't love Hunter..."

"I know. It's hard, isn't it? But we will get through this and he will always be a part of our lives."

I held Alessio until we went to bed. I slept by his side again and we held each other close. I knew I was no substitute for Hunter, but at least Alessio wasn't alone.

***

Alessio and I walked alone on the brick path beside Dunn's Woods. The bell in the clock tower of the Student Building rang out the hour, eight p.m. Most classes had ended for the day and most of the students were in their dorms or out and about in town. The Old Crescent was practically deserted, which is why we'd come at this hour for Alessio and I were about to commit an illegal act.

Hunter had requested that there be no funeral or services, but he did make a request of Alessio and me. He wanted his ashes spread around the Rose Well House. That was the illegal act we were here to perform.

We approached the Rose Well House and checked to make sure we were alone. Once satisfied there were no witnesses Alessio pulled a plastic bag out of his pocket; it held the cremains of Hunter Overmyer, the boy we both loved.

Together, we spread Hunter's ashes around the small limestone pavilion. It was a nice place for Hunter's remains to lie, much better than a cemetery in my opinion.

After we finished, I took Alessio's hand. We stood and gazed at the pavilion in silence for a few moments, and then walked back the way we had come.

Chapter Twelve

"What's wrong Marc?" Laurent asked as he lay naked beside me.

"I feel guilty."

"Alessio?"

I turned on my side to face Laurent.

"It's no secret how you feel about him, Marc. He's all you talk about sometimes."

"I'm sorry."

"It's okay, but you shouldn't feel guilty about us. You are just friends or has something changed?"

"We're just friends."

"But you want to be more."

I sighed.

"Yes. I have since we met in college, but then he got together with Hunter."

"And now Hunter is gone. Perhaps it's time for you to act on your feelings."

"I can't."

"Why not?"

"It's too soon for one thing. I can't swoop in like a vulture the moment Hunter is out of the picture. He died only a week ago, although it seems like ages."

"Okay, I'll buy that it's too soon to start up anything serious, but what else is holding you back?"

"I have this irrational feeling that I'll be betraying Hunter if I allow myself to get close to Alessio in the way I want. I fell for Alessio in college, but then he and Hunter grew close so I had to put those feelings aside. It wasn't easy. I guess I didn't actually put my feelings for Alessio aside, but I didn't act on them. Ever. Seeing them together was hard, but I was also happy for them."

"So you never made a move on Alessio? Ever?"

"Of course not. Hunter was my friend, my brother. I would never have done something that like. When Hunter and Alessio got serious it was the end of whatever could have been between Alessio and me. It was the end of what might have been between Hunter and me as well. I've never been sorry about that because they were happy together. I loved them both. I wanted nothing more than for them to be happy."

"You sacrificed a lot for them."

"Hunter would have done the same for me. If I hadn't waited, if Alessio and I would have become close first, Hunter would have done exactly what I did. I know it."

"I'd say it's your turn for happiness with Alessio."

"I can't shake this feeling of guilt. Maybe I'm acting out of habit. I've distanced myself for so long that's it hard to stop."

"You should tell Alessio how you feel. You're not being fair to yourself or to him."

"Him?"

"Alessio lost someone he loved. You are denying him the chance to experience love again."

"He knows I love him."

"Yes, but it's not the same and you know it. Hunter is gone. Don't you think he would want both of you to be happy?"

"I know he would."

"Do you think he would object if Alessio and you got together?"

"No. Just before he died he put our hands together."

"What more do you want? You're not a vulture. You're not betraying Hunter. All you're doing is getting in the way of your own happiness and you're denying Alessio happiness too."

I sighed.

"You're awfully wise for someone just out of high school."

"Oh, I don't think age has anything to do with it. You can't see the situation clearly because you're too close. Mostly, you're afraid of disrespecting Hunter's memory, but hell, he basically handed Alessio over to you by placing your hands together. He would not have done that if he didn't want you to be together."

"His last words were, "Take care of each other." I think he just wanted us to be there for each other."

"Maybe, but I have a feeling he meant a lot more. Did he know how you felt about Alessio?"

"Yes."

"Then I'm certain he meant more. Think of it this way, if your situations were reversed what would you want for Hunter and Alessio? Would you be angry if they got together after you were gone?"

"Of course not."

"See, you didn't even have to think about it. Tell Alessio how you feel."

"I'll think about it."

"Enough thinking! Act!"

"You're terribly bossy for a freshman."

"Do it or you're getting a spanking."

"You're the one who likes to be spanked."

"Yes, daddy!"

"I can't act on those feelings, not yet. It's too soon. Alessio needs time and so do I. We both have to adjust to Hunter being absent from our lives. It will be harder for Alessio. They shared a life together. After college we kept in touch, but I saw them only rarely. Alessio was with him all the time. I spent a lot of time with Hunter after he and Alessio moved to Bloomington, but that was only a few months. It doesn't measure up to years."

"Okay, so don't act on those feelings—yet, but promise yourself you will when the time is right. Don't delay too long. Don't make the same mistake twice. Someone else will become interested in Alessio soon enough. Hell, I'm intrigued by all you've told me about him."

"Hands off, Laurent."

Laurent laughed.

"Be his friend for now, but be prepared to become more than his friend."

"You give good advice for a kid."

"I'm not a kid as you know well. Let's get some sleep. You've worn me out and I have class tomorrow.

"I wore you out, huh? It's more the other way around."

"Good night, Marc."

Laurent kissed me on the lips.

"Good night."

I closed my eyes and fell asleep thinking about Alessio while holding Laurent in my arms.

I knocked on the door. No one answered. Perhaps Alessio was out, but no; his car was in the drive and so was Hunter's. I took out the key Hunter had given me and unlocked the door.

"Alessio? It's Marc."

There was no answer. I walked toward the bedroom. The door was open. I looked in. Alessio lay on his back with his eyes open. My heart pounded furiously for a moment. What if he was dead? What if he'd downed a bottle of pills because he couldn't live without Hunter?"

"Alessio!"

"Argh! Why did you scare me like that? What are you doing here anyway?"

"You haven't answered your phone for two days."

Alessio shrugged.

"What have you been doing?"

"Laying in bed mostly, watching some TV..."

Alessio was unshaven. I don't think I'd ever seen him when he wasn't freshly shaved. He didn't look good.

"The team is having its first practice of spring outside today."

"That's wonderful."

"Get up."

"Why?"

"You're going to ride with us."

"Uh no."

"That's not a request. Get your ass out of bed, get cleaned up, and dressed."

"Grr."

"Do it."

Alessio reluctantly sat up and swung his legs over the side of the bed, but didn't move. I pulled him up by the arm, aimed him toward the bathroom, and pushed. Once I was sure he was moving on his own I walked to the kitchen.

I made sandwiches out of the ham, cheese, and lettuce I found in the refrigerator, then rummaged in the cabinet until I found salt & vinegar potato chips. By the time I had the drinks ready, Alessio joined me in the kitchen looking much better.

"Miracle Whip or mustard?" I asked.

"Mustard."

I put mustard on his sandwich and Miracle Whip on mine. We sat at the kitchen table and ate.

"We won't push too hard today since it's our first outdoor ride since late last fall. You do have a bike, right?"

"Of course I have a bike, but it's not a single speed."

"That doesn't matter. What the team needs from you is your racing expertise."

"They don't need me. They have you. Need I remind you that you were the best that ever was?"

"I'd start posing for my statue, but there already is one."

Alessio smiled for a moment, but the smile quickly faded.

"You can offer another point of view. I don't know everything and your experiences are different from mine."

"I don't know if I can do this Marc."

"Well, you're doing it anyway. You are not going to stop living because Hunter is gone. Neither of us are going to do that. Hunter would kick our asses if we did."

"It's so hard without him, Marc. It's become harder instead of easier."

"I know it's hard. That's why I'm here. That's why I won't let you lay in bed. Hunter told us to take care of each other."

"He did. Didn't he?"

"Yes and we will honor that wish. Won't we?"

"Yes." Alessio smiled for a moment, but then looked toward one of the empty chairs, Hunter's chair. I reached out and grasped his hand for a moment and then released it.

"You are going to help me train the team. You're going to start going out with me too. Attendance is mandatory."

"You weren't this bossy when I was a pledge and you were my big brother."

"You didn't need your ass kicked to get it in gear then. You were excited and determined to get into Alpha Alpha Omega. Hunter and I were both ready to put up a fight to get you in, but it wasn't necessary. You were so alive then. I miss that Alessio and I want him back. I can't bring Hunter back, but I'm not going to let you slip away. I love you too much for that and I love Hunter too much for that too."

We finished eating, then walked out to the garage. Alessio pulled out his bike. I checked it over.

"You are ready to ride."

"Yeah. Hunter always kept our bikes well maintained."

I glanced at Hunter's bike for a moment and felt a pang of sadness, but didn't let it take hold.

"Come on. Let's ride to the frat. It will be time for practice soon."

Alessio was almost listless as we began to pedal toward AAΩ, but at least he was outside and doing something. That was the most important thing right now.

Our old frat house wasn't far and we were there in minutes. We put our bikes in the rack and I led Alessio inside. Jens was coming down the stairs as we entered.

"We were all very sorry to hear about Hunter," Jens said when he spotted Alessio.

"Thank you for the flowers."

"I've drafted Alessio to help me train the team," I said.

"Great! You raced three years, didn't you?"

Alessio looked surprised that Jens knew.

"Yes. We won two of those years, thanks to Marc."

"I seem to recall other team members on the track. It wasn't thanks to me."

"Be modest all you want, but it's true."

I shrugged.

"Well, I'm heading out, but it was nice to run into you guys. Later."

We walked into the lounge and once more checked out the photos on the wall while we waited on the team.

Austin arrived first, then Baxter, Kang, and Soaring Eagle. Matt, Pierce, and Reece showed up soon after. The last three weren't members of the team, but had ridden with us last fall. I was glad to see them back. Any of them would make a valuable addition to the team next year.

"I'm glad you're all here," I said. "I'm sure you have all been eagerly anticipating this day as much as I have. The Little 500 is only a few weeks away and Quals are coming up fast. Since this will be our first day of training outside we'll take it *somewhat* easy.

"We have extra help now. Some of you may recognize the guy sitting here from the photos of him on the wall. Alessio competed in three Little 500 races and was a member of two winning teams. He was also my little brother back in the olden days when we lived here."

The boys laughed. Even Alessio smiled slightly.

"I only raced for two years, so Alessio has more experience. He can also give you a different viewpoint so take advantage of that. So, let's hit it guys."

We all walked outside and climbed on our bikes. The team members and Reece rode single-speed Roadmasters that met the specs for the Little 500. I rode the Roadmaster that was the team bike for two races back in my day. The others had multi-speed bikes.

We followed our most common route down 3rd Street, up Indiana Avenue, 10th Street, Dunn Street, and then into the countryside. I set a pace a little under that we'd used at the end of last fall, but the guys kept up easily. Even Alessio seemed to have no problem, but then he did have the advantage of a 21-speed.

I upped the pace slightly and then we began to hit the hills. That slowed us down considerably. An inexperienced rider on a one-speed would've been forced to get off and push his bike, but the steep inclines didn't stop us.

"I love being outside again. Perhaps I should sing in Italian!" Austin called out.

"Do it and die!" Kang threatened.

The guys laughed. Alessio looked at me and smiled.

The temperature was cool, but unseasonably warm and we were all quite comfortable riding. I mixed up our training session with face-paced riding and slower uphill sections. We rode about 35 miles before we returned to AAΩ.

"Thanks for making me come," Alessio said as our bikes rolled to a stop.

"We're not done yet." I raised my voice. "If anyone is in the mood for pizza, I'm buying at Mother Bears."

"Hell yeah we're in the mood if you're buying," Baxter said.

The lot of us walked the short distance to Mother Bears. It was just up the street so it didn't make sense to ride. Soon, we were inside and seated at a large booth. Soaring Eagle immediately took out a marker and began writing his name on the wall. It was a tradition at Mother Bears. I pointed to an older set of signatures on the wall where I had signed with Alessio and Hunter on one of our visits to the pizza place during our college years.

"What toppings does everyone like?" I asked.

When the waitress came, I ordered five large pizzas with various combinations of toppings and everyone ordered their own drinks.

"So you raced in three Little 500's?" Reece asked Alessio.

"Yes. I pledged in my freshman year and began racing my sophomore year."

"He rode with the team his freshman year as soon as he became a brother," I said.

"It helped. It gave me much extra practice."

"That's what I'm doing. I didn't make it this year, but I will next year," Reece said.

"Alpha should have a strong team next year if enough of you return," I said.

"And if you coach," Kang said.

"This may be my only year coaching. It's usually done by a senior."

"Oh, you have to coach next year. Screw tradition. You're better," Austin said.

"You already made the team, Austin," I teased.

"I mean it! I say you coach as long as we can convince you to coach."

"Thanks."

"Did Marc really ride nearly the entire Little 500 himself in 1987?" Pierce asked Alessio.

"Oh yeah. That was the race of disasters. Two of us were injured during the first three laps."

"No shit?"

"There were two massive pile ups in as many laps and we lost a rider to each. They were hurt badly enough they were out. Three laps in Alpha Alpha Omega was down to two riders. Then, in the twentieth lap I was clipped and went down hard," Alessio said.

"Fuck," Matt said.

"Yeah, we had a hell of a time getting in our exchanges," I said. "I was the only rider who hadn't been injured."

"What did you do?"

I rode for about thirty laps, then came off and one of the other guys rode a single lap and then I went back in."

"We lost a lot of ground when those of us who were injured did a lap. We weren't in shape to be on a bike," Alessio said.

"But they did it. It was amazing. The entire crowd cheered for each of them during their laps."

"Oh, I can see it now—Breaking Away II!" Soaring Eagle said.

"I wish," I said.

"How many laps did you ride Marc?"

"I did one-hundred-seventy-two out of the two-hundred I think."

Alessio nodded.

"Damn! Has that ever been done before?" Pierce asked.

"Not before or since and we won," Alessio said. "Nearly the entire crowded cheered for Marc at the end."

"And I thought I was going to die," I said, then laughed.

"Let's hope the race this year involves fewer accidents," Kang said.

"Yeah, I'm not fond of pain and don't think I'm up to riding one hundred and seventy-two laps either," Austin said.

"You can do one-hundred-seventy. The rest of us will split up the other thirty," Soaring Eagle said.

"No, thank you. I would like us to win."

"Hey, Marc did it."

"Yeah, but he's a racing god."

"Did you hear that Alessio? I have been proclaimed a god."

"Thanks guys, now he'll be impossible to live with," Alessio said.

When we finished. I had what little pizza that remained boxed up and gave it to the boys to take back to the frat. The lot of us walked back to AAΩ and then Alessio and I rode to his place.

"Practice begins at 6:30 tomorrow evening. See you there?" I asked.

"Um... yeah."

I smiled, then rode away. I knew getting Alessio out of the house wouldn't erase his grief, but at least he was doing something.

I waited anxiously the next evening as time for practice neared. Alessio had shown signs of life the day before, but I feared he would fall back into melancholy during his hours alone in the home he had once shared with Hunter. Shortly before 6:30 Alessio rode in. He showed up for practice the next day too, and all the days that followed. I was relieved. Alessio was beginning to create a new life for himself. It wouldn't be easy, but he had made a start.

***

I sat across from Alessio at his kitchen table. It was the first time he'd asked me over for supper since Hunter's death. We decided to eat in the kitchen because the dining room seemed too big for just the two of us.

"This is great. What is it?"

"Spaghetti."

"I know that. I'm not a complete idiot. I mean the other part."

"You had better be glad Brandon and Jon aren't here. They would have something to say now. It's eggplant parmesan."

"I thought it was some kind of meat."

Alessio laughed for a moment.

"No."

"Oh wait. An eggplant is one of those purple things, right?"

"Yes, they are purple on the outside."

"Well, it's good."

I didn't mind making myself look stupid in front of Alessio. He might tease me, but he was never unkind.

Alessio's features were etched with sadness, but he was moving forward as best he could. This evening was another step in getting his life back on track. He looked so very handsome. I yearned to kiss him, but I knew neither of us was ready for that.

Alessio caught my eyes. I felt as if he knew my thoughts. Not only that, I felt as if he was thinking the same thoughts himself. We had plenty of time, but this time I would not wait until someone else scooped him off his feet. Alessio and I smiled at each other.

We had a wonderful supper, then watched Stargate on DVD. I thought the actor who played Ra was pretty hot, but then I'd always been a sucker for long hair.

Alessio and I sat close as we watched the movie, but I didn't put my arm over his shoulders. The funny thing is I would not have hesitated to do so while Hunter was alive. Things were different now that Hunter was gone. New possibilities existed so the rules had changed. I didn't put my arm around Alessio, but I enjoyed the closeness.

***

"You've got this," I said to the team as Austin pushed our bike onto the track. "I am confident you'll earn a spot and I expect you to come back with a good one."

It was the day of Quals, or Qualifications for those outside the world of Little 500 bike racing. This was the day when the field of potential teams was shaved down to thirty-three. There were forty-nine teams trying out this year, but I meant what I said to my team. Baring disaster, they would earn a spot.

"Remember, it's just like you've practiced. The exchanges must take place between our lines. Make sure your shoes are tied tightly." My thoughts went to Hunter for a moment and my first qual. I wished Hunter was here now, but maybe he was. "Wear your gloves and your helmet. We don't want to forfeit due to forgetfulness or stupidity. We have to take quals as seriously as the race."

"Relax Marc. They will be great," Alessio said to me quietly. I let out a large breath and then smiled.

I knew Alessio was right, but I was nervous, more nervous than I remember being when I was on a bike. The guys were good, but anything could happen and they had never raced in such a big group before. The number of teams trying out at once was limited to the number of lanes, but that was still more riders than they had ever dealt with before.

Our turn came up. I slapped Austin on the back and he moved to his lane. The quals began and the bikers took off, slowly at first since they were beginning from a dead stop, but soon they accelerated. Austin successfully maneuvered to the inside track as I'd taught him. He was currently sixth, but I hoped he could work his way up in the pack.

We had decided to qualify with three riders. The number of riders used to qualify was the least number that could be used on race day. In my day, we had qualified with only two, but then Hunter and I were especially strong riders and we knew we could pull it off. Three was a safer bet. Many used four, but using three was insurance against having to forfeit because we didn't have enough riders to field a team on race day. If one of my guys wasn't able to compete, we could still race.

Austin moved into forth place. Soaring Eagle stood ready for the exchange. Quals were a much-abbreviated version of the race. There were only four laps instead of two-hundred, so exchanges came up quickly.

I watched with eagle eyes as Austin hurtled into our pit, braked hard, and jumped off the bike. Soaring Eagle smoothly replaced him and was off before the bike could even begin to come to a full stop.

"Yes!" I said, pumping my fist. The boys grinned at me. Alessio patted me on the back

Kang was up next. Baxter was sitting out, but only because he'd drawn the short straw. All of the guys were good, but there was no obvious stand out at this point. Any deficiencies had been practiced away. I was already proud of my team.

The bikes whizzed by, eating up lap after lap. Our exchanges went smoothly and there were no screws up or accidents. We finished with a time of 2:28.25, fifth in our pack.

I debated with myself about taking another chance. My first year of racing, our time was 2:23.35. Our time this year was almost five seconds longer. Fifth was not a strong showing in such a small pack.

"What do you think?" I asked Alessio.

"It's a tough call, but I say keep it. We'll almost certainly get a spot with that time."

I thought for a few more seconds.

"Yeah, let's keep it. I want to make sure the guys get into the race. This is a rebuilding year. They need the experience."

"Okay guys. We're going to go with our time. Now, all we have to do it wait."

"That's the hardest part," Kang said.

"I have to agree."

We watched as the other packs raced. With forty-nine teams and a limited number of lanes it took a while to run through them all. Then came additional heats for those trying to better their time. Part of me itched to make the attempt, but I needed to play it safe.

When the final times and places were announced, Alpha Alpha Omega placed 10th. I had hoped for better, but didn't let it show. I don't think the guys would have noticed anyway. They were too busy cheering. I grinned at their excitement.

Several of the current AAΩ brothers came out of the stands to congratulate the team. They were nearly as excited as the riders.

"Good job, Marc," Jens said. "I don't think we would've had a chance to get into the race this year if it wasn't for you."

"I think they could have pulled it off without me. They are a dedicated group."

"Because of you. Are you guys done?"

"Yeah, that's it for today."

"Everyone back to Alpha for the celebration party!" Jens said loudly so all could hear. "That includes you two, too," he said, looking back at Alessio and me. "Thank you for all your help, Alessio."

"Hey, I'm just along for the ride."

"Yeah, right," I said.

The boys took off. I pushed the bike to my Camaro and put it on the rack. Alessio and I climbed in and drove to AAΩ where a party awaited us.

I was taken back several years when we arrived at the frat. There was a big banner that read, "Congratulations AAΩ Little 500 Team!" Smoke wafted off grills where hamburgers and hot dogs sizzled above the flames. There was a keg as well as soft drinks. My old frat knew how to throw a party.

It looked as if most of the current brothers were there. Several congratulated me and I couldn't help but smile.

"Remind you of anything?" I asked Alessio as I handed him a Coke from a tub filled with ice.

"Every AAΩ cookout I ever attended?"

"What do you want to bet it will be the same in a hundred years. The faces and the music will be new, but the rest is eternal."

"Let's hope so."

Alessio and I watched the younger crowd drink and have fun. We weren't that much older, but we were also no longer college boys. I didn't mind. I enjoyed my college years, but I was more settled now and I had my shop.

"I wish Hunter could be here," Alessio said.

"Me too. He will always be with us, but I know what you mean. I would love to share this with him."

Alessio smiled sadly.

"I'm glad you're here. Otherwise it would just be me and all these boys."

"Yeah, I know how you hate young frat boys." Alessio grinned for a moment. Every time he smiled, no matter how briefly, my heart felt lighter.

"That's not what I meant! When I returned to Bloomington I was thrilled and yet I felt like I'd returned home, but everyone was gone. I've made friends, but there is nothing like old friends."

"True."

"Let's get a burger."

I led Alessio to the grills. We each picked up a plate and a bun and then received a burger right off the grill. We moved on to select our condiments and get some chips. We sat at one of the tables with our frat brothers and enjoyed the food, sunshine, music, and companionship.

I laughed as I watched the team. They celebrated as if they had won the Little 500. Then again, I was probably just as excited that AAΩ had earned a spot my first year and maybe even the second. A part of me wished I could race again. There was nothing like being out there on that track during race day. That time would not come again for me, but I had the next best thing and I was glad I could share it with Alessio.

"I hope we can get a good pit location. I need to ask the guys about what colors they prefer. The best will be taken."

"You have 10th choice. That's not bad."

"Not bad, but not that good either."

"Stop thinking about the race, Marc. It's not today," Alessio said.

"You're right, but it's hard to control myself."

"That's because you're a Little 500 fanatic."

"I will admit to a certain fondness for the race."

"Uh huh. I bet you have *Breaking Away* memorized too."

"Hey, stop giving me a hard time or I'll sing in fake Italian."

Alessio made a show of shutting up. I was glad to see him kidding around. Now, if I could get over my intense desire to kiss him...

We remained at the party over an hour. We spent most of our time talking to the boys. Most of them knew Alessio now and all of them knew me. I felt almost as much a part of AAΩ now as I did in my college years. Almost.

"Let's walk over to the well house," Alessio said.

I nodded. We left the party behind and crossed 3rd Street. We stepped onto campus and walked among the familiar buildings. Quite soon, Dunn's Woods came into view. I felt a sense of history as we walked down the wide sidewalk in front of Linden and Kirkwood Halls. Students had walked here for over a hundred years.

We approached the Rose Well House. Early daffodils and tulips were beginning to bloom and the sun shined brightly on Hunter's resting place. I knew he wasn't there, but now it was his memorial, at least in my eyes.

"I come and sit here sometimes," Alessio said as we stepped into the well house and sat on one of the limestone benches that lined the interior. It makes me feel closer to Hunter."

I nodded.

"It's a beautiful place, but I think Hunter is more likely to be wherever you are."

"What do you think happens when we die, Marc?"

"Truthfully, I don't think anyone knows, but I think we go on. I don't think we're this stuff we're made of," I said lightly pinching Alessio's arm for a moment. "I think the real essence of us is our thoughts and feelings. I don't think that goes away when we die. Maybe we're reborn into another body or maybe we exist unhampered by a physical form, but I think we continue to exist. Perhaps we've always existed. I don't know. I have no memories of earlier lives, but then I don't remember most of last week so I don't expect I would. Even if... even if we completely blink out of existence the moment we die it's not so bad because there will be no pain or loneliness or regret."

Alessio sighed.

"I want him back, Marc."

"I know. I do too, but we've had our time with Hunter. Maybe we'll be with him again, but if not at least we had the time with did with him. The pain of losing him is extreme and yet it's worth it. Isn't it?"

Alessio nodded.

"Something else... losing Hunter makes me realize how very lucky we are to know all those in our lives. We get to be a part of their short time here. Even fleeting interactions are something special, like the party we just came from. I don't know the name of most of those boys, but I value getting to experience even the smallest part of their life with them."

"Perhaps you should become a philosophy professor."

"I think not, because all I really know is that I don't know anything."

"That makes you wiser than most."

"Perhaps or maybe it merely means I'm aware of my ignorance."

"I'm glad you're here with me Marc."

I smiled at Alessio. We both stood and faced each other. For a moment I thought we might kiss, but Alessio didn't lean in and I dared not either. I still didn't feel right about it and even if I did, I had the feeling Alessio was not ready.

We walked back to ΑΑΩ, but took our time. We enjoyed the spring day, the beauty of Dunn's Woods, and the easy companionship that existed between us.

Chapter Thirteen

With the warmer weather came increased business at the shop. It had started in the earliest part of spring with eager bikers bringing in their bikes for repair or maintenance so they would be ready to ride on the first warm day. Now, spring was well enough along that there was a considerable increase in the number of bikes we sold. Business was good and I couldn't have been more pleased.

I was busier than I ever thought I would be. The shop consumed my days and the team my evenings. Quite often, a good deal of my night was taken up by shop business as well. I was glad I had taken all those classes at the Kelley School of Business or I might not have been prepared for all the paperwork and accounting. It was definitely not the fun part of owning a bike shop, but I didn't mind—much.

I spent a good deal of my time with Alessio as well. We each had our own life, but we regularly went out together or Alessio had me over for supper. We were just friends and yet there was something more between us. There was something under the surface that neither of us had allowed before. That something gave me hope.

***

"Can I come over?" Laurent asked.

"Yeah. We need to talk."

"Uh oh. Bad?"

"Depends on how you look at it."

"I'll be right there."

I turned off my cell. In a few minutes I heard the bell and went downstairs to let Laurent in the back door. We didn't speak as we climbed the stairs to my apartment.

"So, what's up?" Laurent asked as we sat on the couch.

"We need to stop hooking up."

Laurent actually smiled. It wasn't the reaction I expected.

"Alessio?"

"Yeah, we're spending a lot of time together and we're growing closer. We're not dating or anything like that yet, but I'm beginning to feel uncomfortable about hooking up with you."

"Just me or all your other boys too?" Laurent grinned.

"You are the only one."

"I would be upset because it's really hot with you and I like you a lot, but I figured this was coming. I actually hoped for it. Don't go thinking I'm too noble because this is a rare selfless act on my part. I know what he means to you. I want you to be happy."

"You will make someone a wonderful boyfriend," I said.

"Yeah, but not right away."

"I don't blame you."

"Can we still hang out? Hang out but not hook up?"

"I would like that. You're more than a hookup. I've come to think of you as a friend."

"Cool. I don't mind losing the sex, too much, if we can still do everything else."

"Hey, we can still even hug and hold hands."

"Can I still stay the night?"

"If you can control yourself, yes."

"Don't we have a high opinion of ourselves?"

I laughed.

"It's not that. I used to be you. I know how badly boys your age want and need sex."

"I'll try to drain away my desire by hooking up before coming over. I'm actually good to go for tonight. I got some two hours ago. He was a swimmer. Mmm."

"You hooked up two hours ago and you still called me?"

"Hey, you've always been more than a hookup to me. I wanted to see you."

I smiled.

"Of course, if Dorian ever comes back to visit, I want him!"

"I'll put in a good word for you."

"Deal."

"Hungry?"

"Yeah."

"Me too. I didn't eat much before riding. How about I order a pizza?"

"Perfect."

Half an hour later, we sat at the table eating pepperoni pizza and watching the nightlife on Kirkwood. KOK was busy and cars passed continually on the street below.

"I love your apartment. It's extremely luxurious compared to my dorm room."

"Most apartments are. Remember, I used to live in Briscoe. Collins wasn't much better. Living in a dorm room is kind of like living in a closet."

"No kidding."

"So when Alessio and you get together can we have a three-way?"

"Do you ever keep that thing in your pants?"

"Sure I do. Taking it out during class wouldn't go over well at all."

I rolled my eyes.

"Alessio and I aren't even to the dating stage yet. We're a long way from having sex and I don't know if a three-way will ever be an option."

"Fine, don't share!"

"Hey, you never shared with me."

"You never asked."

"Fair enough."

"I'm not big on three-ways when I'm in a relationship. I did have one with Hunter and Alessio when they were just starting out."

"You never told me about that!"

"You never asked"

"Touché! Now, start talking"

"I'm not giving you details. It was when they were only casually dating, before things got serious between them and it was only once."

"Was it hot?"

"Oh hell yeah!"

Laurent laughed.

"Hunter was gorgeous back then. I'm sure I told you he was on the wrestling team and Alessio... he didn't have Hunter's muscles, but he looked like an angel."

"Oh boy, you're going all school-boy crush on me. You've got it bad for Alessio."

"Hey, you're the school boy, not me, but yes. I have it bad for him. I have since the moment we met."

"It's so sad and pathetic."

"Hey!"

"I'm kidding. I think it's sweet and romantic. Alessio is a lucky guy."

"I don't think he counts himself lucky. He'll never completely get over losing Hunter. Neither of us will."

"I didn't mean that. I meant the way you feel about him and now that I think about it the way Hunter must have felt about him too. He is lucky to have two men love him so much. Many guys don't even get one."

"You won't be one of those guys, Laurent. If it wasn't for Alessio and you were at a settled point in your life I would be very, very interested."

"Arrgh! Don't torment me like that!"

I laughed.

"I don't mean it to torment you. I'm saying that when you are ready for a serious relationship someday, I don't think you'll have much trouble finding someone who is interested."

"Until then I'm going to fuck everything that moves."

"You have such an elegant way of putting things, but I'm sure you're more selective than that."

"Nah, I sleep naked and leave my dorm room unlocked with a sign that reads, "Come in for a free fuck. Everyone welcome" on my door."

"Uh huh and what does your roommate think about that?"

"Oh, he has no problem with it. He fucks me at least twice a day."

"You are so full of shit."

"Actually, I'm pretty damn selective. I don't mind relationships that are hookups only or even one-night stands, but I have to like the guy and find him attractive. Mostly, I stick with the same few guys, although since you're dumping me I guess I'll have to pick up a new one."

"Hey, I'm not dumping you."

"I'm kidding. I wish things could go on as they were and yet I don't. I can live without sex with you if it means you get to be with the one you love."

"We can but wait and see."

Laurent yawned.

"I'm tired. Let's go to bed and not have sex."

"I'm right behind you."

***

I began to breathe harder as we neared the end of yet another training session. I had led the team on a sixty-mile ride through the countryside around Bloomington. My riders were all still in their teens, but I had turned thirty-one on Valentine's Day. I was fit for my age, but that wasn't the same as being young.

I gazed at Alessio. He was a little winded as well. He was a couple of years younger than me and he had obviously kept himself in shape. Knowing Hunter's love for riding as I did, I was sure the pair had spent plenty of time on their bikes, until Hunter could no longer ride. Part of me wished I could have joined in on those rides, but that would have been intruding on the life Hunter and Alessio had together. I also had my own life to live. I was glad Hunter and Alessio had returned to Bloomington. I had several weeks with them I would not have been able to experience otherwise.

Despite being near the end of my reserves I increased speed. The Little 500 was coming up fast and I wanted to push the team to make sure they were as prepared as possible. Pushing them came at a price for I was also pushing myself.

I was winded by the time we reached the frat. Baxter noticed and grinned.

"Don't say it," I warned.

"I wasn't going to say anything. You're in great shape for an old guy."

I speared Baxter with a fake glare. Alessio laughed.

"Hey, I have a brother your age. He couldn't begin to keep up with you. That ride would kill him," Baxter said.

"Coach, are you busy?" Austin asked.

"Alessio and I were going out to eat. What do you need?"

"We have a surprise for you."

"I don't know whether to be intrigued or frightened."

"You'll like it."

Alessio and I followed the boys inside. The projector was set up and the popcorn machine had been rolled out.

"If you can stay, we're showing *Breaking Away*," Austin said.

"He'll stay, believe me. There is no doubt," Alessio said.

I grinned.

"A lot of the brothers will be here. We're ordering pizzas. We have a few minutes yet. You guys want to clean up? I can loan you towels."

"That would be great," I said. Summer weather was far away, but I was still sweaty.

"Come on up to my room."

We followed Austin upstairs.

"This is Marc's old room," Alessio said. "You're a sophomore. How did you score such a good room?"

"The usual way, bribery and blackmail." Austin laughed evilly. "Here are some towels and washcloths. We'll have to pass the shampoo and soap over the wall. You guys can change in here if you like." Austin stripped off his shirt. He had a compact, defined body, but I purposely turned away as I pulled off my own shirt.

The three of us walked to the bathroom with towels around our waists. Alessio's body was as sexy as ever. If anything, he was even hotter than in his college years. He was more muscular than I remembered. Perhaps he'd worked out with Hunter.

Some of the stalls were already occupied. Steam rose in the air and a handful of naked frat boys were coming and going from the showers. I remembered this scene well. The faces had changed, but otherwise I might still have been in college.

Alessio and I took stalls on either side of Austin's. Soon, Austin handed his shampoo over the wall. I squirted some in my

224

hand and passed it back. I loved the lemon-lime scent. The hot water relaxed my tired muscles. I loved a good shower.

Austin passed the soap over next and I lathered up. Showering around so many sexy frat boys, not to mention Alessio, excited me and I was glad we had separate stalls. My mind was still filled with images of the naked boys I'd spotted and of Alessio's sexy, sexy body. He was the most attractive of all, at least to me.

I calmed myself down as I rinsed off and by the time I stepped out to grab my towel there was no evidence of my arousal. I dried off and the three of us walked back to Austin's room.

A few minutes later I was seated next to Alessio with a cup of Coke in my hand and a bag of popcorn. Jens turned on the projector and the familiar scene of Dave Stoller, Moocher, Mike, and Cyril walking to the quarry appeared on the screen. I had watched the movie so many times I felt like I knew those guys personally. When I'd raced in the Little 500 I felt like Dave Stoller. The film had become a part of my life.

I so lost myself in the film I didn't even know the pizza had arrived until Alessio handed me a plate with two slices of pepperoni on it. He smiled at me knowingly.

I turned and gazed at Alessio later when we arrived at the scene that takes place at the Rose Well House on campus. He looked back at me and I took his hand. We held hands for several minutes and smiled at each other when our hands parted. I almost felt like I was back at the beginning when I had first fallen for Alessio.

I grinned to myself when we came to the race scenes at the end. Some of the boys had never watched the film and got so into the race they cheered on The Cutters. I didn't blame them. I became overly excited each time I watched the movie as if it could somehow turn out differently.

"Wow, you're just like Dave Stoller," Pierce said when the film was over.

"More than you know, "Alessio said and smiled.

"Well, I did have useless teammates my second year of racing. I had to make up for all that dead weight," I said.

It took Alessio a few moments to get it.

"Hey!"

"Did you hear Dennis Christopher is coming to start the race this year? Jens asked.

"No. When was this announced?"

"A couple of days ago."

"Oh, I have to meet him," I said.

"A lot of people will want to meet him," Jens said.

"That's very true..." an idea began to form in my head.

"There will probably be an extra large crowd this year," Jens said.

"That means more people will be watching us," Kang said nervously.

"Believe me, when you're racing the crowd is nothing but a roaring blur. It doesn't matter how many people are in the stands. It's the same."

"It's true. You will be so focused on the other riders that the crowd is nothing more than background noise," Alessio said.

"Of course, when you win there are reporters and endless people taking photos and slapping you on the back," I said.

"Yeah. Sheer hell," Alessio said.

Kang smiled.

"This has been wonderful guys. Thank you so much," I said.

Alessio and I departed after we talked with some of the brothers for a while. It was dark out, so we walked our bikes instead of riding. I walked Alessio home and even watched until he was safely inside. I sighed and then walked home.

***

The remaining days before the Little 500 were a flurry of activity. The team trained every evening and I even left my shop in the hands of my employees at times to work in extra training with the boys.

Alessio was as dedicated to the team as me and even acted as coach on a couple of occasions when I could not get away for extra training sessions. I was thankful I had pushed him into getting involved with the team. I think, more than anything else, that had helped bring him back to life. Perhaps, like me, Alessio felt especially close to Hunter as he was riding and never more so than when he was riding with the team. The Alpha Alpha Omega riders benefited as well. Alessio's knowledge of racing gave us an extra edge.

I made a big announcement one week before the Little 500 race. I did so in the form of full-page ads in the Indiana Daily Student and the Herald-Times. Dennis Christopher, the star of *Breaking Away*, would be signing autographs and posing for photos in my shop the day before the race. The university had been very helpful with helping me make it happen. I had ordered a huge number of *Breaking Away* DVDs to sell. The event was likely to create some sales for my shop, but even more it would generate publicity. Besides, it was my chance to not only meet, but hang out with Dennis Christopher. To say I was excited was an understatement.

I was busy, but I still made time for Laurent. We had ceased hooking up, but we went out to eat now and then, watched movies in my apartment, and he still stayed the night when he was at my place late. We had become good friends.

There were not enough hours in the day. Alessio even came to the shop after practice the evening before Dennis Christopher would be making his appearance to help me set up.

"I know I'm forgetting something," I said.

"Relax Marc, you're one of the most organized people I know," Alessio said as we sat up a long table with comfortable chairs behind it. "I will take care of practice tomorrow, then come here to help out with crowd control. All four of your guys are working tomorrow. Right?"

"Yes. All day. Shit! What time is it?"

"It's nearly 8 p.m."

"I have to be at the Showalter House at 8:30 for a reception of Dennis Christopher."

"Have to be?" Alessio grinned.

"Sorry, I'm nervous."

"Go. Get ready. I think we've done all we can here. I'm heading out."

"Thank you for everything Alessio." I hugged him and he didn't pull back.

"Now get moving. You do not want to be late."

Alessio departed. I hurried upstairs, showered, changed, and headed for the Showalter House on the northeastern edge of campus near the golf course.

Despite the name, Showalter House turned out to be much more than house. It was a large, low limestone building with a lobby, offices, and conference rooms. I checked in at a table in the lobby where I was given a nametag and directed to a large meeting room.

There were only some fifty people present which was more than I was expecting since I was told it was a small affair to welcome Mr. Christopher back to campus. There was a large cake, beverages, and hors d'oeuvres.

I didn't recognize anyone until I spotted Herman Wells, whom I remembered from my days at IU. He was the Chancellor then and if I wasn't mistaken, he still was. He smiled when he noticed me looking at him and approached.

"How are you doing Marc?"

"You remember my name?"

"Why is that remarkable? I bet you remember mine." Herman laughed.

"You're better known around campus and I was never the President of IU."

"Well, there's still time for that. You're young. I remember you well. Marc Peralta from Verona Indiana. You are a member of Alpha Alpha Omega and you were a member of two winning Little 500 teams. The last year you raced you won almost single-handedly."

"That's amazing."

"How is Brendan?"

"He's great."

"He was an amazing quarterback, but then all the boys from Verona who played for the university were extremely talented. The Myer brothers were incredible athletes. Oh, how are Casper, Nathan, and... Tristan?"

"They're all fine."

I stood and talked to Herman for quite a while. He kept mentioning names of Verona boys who went to IU and asking about them. I was surprised he had visited Verona himself. He was fond of the antique store in town and had eaten in Café Moffat. I felt as if I was talking with an old friend.

"Oh, I've stood here and talked too long. I'm expected to mingle at these things, but I get so involved with whomever I'm speaking with I forget. To be honest, I just come for the cake." Herman winked. I didn't believe that last bit for a moment.

"Say hello to all the Verona boys when you see them and tell them to visit me the next time they come to Bloomington. Oh, I was so sorry to hear about your Little 500 teammate and fraternity brother, Hunter. That is such a pity. He was a fine young man."

"Yes, he was."

Herman moved on. Everyone smiled when they spotted him. He was a much beloved figure on campus, but he had aged a great deal since I'd last seen him. I hated to think of the day when there would be no Herman Wells on the IU campus.

I started for the refreshment table to get something to drink, but then I spotted *him*. What's more, he was moving toward me. I swallowed hard and wiped my palms on my slacks.

"I'm told you're Marc Peralta."

"Yes, I'm so pleased to meet you Mr. Christopher. This is a big thrill for me."

"Dennis, please. I'm looking forward to tomorrow. I rarely do autograph signings. I was quite flattered when you asked."

"I thought it might generate publicity for my bike shop, but to be honest I mainly wanted to meet you. My friends make fun of me for how often I watch *Breaking Away*."

I couldn't believe I was talking to the actor who played Dave Stoller. He looked different than in the movie because it was filmed close to twenty years before, but it was him.

"So you actually raced in the Little 500?" Dennis asked.

"Yes, twice for the Alpha Alpha Omega team. We won both years."

"I don't see how you guys do it. I did a lot of biking to train for the film, but the race scenes were difficult. I was afraid I'd bump into another rider."

We began talking about bikes, *Breaking Away*, and the signing the next day. The conversation came easier the longer we talked, but we were soon interrupted. Everyone wanted to meet Dennis Christopher.

"I'll see you tomorrow."

"You have my number right? We can sneak you in the back."

"I have it in my wallet."

I smiled and headed for the refreshment table.

I was up early the next morning. I couldn't sleep. Dennis Christopher would be arriving sometime before 1 p.m. when the signing was scheduled to begin and the Little 500 was tomorrow. I hated missing training with the team the day before the race, but Alessio could easily handle it and at this point there was nothing more I could teach my little brothers.

I showered, then fixed myself cinnamon toast. I used raisin bread from Kroger and real butter.

I smiled as I put the bread into my toaster oven. Cinnamon toast was easy to prepare, but I knew Brendan couldn't handle it. His lack of cooking skills was legendary. Casper told he once set a toaster oven on fire while trying to bake biscuits out of a can and I don't think he was kidding.

I ate my toast with hot tea. I had a few special varieties, but some mornings I liked plain old Lipton. This was one of those mornings. I looked out the window at Kirkwood Avenue as I ate. The street was already coming alive. Students passed below on their way to classes or perhaps breakfast and others went about their business. I enjoyed sitting here in the mornings gazing out my window onto life in Bloomington.

I walked downstairs twenty minutes before the scheduled opening time and set up the cash register. I went ahead and unlocked the door and flipped the sign to open. Dennis Christopher would not begin signing until 1 p.m., but I made sure the shelves were fully stocked with *Breaking Away* DVDs. There were more cases of them in the back room. What didn't sell today would in the months to come. It was the only film I stocked, although I did have a few instructional DVDs.

Aaron arrived first and Jake soon after. Travis stumbled in and went straight for the coffee maker we kept in the back room. Todd was the last to show up, but he was still on time. I had a great set of guys working for me. I knew I was lucky.

Business was steady during the morning. This was Little 500 weekend so the hotels were packed with guests. The Women's

Little 500 was today. It didn't pull in the crowd the Men's race did, but it was still popular. The women's race was a recent addition. It didn't exist when I attended IU. In my opinion, there should have been a women's race all along. It wasn't fair that there was only a men's event. I was quite sure women could race bikes as well as the men.

We sold a lot of copies of *Breaking Away* in anticipation of the signing. In fact, people began lining up almost as soon as we opened. Travis took over crowd control and soon the line continued outside. I had a feeling this would be a big event.

I spent much of my morning fielding questions about the signing. The starting time was posted in the window, but customers asked if they could bring in their own items to sign and if there was a charge and so on. The signing was free and I informed all those who asked they were free to bring in anything they wanted to have signed.

My cell rang a little before noon.

"Hello, Marc? It's Dennis."

I gulped.

"Hey. Ready to come over?"

"Yeah, I'm staying in the Biddle Hotel so I'm close."

"I can pick you up out front."

"Great."

"Have you had lunch?"

"No."

"I'll order us sandwiches from Jimmy John's."

"That would be wonderful."

"Okay, I'll be out front in a few minutes. I drive a blue Camaro."

I pressed end.

"Aaron, can you run to Jimmy John's for me and pick up some sandwiches?"

"Of course Boss."

"Order me two of the giant club sandwiches, whatever you think looks good. Get one for all of you guys too, but you can still take your lunch breaks later, and get drinks for everyone. You should probably take one of the other guys with you to carry it all."

"I can take Todd. You know how useless he is."

"Hey!" Todd yelled.

Aaron smiled. I handed him some cash.

"Bring mine upstairs please. Just leave them if I'm not back yet, but I probably will be."

I went out the back and climbed into my Camaro. I almost couldn't believe I was picking up Dennis Christopher and he was coming back to my shop.

I pulled into the circular drive in front of the lobby of the Biddle Hotel. I didn't wait long before the revolving doors moved and Dennis walked out. He spotted my Camaro and hopped in.

"I'm looking forward to this. It should be fun," Dennis said.

"I'm thrilled you're doing it. A couple of my guys are making a run to Jimmy John's. I thought we could eat in my apartment. It's right above the shop."

"Sounds good. Have long have you owned a bike shop?"

"Only a few months. I graduated from IU several years ago, but it's taken me this long to get the money together. Owning this shop is my dream."

"How does the dream measure up to reality?"

"Quite well. It's a lot of work, but I expected that. I studied business at IU. It's not the most fascinating major, but once I set my sights on opening my own shop I knew I would benefit from a business degree. Bikes are my passion, so a bike shop is a great fit."

I pulled in behind the shop and led Dennis through the back entrance and up to my apartment.

"This is my place," I said.

"I like it and I like the view. Kirkwood was a center of activity when we were here filming."

"It still is."

"We spent a lot of time at Pagliai's on the square. They gave the cast and crew free pizza. Actors love free food."

"That's Opie Taylor's now. They have great burgers."

"Knock. Knock," Aaron said from below.

"Come on up. Anyone bringing food is always welcome," I said.

Aaron appeared with two bags and two large drinks.

"This is Aaron. He's a student at IU and he works for me in the shop."

"It's wonderful to meet you," Aaron said as he shook Dennis's hand.

"It's nice to meet you too."

"I'd better get back to work. Oh Marc, since you bought us all sandwiches we've voted you boss of the month."

"Well, if there was more than one I'd feel honored."

Aaron laughed and departed. I set the table with plates and napkins and Dennis and I sat down to eat.

I almost couldn't believe I was having lunch with Dennis Christopher in my apartment.

We had a nice lunch and chatted as if we'd known each other for a long time. I was glad Dennis was such a nice guy. It would have been horrible if I met him only to find out he was a jerk. I told him about driving the team crazy by singing in fake Italian during rides when I was practicing for the Little 500 back in my college days. He thought it was hilarious. We kept talking until our sandwiches were demolished.

"It's a little early, but I might as well get started," Dennis said.

"Sounds great. The bathroom is right back there whenever you need to use it."

"I might do that first."

I tided up while waiting on Dennis to return. We headed downstairs together. When the customers in the shop spotted Dennis, they clapped. He grinned and waved, then sat down at the table.

"If you need anything, just tell me or one of the guys," I said.

Dennis nodded.

Travis guided the head of the line to the table. I propped the door open and was surprised to see how far the line extended when I looked outside. I lost sight of it as it bent around the block.

I watched Dennis sign DVDs and other items as I helped customers. He was friendly and not only signed for each fan, but took a few moments to talk to them. He posed for a photo with any who asked and many did. Even so, the line moved along.

I soon had to go into the back for another case of *Breaking Away* DVDs. I was glad I had ordered plenty. I did not want to run out, not only because of lost sales, but also because of disappointed customers.

One *Breaking Away* fan bought a Roadmaster bike for Dennis to sign. I wondered if he planned to ride it or display it. Others purchased helmets, gloves, and other pieces of biking paraphernalia for Dennis to sign. It would not have occurred to me to ask him to sign a riding glove or helmet.

I spotted a few of those in line with *Breaking Away* movie posters such as the one I had on the wall. I planned to ask Dennis to sign mine before he departed. Others had stills and lobby cards from the film. Everyone in line was quite excited to be there. A couple of girls even cried.

It was an extremely busy afternoon. We sold several bikes. Even without adding up sales, I knew the profits from today would more than cover the costs. Hopefully, the publicity would lead to future sales. Many of those in the shop probably didn't know it existed before they spotted my ad for the event.

As the hours slipped away my mind went to my team. I felt guilty for leaving them to Alessio, but I reminded myself that my presence would make no difference. I had trained them and taught them what I knew about racing. Tomorrow, Alessio and I would both be with them.

Closing time came and went. Dennis insisted on staying until he had signed for everyone, even though he was only scheduled until 6 p.m. My guys agreed to stay too and I promised them bonuses for doing so. I intended to pay Dennis extra for the additional time.

I sent Jake out for pizza. Dennis ate while he signed and the guys ate when they could between helping customers. It was a busy evening.

"You're open 24 hours now?"

I looked up and smiled at Alessio.

"Hey, I'm glad you made it. I hoped you would show up earlier. The line is nearly to the end. I want you to meet Dennis. How was training?"

"Training?" Alessio smacked his head. "I knew I forgot something."

"Not funny."

"Relax. It went smoothly and the guys would have practiced without me I'm sure. We didn't push today as per your instructions. They are in fine shape for tomorrow."

"Anyone feeling ill?"

"No."

"Great. Let's hope they all stay healthy."

Dennis finally signed for the last fan. As soon as the shop was clear I locked the door and turned the sign to closed. I told my guys I would pay them for the extra time and gave them all bonuses in cash on the spot. All four of them left very pleased.

"I'm sure you're tired, but I want you to meet Alessio. He's a close friend and was my little brother in our fraternity. He also competed in three Little 500s."

"I've also watched *Breaking Away* several times, mostly because Marc makes me, but I do like the film."

Dennis laughed.

Before I drove Dennis back to his hotel I got him to sign the *Breaking Away* poster on the wall as well as a photo for me. We also posed together with my bike. Alessio took the photo. Lastly, I wrote Dennis a check.

"This is more than we agreed on," he said.

"Yes, but you also stayed longer than we agreed and I'm very pleased with how today went. This will give my shop a great boost and getting to spend time with you is a dream come true for me. I will never forget this."

Alessio went upstairs and waited on me while I drove Dennis back to his hotel.

"So today went well?" Alessio asked when I returned.

"It went better than expected. It's going to be hard to top."

"I bet. You probably won't get to spend a day hanging out with Dave Stoller again."

"I'm sure."

There was pizza left, so we heated some and sat at the kitchen table and ate. Having Alessio with me seemed right. I wished I could come home to him everyday.

After we ate, I made hot tea and we sat at the table and talked about tomorrow's race.

"I think I'm more nervous than I was when I raced," I said.

"You've invested a lot of time in those boys."

"It's been fun and I'm back in shape now."

"I don't think you were ever out of shape."

"No, but now I'm in racing shape. If I was their age I'd be fit to get out on that track tomorrow."

"Do you think they have a chance to win?"

"They're a good team and I expect them to do well, but winning is another matter. We've both given them the benefit of our experience, but that's no match for actual experience. Then again, my lack of experience didn't hold me back my first time in the race."

"True, but they aren't you."

I shrugged.

"I will be beyond thrilled if they win, but from the beginning I've looked on this as a rebuilding year. I've been working for a win next year. I think they can place in the top ten, but placing in one of the top three spots is a long shot."

"We can but wait and see. Anything can happen during the Little 500."

Chapter Fourteen

"This is it guys," I said, as Alessio, Baxter, Austin, Soaring Eagle, and Kang looked out over Armstrong Stadium. We were early, but there was still quite a crowd in the stands.

The boy's checked in and then we made our way to our pit. The guys looked good in their teal outfits.

"Remember, this is a race, but it's also two-hundred laps. Pace yourself. Those who don't will have nothing left to give at the end. You can give it your all in bursts where you need it, but don't try to maintain it until the end of the race."

More and more of the Alpha Alpha Omega brothers took seats in the stands behind us. There had been a pre-race party yesterday evening, but I didn't attend. I did stop by the party that was going on at the frat this morning, but only because I was picking up some of the riders. Win or lose, I intended to go to Alpha Alpha Omega after the race.

Just as Hunter did in my day, I put one of the riders in charge of checking off exchanges. We needed a minimum of ten. I hoped we could keep the number down to ten because each exchange cost time.

Alessio volunteered to make sure each rider was wearing his helmet and gloves before he went on the track. Failure to wear them could and would result in a disqualification.

I felt a sense of déjà vu as the National Anthem was played and the opening remarks were made. I almost expected to see all my old teammates there beside me, but this was not our race. It belonged to a new generation. Still, I was pleased to be a part of it.

The riders took their positions. Kang was on the track first for AAΩ. The brothers in the stands cheered him.

The bikes stayed in their positions as the pace car made a lap around the track, then the starting gun fired and the race was on.

If the sights hadn't brought back the past, the sounds would have. The loud whir of thirty-three bikes racing past was a sound I had not heard in person since my college years. I felt as if I had been transported back in time.

Kang pulled us into 9th and then 8th place. I was well pleased and not only because he was advancing. He was doing so intelligently instead of powering past the other riders. He watched, waited, and made his move when it was advantageous to do so. He was doing exactly as I had instructed.

I tried to relax as the race progressed, but it wasn't easy. Kang nearly went down when two riders in front of him collided, but managed to avoid becoming involved. No one went down in the collision, but Kang did move up a spot.

The bikers ate up the laps and after twenty Kang signaled for an exchange. Baxter prepared himself under Alessio's supervision. Alessio even made sure Baxter's shoelaces were secured so that there was no risk they might loosen and become entangled in the chains.

Kang came in fast, braked and jumped off the bike. Baxter replaced him a moment later. The bike swerved and looked like it might go down, but Baxter got it under control and took off without the bike ever stopping. I nodded in approval.

I observed as the laps passed and offered what advice I could, but it was up to the riders now. I was pleased with their performance. Half way through the race we were in 7th place, although we had ranged from 14th all the way up to 5th.

Seven teams lost riders to accidents, but one hundred and fifty laps in the AAΩ team was intact. I remembered all too well my last race when collisions virtually reduced the team to me. I still don't see how we managed to win, nor how my injured brothers could endure even a single lap around the track to get in our exchanges. My first year was not free of accidents either. I hoped we remained injury free this year.

The crowd grew increasingly tense as they counted down the laps. At one hundred seventy five the cheering grew louder. Phi Gamma Delta, Zeta Epsilon, and The Cutters battled for the top three places. I wondered if seeing The Cutters race brought back memories of old times for Dennis.

We were currently in 8th place, but Soaring Eagle was making a valiant effort to advance. I cheered along with the rest of the brothers as he quickly moved into 7th and then 6th. Soaring Eagle signaled for an exchange. He was obviously tired and we needed one more exchange to make ten.

"It's up to you now. Watch for your chance. You can expend more energy now, but pace yourself until the final ten laps. Even then, keep something in reserve until the last two laps. Ride smart. Concentrate on moving up place by place. Don't worry about the big picture," I told Austin.

The exchange was perfect. We dropped back a few places, but Austin was fresh and had us back in 7th in a single lap. He was good, which is why we'd saved him for our final rider.

The three front runners were well ahead. The Forest Quad team had moved from back in the pack to take 1st and was ahead by three bike lengths. Phi Gamma Delta was now 2nd, The Cutters 3rd and Zeta Epsilon 4th.

Austin maintained his position and didn't make the mistake of wasting energy by trying to power his way up the right side. It was a temptation, I knew, but while the right side was more open, the distance was greater. A rider might move up only to find he was so tired himself he had nothing left to give.

I cheered as Austin took advantage of a momentary opening to put Alpha into 6th place. The rest of the team and the brothers in the stands echoed my cheer. Alessio looked as if he might burst from excitement.

Soon, there were only fifteen laps to go. Time was running out. I hoped Austin could at least maintain his position. While 6th place wasn't ideal, it was a respectable position and would give the guys confidence for next year. From the beginning, this year had been about rebuilding a decimated team. I had to keep reminding myself about that, but I couldn't help but hope for a win.

I didn't have a clear view of what Austin did, because it happened on the far side of the track, but it looked as if he slipped between the two riders in front of him. His maneuver put us in 4th place!

Austin fell back into 5th place with ten laps to go, but quickly regained his position. The riders in 2nd and 3rd were side-by-side. First one, then the other pulled ahead so that their positions constantly changed. Austin was right behind them and the small group had pulled ahead of the pack. The Forest Quad rider out in front had increased his lead so much that, barring an accident, I didn't think it was now possible for anyone to catch him. There simply was not enough time left.

Five laps later and none of the top positions changed. Most of the crowd was on their feet now. The Forest Quad fans were going crazy. Forest Quad had started in 21th place and had worked its way all the way to 1st. I must admit that even a little part of me was cheering for them. Teams rarely came from that far back in the pack to win.

The leaders zipped past us with only two laps to go. The Forest Quad rider had dropped back a bit. He was clearly running out of steam, but he was still well ahead. Austin was still in 4th, directly behind Phi Gamma Delta and The Cutters. The 5th place rider was far enough behind now I doubted he could catch up and the rest of pack was no longer a danger unless something drastic happened.

Austin made his move with one lap to go. He powered his way to the right of The Cutters and rode even with him and the rider from Phi Gamma Delta. I nodded in approval. It was his only option.

Austin and the other two riders changed position so frequently it wasn't possible to tell who was in what place. As soon as I figured it out, the positions changed. The situation was unchanged with half a lap to go. Forest Quad crossed the finish line and the checkered flag waved with a quarter lap remaining for Alpha Alpha Omega, Phi Gamma Delta, and The Cutters. Sections of the crowd were screaming so loudly the sound was deafening. Most of the noise was coming from behind me. Alessio looked as if he was trying to move Alpha forward by sheer force of will.

The three teams raced across the finish line. I had no idea where we had placed. Neither did anyone else, but the brothers in the stands cheered as if we'd won. I felt as if we had too. While I can't say I never dreamed we'd do so well, I knew it wasn't likely. I was immensely proud of my boys.

While the Forest Quad team and fans celebrated, the rest of us waited for the official times and places to be posted in bright lights on the scoreboard. After less than three minutes, but what seemed an eternity, they appeared: 1st Place: Forest Quad 2:11:31.115, 2nd Place: The Cutters 2:11:35.837, 3rd Place Alpha Alpha Omega 2:11:35.839.

Our section of the stands exploded with cheers as the team, Alessio, and I jumped up and down. I couldn't believe it. Not only had we placed 3rd, we had only missed 2nd by .003 seconds.

I watched with Alessio a little later as the trophies were awarded. Forest Quad was symbolically awarded the huge silver trophy that was on display in the IMU most of the year, then given the still-large trophy they would take back and display in the lobby of their dorm. The Cutters and Alpha Alpha Omega received smaller, but still impressive trophies. I was so happy I nearly cried.

Alessio and I slipped away and left the boys to their fans while we maneuvered through the crowd and made our way back to the Camaro. We were both grinning like idiots.

"Hunter would be very proud of you, Marc," Alessio said with sudden, but temporary tears in his eyes.

My lower lip trembled for a moment, but I did not cry. I hugged Alessio instead.

"He would be proud of *us*. I felt like he was here," I said.

"I think he was."

I drove us back to Alpha where a celebration party was beginning. Poster board signs read "Congratulations on 3rd Place in the 1996 Little 500!"

More and more brothers began to arrive. The grills were fired up and large tubs were filled with ice and soft drinks. Music played a little too loudly. I grinned. It was just like my college years.

The team arrived shortly and the brothers cheered for them. The team immediately descended on Alessio and me.

"Why did you guys take off? You should have posed for photos with us," Kang said.

"No. This is your day. You were on the bike. Not us. I'm so proud of you."

"But we could not have done it without you," Baxter said.

"Who knows what might have been," I said.

"Come on, you're both posing with us now."

Alessio and I were both grabbed by an arm and pulled toward the trophy, which sat upon a table. Austin picked it up and pushed it into my hands. We gathered closely together while brothers took photos of us. I couldn't stop smiling.

The party kept growing larger. There were a lot of people there I did not know, but then brothers from past years often showed up Little 500 weekend. There were girlfriends, some parents, and others as well.

Alessio and I each took a brat, Doritos, a brownie, and a Coke and sat at one of the long tables. The brat was delicious and reminded me of the cookouts Brendan & Casper often had during the summer months at their apartment in The Crossing. We talked with current and past brothers as we ate. Everyone was excited about Alpha Alpha Omega placing in the race.

After everyone had a chance to eat, the music was shut off and Jens picked up a microphone. He had the team stand up and everyone cheered, then he insisted Alessio and I stand up as well.

"Since this trophy is going on display in the lounge we need to make room, so if Marc will come forward, I have something to present," Jens said.

Confused, I got up and stepped toward Jens. He turned around and took a trophy one of the brothers had been holding behind him.

"You might recognize this trophy Marc. It's the 1st place trophy from 1986. Ten years ago you and the rest of the Alpha Alpha Omega team won the Little 500. This year, you took a decimated team and turned them into a winning team. Your Alpha brothers want you to have this trophy as our way of saying thank you."

It was hard not to cry. I accepted the trophy. Jens passed the microphone to me.

"Being a part of this fraternity has always meant a great deal to me and I was excited when Jens asked me to help with the team this year. I've enjoyed every moment of it and I am immensely proud of Baxter, Austin, Soaring Eagle, and Kang. None of them had raced before and by God they actually placed!"

The crowd laughed and cheered. I handed the mic back to Jens. That's when I noticed familiar faces from my past gazing at me. Conner and Jonah clapped along with the others.

I stepped down and sat the trophy on the table where Alessio was sitting. It gleamed in the sun just as it did on the day Hunter, Conner, Jonah, and I posed with it before the crowd.

I turned and smiled as first Conner and then Jonah pulled me into a hug. Alessio was their next target.

"You guys came for the race? Why didn't you tell me you were coming?"

"That would have ruined the surprise," Conner said.

"We were sorry to hear about Hunter. I can't believe he's gone," Jonah said.

"He hung on as long as he could. I wish he could have been here for the race. He would have been so proud of Marc," Alessio said.

"Marc *was* his little brother. You did a great job with the new batch of riders. I heard you had to build a team from scratch. Alessio is right. Hunter would have been proud of you. We are," Jonah said.

"Thanks. To celebrate perhaps I should sing!"

"Uh, no," Conner said.

"Come get something to eat. You know how the Alpha parties work. I'll introduce you to the current crop of brothers," I said.

"Am I invited?"

I turned.

"Adam! I didn't know you were here!"

"I arrived a few minutes ago, just in time too see you receive your trophy."

"Did you watch the race?"

"I watched the second half. I was at the art museum. I donated a piece."

"That's wonderful. I have my bike shop now. I used the money you gave me to help me get started."

"You earned that money."

"I hardly think so." Adam turned to Alessio. "Hi, Alessio."

"It's great to see you!"

"It's the first time I've returned to campus since I graduated. Of course, it hasn't been that long," Adam said.

"I'm glad you came. I live in Bloomington now."

"I know. I'm sorry about Hunter."

Alessio nodded.

"Losing him was hard. It still is."

"I know it's rough for both of you," Adam said looking at me. "Hey, Conner, Jonah. How have you guys been?"

"Great."

"Awesome."

"So what did you donate to the museum? It's not another statue of Marc, is it?" Jonah asked.

"No. It's a painting, a birds eye view of campus seen through the clouds."

"Oh, I must see it. When is the unveiling?" I asked.

"Next month, but I can't be here. I already have other commitments."

"That's too bad."

"I timed delivering the painting with Little 500 weekend. I thought it was a good time to visit Alpha Alpha Omega. It looks like I was right."

"You still have time for us little people now that you're a famous artist?" I asked.

Adam grinned.

"The fame does not matter. Only the art matters. I would sculpt and paint if no one wanted my work, but this way I get to do it full time."

"I'm happy for you, Adam."

"And I for you."

The five of us talked while we ate and for a good long time after. One of the brothers interested in art recognized Adam and soon Adam had quite an audience as he talked about his artwork. It hardly seemed possible this was the same guy I had so dreaded rooming with all those years ago.

We remained at the party for a couple more hours. We didn't depart until Conner and Jonah left and Adam told us he had to leave to catch his flight in Indy. Alessio and I hugged each of them goodbye and then I drove Alessio home.

I placed the trophy on my kitchen table and admired it. I was immensely proud of it; not only because I was part of the team that won it a decade before, but because the current brothers of my fraternity presented it to me. I was glad I had returned to Bloomington.

***

"Marc, would you like to come over for supper tonight?" Alessio said when I answered my phone.

"I suppose I could reschedule my macaroni & cheese for tomorrow evening."

"Oh good Lord."

"I would love to come. What time?"

"Let's make it 6:30."

"Sounds great. I will be there."

With the Little 500 over, I had more leisure time in the evenings, although my shop kept me busy. Alessio and I spent quite a bit of time together, but we had not crossed the line and become more than friends. Each time I was near him I wanted to take him in my arms and kiss him, but I feared his reaction and even more a little part of me still felt as if doing so would betray Hunter. The shock of losing Hunter was past, but I would always miss him.

The shop was busy right up until closing time. Little 500 weekend was two weeks behind us, but we were still experiencing increased sales. I even had to reorder more *Breaking Away* DVDs because my stock of them was nearly wiped out the day Dennis was signing. I was glad I had over-ordered because as it turned out too much was just enough.

I locked up and turned the sign to "closed" as soon as Jake departed, then walked upstairs to clean up. Alessio and I didn't have the relationship I wanted, but I enjoyed every moment I had with him.

I put on a purple polo and some cologne and then headed out. The weather was pleasantly warm so I walked. I could have ridden my bike, but I didn't want to arrive too early and sometimes it was nice to see Bloomington at a slower pace.

I took an indirect route so that I could arrive right at 6:30. Alessio answered the door and smiled.

"I hope you didn't go to too much trouble," I said.

"I put in more effort than what's required for your macaroni & cheese, but remember I like cooking. I made shrimp Creole."

"That sounds difficult."

"It's really not. I also baked a chocolate cake."

"I love you!"

Alessio laughed.

We ate in the dining room. It was the first time we had done so since Hunter died. The shrimp Creole was delicious, but then so was everything Alessio cooked. The chocolate cake was wonderful too, although even bad chocolate cake is good.

"I received something in the mail today." Alessio paused before continuing. "It's from our lawyer, I mean my lawyer, the one who drew up wills for Hunter and me. He sent me a videotape. It's from Hunter. He recorded it before he died and asked that it be sent to me two-and-a-half months after his death. The note says it's for us to watch together."

I felt myself go pale.

"Are you ready to watch it?"

I nodded. I followed Alessio into the living room. He turned on the VCR under the DVD player and inserted the tape. He turned on the TV and we sat together on the couch. The tape began to play. Hunter appeared on the screen, sitting on the very couch we were sitting on now.

"This is Hunter contacting you from the grave. Bah-ha-ha-ha. Okay, you probably don't think that's funny, but what can you do to me?"

Hunter grinned. The tape was recorded early enough in his illness that he still looked good.

"I'm sure you have been there for each other since I've been gone. I've never worried about that for a moment and it's a great comfort to me, but there is something more. I know you love each other. You always have. The two of you could easily have been a couple instead of Alessio and me. I know I did nothing wrong, but I've always felt a little guilty for taking Alessio away from you Marc. What I mean is, if I hadn't been in the picture, the two of you would have been together.

"I know neither of you acted on your feelings when Alessio and I were together and I'm sure it was difficult at times, especially before we graduated and after Alessio and I returned to Bloomington. I appreciate your faithfulness, although I would have forgiven you if you had slipped. You are both my best friends and I love you both dearly.

"I'm sure you've been drawn together since I died and I'm just as sure you haven't been able to bring yourselves to act on those feelings. If I'm mistaken and you have, it's fine. In fact, I hope that's what has happened, but I know the two of you too well. Some little part of you will feel like you're betraying me. It's nonsense, but I know that's how you feel."

Alessio and I looked at each other. Hunter was right.

"I wish I could have stayed with you longer. I'm thankful for every moment I had with each of you, but I'm gone and I'm not coming back. You love each other and I want you to be together. I want you to hold hands and kiss and fuck like bunnies."

I couldn't help but laugh as Hunter did on the screen.

"I want you to be together, love each other, and make love to each other. Do your best to make each other happy knowing it is what I want. I love you both and I know you love me. Goodbye."

The tape ended and I began crying. I wasn't alone. Alessio cried too. We clung to each other for several moments until our tears slowed, and stopped.

"I guess he couldn't have made it more clear that that," I said.

Alessio smiled, then leaned in and kissed me.

Made in the USA
San Bernardino, CA
10 September 2016